W9-BSE-288

GATEWAY

BOOKS BY SHARON SHINN

GATEWAY

SHARON SHINN

Viking

An Imprint of Penguin Group (USA) Inc.

VIKING

Published by Penguin Group

Penguin Group (USA) Inc., 345 Hudson Street, New York, New York 10014, U.S.A.

Penguin Group (Canada), 90 Eglinton Avenue East, Suite 700, Toronto, Ontario,
Canada M4P 2Y3 (a division of Pearson Penguin Canada Inc.)

Penguin Books Ltd, 80 Strand, London WC2R 0RL, England

Penguin Ireland, 25 St Stephen's Green, Dublin 2, Ireland
(a division of Penguin Books Ltd)

Penguin Group (Australia), 250 Camberwell Road, Camberwell, Victoria 3124, Australia
(a division of Pearson Australia Group Pty Ltd)

Penguin Books India Pvt Ltd, 11 Community Centre, Panchsheel Park,
New Delhi – 110 017, India

Penguin Group (NZ), 67 Apollo Drive, Rosedale, North Shore 0745, Auckland,
New Zealand (a division of Pearson New Zealand Ltd.)

Penguin Books (South Africa) (Pty) Ltd, 24 Sturdee Avenue, Rosebank,
Johannesburg 2196, South Africa

Penguin Books Ltd, Registered Offices: 80 Strand, London WC2R 0RL, England

First published in 2009 by Viking, a member of Penguin Group (USA) Inc.

1   3   5   7   9   10   8   6   4   2

Text copyright © Sharon Shinn, 2009
All rights reserved

LIBRARY OF CONGRESS CATALOGING-IN-PUBLICATION DATA
Shinn, Sharon.
Gateway / Sharon Shinn.
p. cm.
Summary: While passing through the Arch in St. Louis, a Chinese American teenager
is transported to a parallel world where she is given a dangerous assignment.
ISBN 978-0-670-01178-0
[1. Space and time—Fiction. 2. Chinese Americans—Fiction.] I. Title.
PZ7.S5572Gat 2009
[Fic]—dc22
2009014002

Printed in U.S.A.
Set in Kennerly
Book design by Kate Renner

For Sydney Xiang Prow and Molly Yang Prow,
who came to St. Louis from a far land.
I hope your lives hold many adventures.

—Sharon Shinn

 # ONE

DAIYU LOOKED OVER the assortment of jewelry at the old woman's booth and didn't see anything she liked. She'd spent nearly an hour wandering outdoors around the Arch grounds, investigating the stalls being set up for Fair Saint Louis, and she'd been so surprised to see a jewelry vendor among the food booths that she'd stopped to look over the merchandise. But now she wished she hadn't. The necklaces were cheap, the summer heat was overwhelming, and in a minute she was going to be late getting back from lunch.

"I'm sorry," she said to the old woman standing on the other side of the rickety table. "I don't think I'll be buying anything today."

The vendor was so tiny, she had to look up at Daiyu, and Daiyu was the shortest girl in her class. The old woman was so old, even her wrinkles had wrinkles. But her black eyes were shrewd and calculating. "You like rings?" she asked, reaching for something under the table.

Daiyu shrugged. "I usually don't wear one." In fact, she rarely wore anything except a watch, hoop earrings, and the necklace her parents had given her—a gold chain hung with a gold charm that spelled out her name in Chinese characters.

"You'll like this ring," the old woman promised, bringing out a small box wrapped in red silk.

She flipped open the lid to reveal a jet-black ring nestled in a snug slot of red velvet. The old woman teased it loose and held it out in her narrow palm, and Daiyu bent closer to see. It was a single piece of stone carved in the shape of a dragon, head thrown back, talons extended, tail whipping around to touch its nose. Daiyu had a sudden, intense, and most uncharacteristic impulse to snatch it up and then go running from the fairgrounds.

"Try it on," the old woman urged.

Why not? Daiyu picked it up and slid it onto the ring finger of her right hand. Smooth and cool as glass against her skin, the ring was a perfect fit.

"Do you like it?" the vendor asked.

"I do," Daiyu said, holding her hand up to get a better look. Her spread fingers seemed perfectly framed in the elegant chrome curve of the looming Arch. "It's beautiful."

"Very reasonable," the old woman said. "Twenty dollars."

Daiyu had expected to hear that it was a hundred dollars, so that was reasonable indeed. Maybe the ring was glass after all, though the material looked so dense that she'd just assumed it was carved out of some semiprecious stone. "I'm saving all my money for college," Daiyu said, feeling a surprising sense of reluctance as she pulled off the ring, "so I really can't."

"Fifteen dollars," the old woman said.

Daiyu smiled. "I don't even have five on me."

"I could wait," the woman offered. "Will you come back tomorrow?"

Daiyu hesitated. "Maybe," she said. "But—you shouldn't hold it for me. I don't think I can buy it."

The woman's bright eyes looked pleading; her voice took on a tone of urgency. "But it's black jade," she said. "It's meant for you."

Daiyu felt a little chill go down her back, despite the relentless heat. "Why do you think it's meant for me?"

The woman pointed at her. "Daiyu. That's your name," she said. "It means black jade."

Daiyu put her finger up to the boatneck collar of her sleeveless shirt, but the gold pendant with the Chinese characters was still tucked safely inside, against her skin. Maybe it had slipped free while she was leaning over the booth. Otherwise, how could the old woman know her name? "It's beautiful," she repeated, "but I really can't buy it."

"Come back tomorrow. I'll be here waiting."

A car sounded an irritable horn as traffic on Memorial Drive snarled up, and Daiyu quickly glanced at her watch. She was officially late. "I've got to go," she said by way of apology and farewell. Taking off at a half run across the fairgrounds, she left behind the Arch standing guard over the Mississippi River and the mayhem of the merchants setting up their booths.

She looked back once to find the vendor was watching her. The old woman's face was fierce, and even from a distance her eyes seemed to burn. Her fingers were balled into fists. Daiyu couldn't tell from this far away whether the ring was still lying on the rough counter or if the old woman was clutching it in her hand as if protecting it from the sight of any other curious visitors who might wander past.

The rest of the afternoon dragged by. Until this week, Daiyu had been kept pretty busy during her summer internship at the Executive Edge Employment Agency, but there wasn't much to do on this Friday before the Fourth of July holiday.

"Are you as bored as I am?" Isabel demanded at around four in the afternoon as she came stalking out of her office. Isabel, who owned the agency, was a tall, thin, intense woman of uncertain age and immense energy. When Isabel got worked up over some cause or another, Daiyu sometimes thought her soul might vibrate right out of her body. "You're always so calm that it's hard to tell."

Daiyu laughed. "There isn't much for me to do right now," she admitted.

"Then let's just beat the traffic and go on home," Isabel said. "Are you coming down for the fair over the weekend?"

"Probably."

"I'll be at the voter-registration booth, if you want to drop by and say hello." Isabel was passionate about politics and always trying to interest Daiyu in attending some rally or debate.

She'd already made Daiyu swear that she would register to vote the minute she turned eighteen.

"I don't know," Daiyu said vaguely as she gathered up her purse. "Maybe."

They rode together down the elevator of the Metropolitan Square Building, into the grand foyer with its huge murals of St. Louis history, then Isabel waved good-bye and headed for the garage. Daiyu made her way back out into the stifling heat to await the Soulard bus. Traffic was already clogging the roads, and horns were sounding up and down Olive Street. Naturally, the bus that arrived ten minutes later was not air-conditioned.

Daiyu sighed and slipped into an empty seat, feeling the vinyl stick to the bare skin on the back of her arms. She pried open a window, hoping for a little fresh air, and watched the crowds filing in for the night's baseball game at Busch Stadium. Everyone was dressed in red in honor of the Cardinals; red birds adorned everything at the stadium from flags to awnings to electronic signs. Fredbird, the Cardinals' mascot, capered on the sidewalk and posed for pictures with kids. The bus inched on by.

Traffic cleared once they were in the historic district of Soulard, and Daiyu got off the bus to walk the last few blocks home. This particular street was a little more rundown than the one in Lafayette Square where Daiyu and her parents had lived last year. A few of the old redbrick buildings had been lovingly restored, and some of the tiny front lawns had been carefully reseeded, but more often than not the townhouses looked bedraggled, unkempt, like an old homeless woman with an interesting history but a perilous future.

Daiyu pushed open the door to their new place and instantly inhaled the scents of paint and turpentine. She heard the whine of a saw coming from upstairs and then the thump that meant someone had dropped a tool.

"Dad! I'm home!" she called from the foot of the steps. "Do you want me to make dinner?"

"That would be great!" he called back. "Make enough for three."

The kitchen was cramped and falling into disrepair, and it was always a challenge trying to maneuver around the piles of lumber and stacks of paint cans that her father seemed to think were best stored right inside the back door. Still, Daiyu was rarely bothered by turmoil or disorder; her father said her ability to function even in the midst of chaos was her single most valuable personal skill. Within forty-five minutes she had cooked the meal, set the table, and stored some of the paint cans in a more convenient spot.

"Dinner's ready," she announced, and two men tramped down the stairs to join her in the dining room.

Her father had to bend way down to kiss her on the cheek. He was a good six feet three inches, lanky and loose limbed, with hair as black as hers but eyes so blue people always remarked on the color the first time they met him. "Honey, this is Edward," he said, introducing his companion.

"Hi, Edward," she said. "I hope you like pasta."

Edward smiled. He was missing a few of his teeth, and his skin was bad, but his hair was washed, his clothes were clean, and he'd shaved that morning, so he looked pretty good compared to many of her father's itinerant workers. Her father hired a lot of them from local homeless shelters or work-release programs, but he'd also been known to pull to the side of the road when he saw someone holding up a sign proclaiming WILL WORK FOR FOOD. Daiyu couldn't remember a holiday or a renovation project during which her family hadn't been offering hospitality to some stranger down on his luck.

"I like pretty much anything someone is willing to put on the table in front of me," Edward said.

"How much did you get done today?" Daiyu asked as they sat down and began dishing out the food.

"Put up the crown molding in that third-story bedroom," her father answered. "Edward's exceptionally handy with a saw."

"Used to be a carpenter," Edward said.

"How about you, honey?" her father asked. "Did you have a good day?"

"Kind of slow at work, but I walked around the Arch grounds at lunch. It's almost all set up for the fair. Are we going tomorrow?"

He looked briefly dismayed. "I can't! I promised Jordan I'd be at church all day tomorrow working on the new addition." He glanced at Edward. "You could come help out, if you like. No money in it, but you'll get lunch and dinner."

"I'll take you up on that," Edward said.

Her father looked back at Daiyu. "We could go Sunday."

She shook her head. "I don't care. If I feel like it, I'll head down tomorrow afternoon by myself."

Daiyu was serving Oreos for dessert when Mom called, and Dad took the cordless phone upstairs to have a private conversation. Edward dunked his cookie in his coffee and gave Daiyu an appraising look.

"Are you one of those Chinese babies?" he asked.

She smiled. "I'm hardly a baby anymore, but yes, my parents adopted me from China when I was six months old."

"You think you might go back to China someday?"

"I'd like to," she said. "Maybe after I'm out of college. At least once in my life I'd like to travel someplace exotic. The farther away, the better."

Edward helped her clear the table, but they weren't quite done with the dishes when her father came back downstairs and handed her the phone. Daiyu carried it halfway up the stairs and sat down on one of the worn-out risers.

"Hi, Mom," she said. "How's Gramma?"

"Pretty good," replied her mother. "She's getting stronger and less cranky every day."

Gramma had had hip-replacement surgery, and Daiyu's mother was out in California for the summer overseeing the recovery.

"Well, tell her she has to get well enough to climb steps, because she has to come visit us and there's no bathroom on the bottom floor. Or tell her if she doesn't want to climb the steps, we'll just have to get her a bucket."

Her mother laughed, and Daiyu imagined her face lighting up in amusement. Her mother was a calm, big-boned woman with wide brown eyes, thick brown hair, and an inexhaustible sense of humor, and amusement was her most common expression.

"Hey, I made do with a bucket when your dad and I
were first dating and he was fixing up that dreadful place on
Jamieson. I always told him he only married me because I had
a functional toilet."

They talked for another fifteen minutes before hanging up.
Her father had already left to take Edward home—or, more
likely, to one of the shelters downtown—so Daiyu finished up
the dishes and then headed up to her room. It was long and
narrow, with high ceilings and leaded glass windows, and once
it was restored it would be a beautiful space, she thought. But
right now the paint was peeling, the floor was in bad enough
shape that she'd gotten splinters twice, and there was a faint
scent of mildew. She knew that within a year, it would be airy
and charming and full of light. That's when they'd sell the
place and look for a new project to renovate.

She spent the next couple of hours talking on her cell phone
and sending text messages. Three of her close friends were out
of town for the holiday, and the other two didn't want to go
to Fair Saint Louis. Fine. Daiyu decided she wouldn't go either.
No reason to revisit the jewelry booth. No reason to look at the
jade ring again and then realize she didn't want it. Because she
really didn't. She told herself she couldn't even remember how
it had felt on her hand.

TWO

DAIYU WAS STILL in bed the next morning when Isabel called her cell phone. "What's going on?" she asked in a sleepy voice.

"Would you be willing to work for a few hours this afternoon? There's a career fair at the Fox Theatre today. I'm going to give a presentation and hand out fliers. My daughter was supposed to help me out but she's got the flu. I'll pay you thirty dollars for the afternoon."

"They do career fairs at the Fox?" Daiyu said, pulling herself out of bed and hunting through her closet. She didn't have too many outfits that qualified as professional, and most of them had already been worn this week. "That seems weird."

"It's some special event for a women's networking group. After the presentations, there will be a concert, I believe, but we won't stay for that. Would you be willing to help me out?"

"Sure," said Daiyu. "When do you need me there?"

"I'll pick you up at three."

After lunch, Daiyu put together an outfit of narrow black

pants, a sleeveless gold top, and a pair of black Skechers. She'd learned the hard way that while it was important to look good at events like this, wearing comfortable shoes was even more critical. She was standing outside the townhouse when Isabel pulled up.

"You're my favorite summer intern *ever*," Isabel declared. "I can't think of a single other high school girl who would have been willing to work on a Saturday, especially on such short notice."

"I need the extra money," Daiyu said, surprising herself. "I want to buy a ring."

It was always a treat to go down to Grand Avenue and visit the Fox, an eighty-year-old restored movie theater that was now a prime venue for concerts and plays. The cavernous, high-ceilinged lobby was lined with massive terra cotta–colored pillars that seemed to hold up the intricately detailed ceiling; the floor was a slick, reflective marble. Daiyu always thought it deserved its nickname of "The Fabulous Fox."

About fifteen booths were set up in the lobby. Daiyu stood behind the Executive Edge table and handed out brochures to the smartly dressed women who circled through, looking for better jobs with higher salaries. Isabel spent her time working the floor or slipping up the wide stairs into the theater to hear her competitors deliver speeches. At five, she disappeared for half an hour to give her own presentation. By six, the networking women were filing over to a buffet line for dinner, and Isabel and Daiyu were headed back out to Isabel's car.

It felt like it was 120 degrees inside the black Lexus, and even the high-powered air-conditioning wasn't going to have an impact anytime soon. "Do you want me to take you back home?" Isabel asked as she pulled out of the parking lot. "Or do you want to come help out at the voter registration booth with me? But that's strictly volunteer work."

Daiyu laughed. "I don't want to work, but I do want to go to the fair, so if that's where you're going—"

"I have a guaranteed parking spot at the Mansion House," Isabel said with satisfaction.

They parked five levels down in the dungeonlike lower recesses of the Mansion House, then climbed up the spiral ramps to the exit and welcome fresh air. As they were crossing Memorial Drive toward the fairgrounds, Isabel lifted her eyes to gaze up at the top curve of the Arch, glistening silver even in the waning light of the summer evening.

"Gateway to the West," Isabel said. "Prettiest landmark in the whole country, I always think. And I love the view you can get of the city when you ride up to the top."

"I never go up in the Arch," Daiyu said. "I'm a little afraid of heights."

Isabel handed Daiyu a twenty and two fives, then strode off confidently toward the north end of the fairgrounds. Daiyu moved more aimlessly. Today there were thousands of people milling around among the tents and booths, eating cotton candy, sipping beer, sweating in the heat, talking, laughing, quarreling, strolling. It would get even more unbearably crowded near true dark, right before the spectacular fireworks displays over the

Mississippi that ended the fair every night. Daiyu loved the great constellations of color that reflected in the silver of the Arch and painted moving patterns on the broad and restless river.

She was trying to decide if she was hungry enough to buy herself dinner when a soft voice from the shadows asked, "Got a dollar to spare, miss?"

Daiyu turned to see an old man standing a few feet away, clearly not wanting to get close enough to alarm her. He was white skinned but smudged with dirt, bald but bearded, wearing way too many clothes on such a hot day. She could catch the odor of urine even though he kept his distance.

"I do," she said. Her father encouraged her to give away five dollars to some charitable cause or homeless person every week, and she usually kept one-dollar bills in her pockets, ready to hand out. But she'd dispensed her last single Friday morning, so she handed him one of Isabel's fives. "There's a lot of good food at the fair, isn't there?"

A smile magically transformed his face. "There is," he agreed. "I want one of those hot dogs."

She laughed. "That sounds pretty good. Maybe I'll get one too."

"Thank you, miss. God bless you."

As soon as he left, she checked her wallet and realized with dismay that she didn't have any money except the bills Isabel had given her. Fair food could be pricey—she might easily spend ten dollars on a burger and a soda—and would the old woman really sell her the black jade ring for fifteen dollars? Maybe she should buy the ring before making any other purchases.

She tried to tell herself that she didn't want the ring, and if someone else had already bought it, she didn't care. She tried to make herself stop to buy a hamburger before looking for the old woman's booth, but the line was long and she couldn't keep her feet still. Before she knew it, she was drifting through the fair again, trying to be courteous as she pushed her way past strangers, stepped around baby carriages, and hurried past all the other booths that lined the fairgrounds.

There. Sandwiched between a lemonade stand and a funnel-cake vendor. There was the jewelry booth, hardly more than a battered table and a tattered yellow awning. The tiny old woman stood motionless behind the counter, dressed all in black even on this hot evening. She was staring at Daiyu as if she had not taken her eyes off her since Daiyu left the grounds the previous afternoon.

For a moment, Daiyu felt peculiar again. For a moment, she had the sense that this wrinkled old lady was more dangerous to her than the polite beggar would ever have been. Her hands curled into fists. She remembered the cool, silky weight of the ring against her finger. She stepped over to the booth.

"You came back," the old lady greeted her.

"I guess I did," Daiyu said. "Do you still have the ring?"

"Fifteen dollars," the vendor said.

The red silk box was already in the woman's hand.

As if she had been standing there since the fair opened this morning, waiting for Daiyu to return.

Wordlessly, Daiyu handed over the twenty-dollar bill that Isabel had given her. She waited until the old woman had given back her change before she slipped the ring on her finger. As she remembered, it was a perfect fit, heavy on her hand, but in a pleasing fashion, calling her attention to it, making her pause to admire it. She twisted it slowly in one complete circle to study the detail of the carving, the dragon's precisely rendered head, its sleek scales, its stylized feet.

"I do love this," she said under her breath. "I don't know why."

"It was meant for you," the old woman said.

Daiyu laughed softly. "That's what it feels like. Well. Thank you. Now I'm going to get myself something to eat and then go home before it gets any more crowded here."

"You could do me a favor," the old woman said suddenly.

Daiyu blinked at her. How odd. "What?" she asked warily.

The woman pointed to a tent about twenty yards away if Daiyu walked straight under the great silver wicket of the Arch. "A woman in that booth was interested in one of my necklaces. I told her she could wear it tonight and see if she wanted it. I don't like to leave my table. Just take it to her—that's all you have to do."

"I suppose I could do that," Daiyu said.

"I'd be very grateful," the old woman said.

She held up a long silver chain hung with a pendant that looked as fiery as an opal but with a pinker cast. "That's pretty," Daiyu said, cupping her hand to take hold of the stone. Oh, what was wrong with her? The instant it rested against her skin, she wanted this piece, too. It felt lighter than the black jade, as if it was porous or constructed of molecules of some lower specific density, and as if those molecules were dancing in her palm. "What kind of stone is this?" she asked.

The old woman waggled her head from side to side. "Some funny name. I don't remember."

"How much is it?"

The old woman smiled. "It might not be for sale," she said. "Ask me again if my friend decides not to buy it."

"Maybe I will," Daiyu said, though she couldn't imagine that this bauble would go for the ten dollars she had left. But Isabel would probably give her a loan, if Daiyu helped her register voters for a couple of hours. She started to add, *Maybe I'll see you later,* but just then there was a shrill whizzing sound and then a loud boom that reverberated off the downtown skyscrapers. Daiyu shaded her face with her hands.

"Fireworks already? It's not even seven o'clock."

The old woman shrugged. "Practice rounds. You go see my friend. Give her the necklace."

Daiyu waved in lieu of farewell. She had taken three steps away when she heard the woman add, "You be careful, now." Daiyu turned back in surprise, but the old vendor was crouched under the table, digging through boxes of merchandise. Either Daiyu had imagined the voice, or she'd heard someone else speaking. She shrugged and, holding the pink stone covetously in her hand, she passed under the Arch.

The world fell apart.

# THREE

THE GROUND SURGED and shattered under Daiyu's feet. The twilight sky bloomed to nuclear brightness, then went utterly dark. Blind, she cried out and stumbled to her knees, cutting her palms on a stony surface. She whimpered, but the sound was lost under the ongoing percussion of urgent explosives.

Then suddenly her vision cleared and the booming noise stopped, and Daiyu lifted her head. Had that been an earthquake? Had a barge on the river blown up when its fuel tank caught fire? Where were the sirens? Where were the frantic onlookers? Why was no one screaming?

Instead, all she heard was the comfortable, indistinguishable mutter of a cheerful crowd—a few giggles, a high-pitched squeal, the sound of another firecracker detonating, and some appreciative cheers. Someone tripped over her and hastily apologized. A woman's voice asked, "Is she all right?" and a man's voice answered, "Drunk, I suppose."

Daiyu pushed herself to her feet and gazed around.

For a moment, she thought she was still at Fair Saint Louis. Here was a brightly colored mob of people gathered on a summer evening on a stretch of land overlooking a river. But . . . but . . . the river was so small, not even half the width of the Mississippi. There were no booths selling sandwiches and soda; there was no smell of roasting meat and fried dough. And the people! Everyone was oddly dressed—not in shorts and halter tops, but in brightly colored shirts over formal black skirts and trousers.

Everyone was Chinese.

Daiyu looked around slowly, not believing her eyes. But everyone *was* Chinese.

She pivoted swiftly to glance behind her and clapped a hand to her mouth to silence the scream. *The Arch was gone!* In its place was a towering pagoda-shaped gate made of some sleek material that looked like red lacquer. It was maybe half the height of the Arch, but its gorgeous color made it equally impressive. More brightly dressed Chinese men and women stood near it, laughing and talking.

A short report in the air made her gasp, but the whipcrack of sound turned out to be another firecracker bursting over the diminished river. The mob of people murmured and applauded as streaks of green and blue and red rained down.

"What's happened to me, what's happened to me," Daiyu whispered, turning in a slow circle to take in the rest of her surroundings. The familiar tall buildings of downtown St.

Louis—gone—replaced by a crowded, crazy-quilt collection of buildings in stone and wood and steel. The well-tended lawns of the Arch grounds—gone. In their place was a swath of green grass bordered by a broad expanse of gravelly stones laid out in interlocking patterns of light and dark. *Yin and yang,* Daiyu thought wildly. *I'm in China.* Somehow she had been flung across thousands of miles to the country of her birth— but that was ridiculous—that couldn't happen—she must have fallen, she must have hit her head, perhaps she was still dreaming, no part of this day had actually occurred—

She shook her head but could not shake herself awake. Unaccustomed panic began building inside her chest, crowding the air out of her lungs. She started pushing her way through the throngs, not sure what to do, where to go, but feeling the need for motion. "This is crazy, this can't be happening—"

With each phrase, her voice got a little louder. In a minute she would be shrieking and running. Where was she? What cataclysm had overtaken her? "Someone help me," she panted, pushing past staring girls and curious couples, not pausing long enough to allow anyone to offer comfort or reassurance. "Someone—anyone—I don't know what's going on—"

Behind her, from the direction of the river, came a single resounding boom, so loud that Daiyu froze and let out a little cry. It was followed by such a flurry of explosions that everything else was drowned out. She clapped her palms over her eyes and screamed as loud as she could.

A hand slapped itself around her right wrist and pulled it

away from her face. She was so startled, she stopped scream-ing and opened her eyes. She was staring at a tall young man, who leaned close enough to yell into her ear over the sound of fireworks.

"I know you're terrified," he called. "But everything will be all right. I'll take you home."

And just like that, Daiyu stopped being afraid.

For a long moment, Daiyu simply stood there, trying to recover her habitual composure. She stared up at the young man. He was thin, Caucasian, and serious; his brown eyes were framed by thick lashes. His hair was dark and curly, his mouth gener-ous, and he wore a single gold stud in each ear. She knew she had never seen him before, and yet he looked familiar to her, as if someone had told her about him and she had been waiting all this time to meet him.

"Who are you?" she whispered. Her throat felt too raw for normal speaking. "What's happening to me?"

"I'm Kalen," he said. "And you've stepped through one of the gateways into another world."

Her breath caught, and for a minute she felt panic make an-other hard charge against her ribs. Another world? *One* of the gateways? "I don't understand," she said, still in that whisper-ing voice. He leaned close enough to hear it over the noise of the crowd and the fireworks.

"It's complicated," he said. "This isn't the place to explain. Are you hurt? Can you walk?"

"I fell," she said. He still gripped her right arm, but she held up her left hand to show him the scrapes.

"Ouch," he said. He released her wrist to pull items from a nondescript bag he carried over his shoulder. In a moment he was dampening a scrap of cloth with the contents of what appeared to be a water bottle.

"There," he said, gently daubing at her palm. The water was soothing to her raw skin and his voice was soothing to her jangled nerves. "Does that feel better?"

Only marginally, but the act of compassion lifted her spirits just a little. "Yes, thank you," she said.

He dropped his rudimentary first-aid kit into his bag, took hold of her arm again, and urged her forward. They stepped toward the green area, away from the river, away from whatever celebration was going on around the red gate. "I'm sorry I wasn't there when you arrived," he said. "We only just realized you'd be coming tonight."

All her goodwill vanished and she stopped dead. "You were expecting me?"

He glanced down at her. "Aurora and Ombri have been looking for someone like you for a long time," he said.

She jerked her hand free. "Who are Aurora and Ombri? Who are *you*? What's *happening*?"

"Daiyu—"

"And how do you know my *name*?"

"People have crossed from this time and place to your world, looking for someone like you to make the journey here."

She shook her head and put her hands to her face again. "I still don't understand."

"No," he said, surprising her, "I don't really understand it either. Aurora and Ombri can explain it better than I can. Let me take you to the house and get you something to eat. I promise you, everything will be all right."

For a moment she hesitated. If she truly was in a different world—however impossible that seemed to be—how would she know whom to trust, what to believe? If she followed this stranger to some isolated location, would she suddenly be in mortal danger?

"I promise no one will hurt you," he said, as if he could read her mind. "Truly, it will be better if I can get you to the house."

She had no reason to trust him. And yet she couldn't bring herself to summon fear. He watched her gravely, and something in his expression struck her as simply kind. Again she experienced the sense that she knew him already, that he had watched over her at some point when she was injured or in danger. Daiyu was used to meeting strangers; her father brought them home all the time. But she had never before met a stranger who had made her feel this instant sense of connection. She put her hand out again, and he took it with great care.

"All right," she said. "Let's go."

He led her across the greensward and onto one of the streets cluttered with a mishmash of buildings. Traffic was heavy, but it consisted mostly of people on foot or riding contraptions that looked like bicycles crossed with carts. There seemed to be thousands of people crowded into the streets and on the sidewalks. By the time Kalen had turned a couple of corners, Daiyu was hopelessly lost; she couldn't even orient herself by the placement of the river. She hoped they didn't have to walk far. She was feeling pretty worn.

A clattering sound caught her attention, and she looked up to see a long, narrow trolley heading their way, slowing down as Kalen raised a hand to signal it. She couldn't tell what powered it—not horses, at any rate, and she couldn't smell gasoline fumes—but she didn't greatly care. She climbed on behind Kalen and sank gratefully onto a hard wooden bench between Kalen and an older woman.

"It's not that far," he told her in an encouraging voice.

She nodded wearily and looked around. Her fellow passengers were almost all Chinese, most of them more shabbily dressed than those who had been at the red gate. Of the other thirty or forty people crammed onto the trolley, Daiyu saw only five besides Kalen who were Caucasian and two who were black. One of the white women was middle-aged, dispirited, and dressed in layers of ill-fitting clothing. If she'd been back in St. Louis, Daiyu would not have been surprised if this woman had come up to her asking for a handout.

If she'd been back in St. Louis. . . .

Where *was* she?

The trolley made a cheerful racket but fairly slow progress

as it wound its way through a maze of streets, stopping every few blocks to pick up or drop off passengers. As it moved into an increasingly residential district, the makeup of the ridership changed, and soon almost all the passengers were white. It was quickly clear that this particular neighborhood was not for the affluent. Most of the buildings were small and squat, built out of a dull gray stone or an even drearier brown material. Here and there, filling in gaps between sturdier structures, Daiyu spotted what looked like tents—heavy cloth strung over a variety of makeshift supports.

"People live there?" she asked Kalen.

He nodded. "Most of the *cangbai* laborers make their homes in this district."

"The what?"

"*Cangbai.* Like me. Pale." He gestured in an indeterminate direction. "Across the river is where most of the Han live."

"Han?"

"Like you," he said.

Chinese, she thought. What kind of world had she stumbled into?

He smiled as if a thought had occurred to him. "Well, the *poor* Han live across the Zhongbu River. The rich ones live in big houses on this side of the river."

She offered no answer, and they made the rest of the journey in silence. They finally got off at a tumbledown street corner and walked three blocks to a one-story building of tired white stone. The two windows that she could see were open to allow in the sultry air. It was pretty clear there wasn't going to be air-conditioning inside.

There wasn't—and not much else, either. Daiyu stood just inside the doorway and took a long, comprehensive look. There was one main room that seemed to serve as kitchen and common area. Three doors, all closed, probably led off to other rooms, and she hoped one was a bathroom. The furnishings seemed to consist mainly of rag rugs over a scarred wood floor, a couple of benches close to a sturdy table, and shelving units holding an unclassifiable assortment of objects. If there had ever been any paint on the interior of the stone walls, it had long since peeled off. Her father would be absolutely in his element trying to rehab this place.

The thought of her father gave her a sharp stab of pain, and she turned rather fiercely on her new acquaintance.

"My parents—they'll be so worried about me," she said. "I don't know why I was brought here, but I don't want to *be* here. How can you just take people away from their homes? What do you *want* with me?"

"Your parents will have no reason to fear for you," said a deep, rich voice, and Daiyu spun around to see a black man stepping in through the door behind them. He was shorter than Kalen and at least fifty years older, with closely cropped hair that had turned entirely gray. He was dressed in black pants and a sleeveless black shirt that showed off powerful arms. "You will be returned to them unharmed, only seconds from when you saw them last. Your iteration does not vibrate in synchronicity with this one. You exist here, as it were, outside of time."

Daiyu pressed the heels of her hands to her eyes. "What?" she said faintly.

"This is Ombri," Kalen said helpfully. "He can explain everything."

Daiyu dropped her hands to glare at Ombri. "Are you the one who brought me here?" she demanded.

"I would more truly say I invited you here and you accepted," Ombri replied.

"There was no invitation! There was no acceptance! How can you say that?"

He pointed to her hand. "You wear the dragon ring. Only someone who is willing to sojourn between iterations can wear the ring on her finger."

"I'm *not* willing to—to sojourn between worlds!" she said. She tugged the ring off and flung it across the room. "There. It's gone. Now, take me home."

Kalen loosed an exclamation of dismay, looking between Daiyu and Ombri as he spoke in some rapid, unintelligible language. Ombri kept his dark eyes on Daiyu as he responded, his voice much calmer than Kalen's, though equally impossible to understand.

Daiyu threw her hands in the air. "I have no idea what you're saying. I don't care. Just take me home."

Kalen turned to her with a pleading look and spoke even more urgently. Again, she couldn't make out a word. Now Daiyu felt another spike of fear. It hadn't even occurred to her to wonder how she was able to understand these strange people in this utterly strange place. If she had somehow lost the ability to communicate with them—

Kalen dove across the room to search the pile of shoes and papers where the dragon ring had landed. As soon as he found it, he hurried back to Daiyu, offering the black jade circlet to her with a single pleading word.

"I don't want it," she said.

Kalen slipped the ring on his finger and then spoke into it as if it held a concealed microphone. Then he held it up to his ear and his expression of exaggerated bewilderment cleared up. "Oh!" he exclaimed, followed by a few more happy words.

The ring appeared to be a translator. Daiyu could certainly use some translating right about now. She slipped it back onto her finger, where she was annoyed to find it made her hand feel just right.

"I'm not wearing this to tell you that I accept your invitation to travel to your world," she said icily. "But if it lets me have a conversation with you—"

"Yes, that is exactly what it does," Ombri said, and Daiyu felt a rush of relief when she was able to understand him again. "We also have a pair of black jade earrings, if you would be more comfortable wearing them."

"I don't want to wear your jewelry!" she exclaimed. "I just want to understand what's happening, or I would take the ring off right now!"

"For now, we will agree that the ring does not constitute any kind of offer or acceptance, and let it serve only its more practical purpose of interpreting speech," Ombri said. "As long as you wear it, you will be able to understand any of the dialects in our iteration, and your speech will be comprehensible to any individual you encounter."

"Why do you keep saying that?" she demanded. "What's an iteration?"

Ombri gave her a sober smile. "That, Daiyu, is the very essence of existence. Let me tell you our story."

FOUR

"ONCE, MILLENNIA AGO, the world was formed, and it was perfect," Ombri said in his resonant voice. He and Daiyu had seated themselves across from each other at the table, while Kalen made tea in the tiny kitchen.

"Let us not concern ourselves with the myriad gods who had a hand in its creation," Ombri went on. "But there were factions among the gods—those who believed they could have created a better model—and they produced their own worlds. And more factions arose, and more, and each designed their own version, always taking as their template the original pattern. Eventually, the gods reached a truce and no more worlds were called into being, but by then there were at least a dozen copies, all variants of the original model. We call them iterations. Some were designed by spiteful gods, some by playful gods, some by sober gods, and no two are exactly alike, although all of them bear a great resemblance to each other, as if they were siblings born to the same two parents."

Daiyu stared at Ombri. It was too bizarre to believe. "Is my world the original template?"

He smiled. "Hardly. It was constructed by one of the gods who has a—shall we say—streak of whimsicality. Your iteration is one of the most unstable of them all. Though I have to admit it is one of the most intriguing as well."

Daiyu folded her hands and did not answer.

"In the normal course of events," Ombri continued, "people do not travel between worlds. There are a few of us—servants of the gods—who move freely between iterations, carrying messages or watching over the native peoples. Although we monitor and report on the evolution of each iteration, we do not interfere with the way history unfolds in any of these worlds. Most of the time."

Kalen brought over a tray holding a teapot, three cups, and a pile of what looked like scones. Daiyu realized that she was starving. Kalen sat on the bench beside Ombri, and they all took a moment to serve themselves. The sconelike bread was delicious. The hot tea was sweeter and more flavorful than the tea back home, but it was aromatic and soothing, and Daiyu took a couple of cautious sips before she said, "Go on."

"It seems that one or two of the gods chose unwisely when they selected their servants," said Ombri. "And these individuals—with the ability to slip between dimensions, as it were—have upon occasion moved from iteration to iteration and created great havoc. It has fallen to the rest of us to chase them down and return them to our original world. Most of them are now safely contained, but one or two remain unfettered." Ombri blew on his tea to cool it, and then took a swallow. "One of them resides in this world. His name is Chenglei. We want to send him home."

"We?" Daiyu said.

"Aurora and I. You will meet Aurora soon."

Daiyu shook her head and then she laughed. "Everything you say sounds utterly ridiculous."

Kalen looked up from his cup and asked diffidently, "I know it's all very hard to accept, but how else do you explain what's happened to you?"

She put a finger to her temple. "Concussion. Coma. At the very least, a bad dream. I figure I'll wake up tomorrow and I won't be in Oz any longer."

"Oz?" Kalen said in a puzzled voice.

"It's an imaginary place where someone went after she suffered brain trauma," Daiyu said.

"If you believe that none of this is real, then you may as well accept everything I'm telling you as absolute truth," Ombri said mildly. "It would at least be true within the logic of your dream construct."

Daiyu took a deep breath. "Even if it *is* true," she said, in a voice of exaggerated politeness, "what does it have to do with me?"

Ombri took another sip. "We cannot capture Chenglei without your help."

She laughed in disbelief. "You're a servant of the *gods?* You can move between *parallel dimensions* anytime you choose? And you need *my* help? I'm sorry, but that doesn't make sense."

"Chenglei is much too wily to allow Aurora or me to get anywhere near him," Ombri said, unruffled by her scorn. "He surrounds himself with the affluent Han of this iteration, and so we need someone who looks like they do to approach him on our behalf."

"I saw plenty of Chinese people on the trolley tonight," Daiyu said. "Why don't you recruit one of them?"

"Most of the people of this world are practically transparent to Chenglei—and to Aurora and to me," Ombri said. "We have little difficulty reading their thoughts and emotions. If we tried to recruit some of the locals, Chenglei would almost certainly be able to read their intentions when they drew near to him."

"But he won't be able to read *my* mind?" Daiyu asked skeptically.

Ombri smiled at her over his teacup. "Well," he said, "*I* can't. People from your world tend to be more opaque, even to the servants of the gods."

"If he can't read my mind when he meets me, won't that make him suspicious?" Daiyu said. She could hardly believe she was buying into this fantasy enough to ask the question. "Won't he guess I'm from another world?"

"No, for now and then even Aurora and I encounter natives whom we cannot scan. Chenglei will believe you are merely more complex than most of the individuals he has met so far. He may even be drawn to you for that reason—because he will see you as a puzzle, or possibly a challenge."

Daiyu remembered the vendor from Fair Saint Louis, the one who had sent her on this journey to begin with. "Is that why that strange old woman extended the invitation to me? Because she couldn't read my mind?"

"That was an important consideration," Ombri acknowledged. "But that 'strange old woman' is another servant to the gods, and she has a knack for sensing who might be open to making such a crossing. You have already journeyed a long distance in your short life, from China to the United States."

"I was a baby!"

He shrugged. "There is a part of your soul, no matter how deeply buried, that responds to the call for more adventure. That is what our friend saw in you when she offered the ring."

"And then, how did I get here? One minute I was standing under the Arch—"

"You were at a gateway," Ombri interrupted.

"What? You mean the Gateway to the West? But—"

"The Arch you know is more than a symbol of man's exploration of the western reaches of your continent," Ombri said. "It is a magical portal to worlds beyond worlds. Every iteration constructed by every god contains a doorway in that very same spot."

"The red gate," Daiyu whispered. "I saw it when I first looked around."

"Exactly. In another world it is a small wooden framework that leads between two simple gardens. In another, it is a massive gate built of towering stone. In every case, for wayfarers who know how to traverse it, it leads to other worlds."

"That doesn't make sense," Daiyu objected. "I've walked under the Arch a hundred times—"

"You have to be carrying the talisman that will bring you to the world you want to visit," Ombri said.

Suddenly, Daiyu remembered the necklace that the old woman had asked her to deliver to "her friend" at the fair. "The pink stone . . ." she said, and glanced around as if looking for it. "I must have dropped it when I came through." She opened her eyes wide. "Does that mean someone else might find it? And go through the gate and end up in my world?"

Ombri shook his head. "That particular talisman can only bring someone to this specific iteration, and only if that person walks through a gateway. In this world, no matter who picks it up, it is harmless—just a pretty bauble. Though an expensive one."

"And how do I get back to my own world? Is there a talisman for that?"

Ombri nodded. "Normally we would give you a small piece of rose quartz, a stone that is only found on your world, and send you through the gateway. You would arrive back on Earth in the place where you left, with no memory of your experience here—"

Daiyu blinked at him. "Wait. You mean I won't remember any of this?"

Ombri waved a hand. His dark fingers were long and elegant. "One of the peculiar attributes of planet Earth is that it erases your memory of previous iterations. Every sojourner who goes there arrives with his mind blank of time spent anywhere else. Even the servants of the gods have trouble crossing to your iteration. We adjust, but the effort is immense. It is unlikely that you will remember anything more of your time here than an image or two, dreamlike indeed."

"That's not going to bother me," Daiyu assured him. "So you'll give me a piece of rose quartz and send me through the gate—"

"That is what we would normally do," Ombri corrected. "But because we think it is possible you might be in danger when you confront Chenglei, we will craft a powerful talisman that will instantly transport you back to your world, no matter where you are in this one. You will not need to go through the gateway to activate it."

"That sounds good," Daiyu said, holding her hand out. "Let's have it."

"It's not ready yet. Aurora must shape it to the unique make-up of your particular body. If you would entrust me with a few strands of your hair—"

Daiyu closed her eyes for a second. Now he was asking for DNA. It was getting more and more surreal. But . . . "Anything to be able to go home again," she said, opening her eyes and quickly yanking out a couple of hairs. Ombri took them carefully and folded them into a piece of paper that he stowed in a pocket of his black pants. Daiyu said, "So where is this Aurora?"

"She's working," Kalen answered.

"If you're really who you say you are, it seems odd that any of you would need a job," Daiyu said.

Ombri gave her that serious smile. "We don't need money," he said. "We need entrée into the society that governs this particular city in this particular world. Aurora works for a childless woman who has great personal ambition. This will serve us well now that you have arrived."

Daiyu leaned her elbows on the table. "Okay. I guess it's time to talk about why exactly you brought me here. What you want me to do."

"They want to send Chenglei back to where he belongs," Kalen said.

"I heard that part already. How can I do anything about it?"

"First let me tell you a little about Shenglang, the city where you now reside," Ombri said. He waved vaguely toward the windows, through which only darkness was now visible. But the coming of true night had cooled off the air a little, and Daiyu felt a welcome breeze tiptoe in. "Like your own St. Louis, Shenglang is located in the middle of a large continent. It is arguably the most important city in the nation. Chenglei has managed to get himself elected prime minister of Shenglang, and so he might be considered one of the most powerful men on the planet. He has used that power unwisely."

"Some people like him," Kalen said. "Mostly people with money."

Ombri nodded. "He has done a great deal to enrich the highest social class of the city and a great deal to destroy the precarious well-being of the poor," Ombri said. "So far his scope has been fairly limited and local, but he will soon be signing pacts with neighbor nations on Jia that will extend his most onerous policies. There will be a great deal of suffering, and those who will suffer most are those who can least afford to sustain another loss."

He could not have said anything more calculated to catch Daiyu's interest. Maybe he knew that; maybe he had studied her life and her family before he found a way to get that dragon ring onto her finger. Oddly enough, that made her begin to distrust him, an emotion that resided uneasily beside her ongoing disbelief. "But what can *I* do to stop him?" she said.

"You merely need to place a bracelet on his wrist," Ombri said.

Daiyu stared at him. It was the last thing she had expected him to say. "Couldn't anybody do that?" she said.

"Nobody can get close to him," Kalen muttered.

"A select few are admitted into his presence," Ombri explained. "None of them are *cangbai*, like Kalen, or *heiren*, like me."

Heiren, Daiyu thought. *Must mean black.*

Ombri was still talking. "Chenglei only associates with Han—and Han of a certain social circle. If we can insinuate you into that circle, you will inevitably be introduced to him. You will place the bracelet on his wrist, and he will be flung back to the original template of the universe."

"That doesn't sound so hard," Daiyu said. "So why do you think I might be in danger?"

"If Chenglei discovers who you are, he will be— displeased."

Daiyu widened her eyes and raised her eyebrows, but she didn't really want a description of what Chenglei might do to her to express his displeasure. She guessed punishment and torture were pretty much the same from world to world.

"That is why we want you to have the talisman," Ombri continued. "So that if you ever feel threatened, you can instantly transport yourself to home and safety. We would then look for some other sojourner who is young and Chinese and potentially able to introduce herself to Chenglei."

"Is he Chinese?" she asked.

"Part Chinese, part *cangbai*," Ombri said. "Here on Jia, he pretends to be full-blooded Han."

"When I came through the gate," Daiyu said slowly, "everyone I saw was Han."

Ombri nodded. "In this iteration, it is the Han who colonized the Western hemisphere, not the nations you know as Europe. The races are not absolutely identical from world to world, but you will fit in with the Han. You will be accepted. The language they speak will deviate a bit from what you understand as Chinese—"

"I don't speak Chinese," Daiyu said, putting up her fingers to rub her temples. Her head was beginning to swim; it was too much information to take in all at once. "I don't think I can hear one more detail," she said. "Is there someplace I can lie down? I'm so tired."

"Of course. It was discourteous of me to talk so long," Ombri said, rising to his feet. He gestured at Kalen, who jumped up. "It is difficult for any ordinary human being to make the transition between worlds—it takes a great physical toll, and exhaustion is commonplace. We have prepared a room against your arrival. Sleep as long as you like."

She glanced around again, embarrassed to ask about a bathroom in front of two men. "Is there—a place to clean up first?"

"Of course. Kalen, please acquaint her with the amenities."

The small room that Kalen showed her to looked enough like the facilities Daiyu was used to that he didn't have to explain the faucets or the rather strange toilet, which was more like an open-bottomed throne contained behind a low enamel wall. It was quickly clear that there was no such thing as a toothbrush, but Kalen demonstrated how she should use her finger and some gritty paste to scrub her teeth, and the soap was completely familiar.

"Aurora left you some clothes," Kalen said a little awkwardly as he stepped out of the small room into the hallway. "She was just guessing what might fit you, but—Should I bring them in?"

"Is there something for me to sleep in?" Daiyu asked.

"A nightshirt. Let me get it."

He disappeared and returned moments later with a voluminous blue shirt made of some soft, brushed material. "It's kind of big," he said with a grin, holding it up by the shoulders.

She smiled as she took it from his hands. "I'll probably be all tangled up in it by morning. Thank you, though."

He lingered in the doorway as if he wanted to say something else. She raised her eyebrows in inquiry. "I just—I don't want you to be afraid," he said. "Here in such a strange place. Is there something I can do to make you feel better?"

Bring me that talisman that will send me straight home, she thought. "I don't think so."

He pointed toward the main room. "I'll be sleeping right out there. If you wake up in the middle of the night and you need something—or you hear a sound that frightens you—come get me. Or just call my name. I'll hear you. I'll be there in a second."

His sweet earnestness made her smile again. "I'll keep that in mind," she said. "Good night."

Twenty minutes later, she was clean, wrapped in the oversized shirt, and stretched out on a thick mattress on the floor of a tiny room. The mat was surprisingly comfortable, especially since it was augmented with piles of pillows. The window was open, and some of the scents coming through were familiar and reassuring, while others were utterly strange.

Daiyu snuggled her head on one of the pillows and thought, *I will wake up in the morning and I will be in my own bed. And I will call my father and say, "Daddy, I have just had the strangest dream." Everything will be fine in the morning. I'll be home.*

 FIVE

THE SMELL OF cooking tickled her nose, and Daiyu turned over in bed, trying to figure out what her father was making for breakfast. Something flavorful, maybe sausages. She was starving.

She opened her eyes and immediately lost her appetite.

She was on the low mattress in the small room in the white stone building where she had arrived the previous night. If she was still dreaming, it was the longest and most detailed dream she had ever had.

Clothes had been laid out for her across a stool—a red top and wide-legged black pants, as well as a pair of black cloth ballet flats that didn't look all that different from her Skechers. She scooped them up and scooted into the bathroom before anyone could see her. Once she had dressed and combed out her hair, she felt a little more prepared to face the day. There didn't seem to be a proper mirror in this place, but a shiny chrome square hanging on the bathroom wall gave her a wavering reflection.

Her chin-length black hair seemed lustrous as always, her dark eyes thoughtful and measuring. Her face was deceptively serene, belying her inner disquiet.

She took a deep breath. If she could make her interior match her exterior, she might yet sail through this adventure without a total meltdown.

She stepped out into the main room of the house. "What's for breakfast?" she asked.

Kalen was the only other person home, and he turned from the kitchen to give her a hopeful smile. "How did you sleep? How are you feeling?"

"I slept wonderfully and I feel pretty good," Daiyu said, settling at the table. "But I'm still . . . well, it's all pretty weird, you know."

"I know," he said. "Or, at least, I guess. It must be even stranger for you than it was for me." He brought over a casserole pan holding what looked like potatoes and eggs and crumbled bits of meat. "Are you hungry?"

"*Starving*," she said. "Do I eat with my fingers or what?"

He laughed and fetched flat wooden boards that served as plates and large spoons that appeared to be the only eating utensils. Juice completed the meal—definitely not orange juice, but something pulpy and sweet, and Daiyu gulped it down—and for a few moments they ate in companionable silence.

Then Daiyu remembered what he'd just said. "What do you mean about things being strange for you, too?" she asked. "Aren't you one of them? A servant to the gods and all that?"

He laughed. "Me? Hardly. I'm just a *cangbai* workingman."

She gestured around the room. "So this is your world? Jia?" When he nodded, she said, "How did you meet up with Ombri and his friend?"

"Ombri and I were both stonepickers on the river, and we talked now and then while we were working. One day he said he and his wife wanted to buy a house, but they'd have to rent out a room to be able to afford it. Did I want to be a boarder? I was living in a tent at the time, and winter was coming, so I didn't even think about it. I just said yes."

Daiyu filed away the question about what a stonepicker was. "How did you know they wouldn't steal your stuff?"

He shrugged. "I don't have any stuff. I wasn't risking much."

Daiyu propped her chin on her hand and looked him over. She had originally thought he just had a slim build, but now that she paid more attention, she could see that his was the slenderness of lifelong hunger. His face was bony, his wrists thin; his eyes were kind because they had looked upon a lot of misery and empathized with pain.

"What's your story?" she said presently. "Where's your family?"

He shrugged again. "My father was never around. My mother died when I was little," he said. "I've been on my own most of my life." He grinned. "Meeting Ombri and Aurora is about the most exciting thing that's ever happened to me."

"Well, it's certainly been exciting for me so far too," Daiyu said dryly. She hesitated and then said, "I have to admit, even after this morning, when I woke up and I was still here, I'm having a hard time believing that anything Ombri said was true."

"This is where I've lived my whole life, so I can't really judge," Kalen said. "But you seem to think you're somewhere that you didn't expect to be. So you tell me. Is this a different world?"

"Going by what I saw last night, yes," she said. "But I just don't know how that could be possible." She gave him a straight look. "What did they tell you to make you believe that they were from another universe?"

"To tell you the truth," he said, "at first I *didn't* believe them. But I didn't care. They were generous and they were thoughtful and they made sure I had enough to eat. If they wanted to pretend they were sent here by the gods, it didn't matter to me."

"What changed your mind?"

He tapped his flat wooden plate with the bowl of his spoon. "Little things. Ombri can see in the dark. Aurora knows when the weather is going to change. And—like he told you last night—they're both able to read people as if they can see the thoughts in their heads. It's like nothing in this world is mysterious to them. I find that pretty convincing."

"So what did they tell you about why they came here?"

"Pretty much what Ombri told you last night. That they wanted to find a way to send Chenglei back to his own iteration."

She toyed with her spoon. "And did that make you—curious? Uneasy? Did you wonder why *they* should have the right to decide who gets to live here and who has to go home?"

Kalen just looked at her, his expression startled. "Not really," he said at last. "I've come to trust them, so I believe they have good reasons for what they want to do."

Daiyu nodded and let it drop, though her own uneasiness remained. She glanced around. "So where is Ombri now? And Aurora?"

"I don't know, but I think they'll both be back by dinner tonight." He gave her a tentative smile. "So what would you like to do today? If you're feeling rested enough to leave the house—"

Rested and deeply curious. "I am," she said. "Why don't you show me your world?"

By daylight, Kalen's neighborhood didn't look any more impressive than it had by twilight. Daiyu followed him to a rundown intersection, where they hailed another of those clattering trolleys. This one held riders who were mostly whites and blacks—*cangbai* and *heiren*—and was even more crowded than the one the night before. When the trolley made a ninety-degree turn, Daiyu realized that they were on a broad avenue that was parallel to the river. If this had been the Mississippi, they would be heading north away from Soulard, a district that had been built a century ago to house the working poor. . . .

"Hey," she said, "I think you live really close to where *I* live back on Earth." Her voice trailed off. "That is so *weird*."

"Ombri said there would be a lot of points in common between our worlds."

"Yeah, but I didn't think that I'd be staying in practically the same neighborhood where I live back home."

Kalen smiled down at her. "Does that make you feel a little better?" he asked. "Like you're where you're supposed to be?"

She couldn't help a slight laugh. "Kalen," she said, "nothing will make me feel like this is where I belong."

Once Daiyu was oriented to the river, though, she did start to develop a better sense of how Shenglang was laid out, which made her more cheerful. They disembarked from the trolley within sight of the red gate and slowly strolled toward the river, their shoes crunching over the yin-and-yang pattern of the decorative stone mosaic. The riverfront was crowded with workers hauling cargo to and from small boats and idle onlookers watching the water slip by. A steady stream of pedestrians crossed a series of narrow bridges that led from the eastern side of the river, where the land appeared to be dense with houses, vehicles, and commercial buildings. Daiyu thought it might be even more populous than the city on this side of the river.

She automatically looked north, where she would have expected the symmetrical scallops of Eads Bridge to connect Missouri and Illinois. Instead there was a high, thick structure spanning the river that looked like a combination dam and sluice. Three monstrous gates had been lifted from the central portion of the bridge so that water streamed unimpeded past the remaining supports, carrying the occasional boat on its surface. Daiyu guessed that when the gates were lowered, the river slowly filled up behind the dam. She couldn't imagine why.

She looked up at Kalen. "Okay. This is where you explain everything you've said about working on the river."

He guided her toward a stone bench that overlooked the water. She settled beside him and was grateful for the erratic breeze that wandered off the river. It wasn't even noon yet, and already the day was heating up.

"The Zhongbu River washes down from mountain ranges way up north," he said. "It brings all sorts of minerals and stones with it—particularly *qiji* gems."

"What gems?"

"*Qiji*," he repeated. It sounded like he was saying *scheet-schee*. He went on, "The word means 'miracle.' Whenever they dam the river, stonepickers—like me—wade out into the muck and pick up every stone we think might be a *qiji*—"

"You mean you can't tell?" Daiyu interrupted.

He shook his head. "In their raw state they look like any common river rock. So we bag up as many as we can, and we take them to the vendors to be tested, and they pay us for the ones we find."

"How many *qiji* gems do you find on an average day?" she asked.

"Maybe two. A good day would be five."

She appraised him. "And I'm guessing two stones don't pay all that well."

"Enough to live on," he said.

"How often do they dam the river?"

"Usually two or three times a week." He pointed at a rickety tower set about ten yards back from the river. It looked like a lighthouse made of scaffolding, but at the very top, instead of a light, Daiyu could see a huge bronze bell. She glanced across the river to see its twin on the eastern bank. Kalen said, "They ring the big bells the night before so all the stonepickers know to come work the next morning."

"And how long does the dam hold? Because I'd think that the water would start pouring over pretty fast."

"Generally you get about half a day. But when it's time to get out, they ring the small bells—you probably can't see them from here. The whole time you're working, you're listening for that sound, because they wait till the last possible moment to send the signal. Sometimes there's already water spilling over the top of the dam."

"I think I'd be working as close to the riverbank as I could!"

He shook his head. "Most *qiji* gems can be found in the middle of the river. You'd starve if you only worked the shallow ends."

"I'd probably starve anyway if I was stranded in this world," Daiyu said under her breath.

"Not now that I've found you," he returned with a smile.

A young *cangbai* man about Kalen's age had approached while they talked. "Hey, Kalen," he said. "Can't stay away from the river, can you?"

"Neither can you," Kalen said, grinning. They stood up, and Kalen made introductions. "Gabe, this is Daiyu. She's a friend from another city."

She saw Gabe give her a quick appraisal, note her Chinese heritage, and decide that she couldn't be wealthy Han or she wouldn't be with Kalen. He gave her a conditional smile.

"How long are you here visiting?" he asked.

"I'm not really sure yet," she replied.

Gabe's smile widened a little. "You could go stonepicking with Kalen next time they shut off the river. You wouldn't have to be nervous. I'd make sure the bells called you back before the river ran free."

"Gabe's the ringer on this side of the river," Kalen explained.

Gabe turned to Daiyu, his eyes alight. "Hey, you want to see the bells?"

She glanced at the open tower. "I *can* see them. The big one, anyway."

"No, I mean up close. Come on. I'll show you."

She looked at Kalen, who nodded an affirmative, so she said, "Why not?"

It was a short walk to the bell tower but it was a long climb to the top, up a truly terrifying set of circular metal steps that spiraled around the outside of the scaffold. "Are these safe?" Daiyu demanded as she took her first few steps behind Gabe. She clung to the rail, convinced that the whole tower had just swayed under their combined weight.

"Sure, of course they are," Gabe said. "Just make sure you hold on."

So, fighting vertigo the whole way, Daiyu slowly followed him up. The top portion of the tower was almost a room, with a half wall, a roof, and a narrow catwalk circling the interior to serve as a floor. It was barely wide enough to stand on, with no interior barrier to keep any careless visitor from tumbling down the center of the tower to the ground below. Daiyu stood on the top step and refused to release her hold on the railing.

Kalen passed her and moved with care around the catwalk, but Gabe skipped across the boards with the agility of the fearless. He pointed to a thick woven rope that stretched from the monster bell to an iron tether embedded in the far wall.

"That's the rope that starts the bronze bell clanging," he said. "It's heavy, so you need a few good pulls before the clapper hits, and you'd be surprised how much strength it takes to keep it moving. Once it pulled me off my feet and I was swinging back and forth over the open ground, trying to land on one side or the other."

Daiyu figured this story had an equal chance of being true or false, but she didn't really care. She didn't like heights, and she was pretty sure the whole tower had trembled again. "What about the little bells?" she asked.

Gabe danced even farther away, hopping over what appeared to be a small break in the continuity of the catwalk, to point at a much thinner rope tied to a second hook. The other end was attached to a circle of small bells that looked as if they were made of chrome swirled with crystal. "They don't weigh hardly anything at all," he said. "A little kid could pull them. A girl. *You* could."

She smiled faintly. "Why didn't somebody design the tower so you could reach these ropes from the *ground*?"

"Then anybody could come along and pull them just for a prank. You'd have people rushing out of the river when they had half a day of work left."

"Well, they could do that *now* if they felt like climbing a

SHARON SHINN ✳ 51

hundred stories and maybe breaking their necks," Daiyu said.

Gabe shook his head and grinned. "The gate at the bottom of the stairs is supposed to be locked. Everyone thinks it is, but I know the lock is broken."

She didn't answer. She was starting to get nauseated, and she really wished she was back on level ground.

"Are you feeling all right?" Kalen asked, and Daiyu shook her head.

"No. I think— This is kind of making me sick."

Abruptly, she sat down on the top step, quickly transferring her hold to one of the metal posts that supported the railing. She heard Gabe exclaim, "What's wrong with her?" but Kalen didn't bother asking questions. He just crossed to where she was sitting and crouched beside her, putting a hand on her wrist.

Just as he had the night before. Taking hold of her so she wouldn't be afraid.

"Maybe breakfast upset your stomach," he said. "All that food you're not used to."

She tried to smile at him. "I think it was the climb. And maybe the travel yesterday."

"Can you get back down?" Gabe wanted to know.

"Well, I hope so," she said. "Maybe I'll just go down on my butt, one step at a time."

Still holding her hand, Kalen slipped past her and carefully stood up. "I'll go down first," he said. "You can hold on to me."

A little uncertainly, she came to her feet, clutching the

railing with one hand and resting her other on Kalen. His bony shoulder seemed so much more solid and reliable than the thin railing. She quickly figured out how to synchronize her steps to his, and they eased through the descent. Daiyu was shaky but grateful when she was finally back on solid ground.

Gabe bounded down the last three steps without touching his feet to one of them. Daiyu attempted to smile at him. "Thanks for showing me the bells, even though I got sick," she said. "I hope I hear you ring them sometime."

"You will, tonight or tomorrow," Gabe said. He looked at Kalen. "Are you going to work the next time? Or will your friend still be here?"

Kalen gave a convincing shrug. "She'll probably still be here, but she might be busy. If she's got something else to do, I'll come to the river."

"Don't miss work because of me," Daiyu said.

He smiled. "It's all right. I can work in the river any day, but you won't be here very long."

She laughed, but the sound was a little rueful. "Well, I don't think I will be," she said. "I suppose you never know."

SIX

ONCE THEY LEFT Gabe behind, Kalen showed Daiyu around the shops that clustered on the streets a little west of the river. She figured they were roughly in the area where Isabel's office was located in St. Louis, but how different the cities!

Where downtown St. Louis had a diverse but orderly collection of office buildings lining the parallel streets, the central district of Shenglang was built around winding avenues that spilled into circular drives and meandering boulevards. The small buildings were all crammed together like parade watchers determined to be at the very front. The streets were noisy and crowded, trolleys jostling for space with vehicles that looked like fancy Model T's and those contraptions that seemed to combine bicycles and carts. The sidewalks were thronged with people, overwhelmingly Han with *cangbai* and *heiren* individuals mixed in. Almost everyone, male and female, wore outfits similar to Daiyu's—wide-legged black trousers and brightly colored tops.

"I can't believe that the clothes I picked out yesterday when I was still on Earth turned out to be perfect for wearing on Jia," Daiyu said.

Kalen smiled. "Somehow you knew you were coming here."

"Somehow I don't think so," she retorted.

When she was thirsty, Kalen bought her a bottle of some sweet-flavored juice that tasted like apples and cinnamon and ginger ale. "Ice costs more than the juice does," he told her. "We'll have to drink it warm."

She practically gulped hers down anyway. "I don't care," she said. "I love it."

By this time they had wandered to a street that was wider and straighter than most of the rest, and both the foot traffic and vehicular traffic were heavier. Twice, Daiyu and Kalen got separated when careless pedestrians pushed between them, and the second time, Daiyu felt a surge of panic as strong as the one she'd felt when she first arrived. She looked around wildly for Kalen.

He was right behind her. "I'm here," he said, putting a hand on her shoulder.

She reached up to take his hand in hers, and he moved around so they were side by side. "Stay close," she said. "I don't want to get lost."

"Don't worry. I'm not planning to lose you."

He looked like he was going to add something else, but then a low murmur from down the street caught his attention. He shaded his eyes to look in the direction of the noise, which was building to a muffled roar.

"That's Chenglei's car," Kalen said. "He's going to pass right by us. You want to see him?"

"Chenglei?" Daiyu exclaimed. "Of course!"

Still holding hands, and trying to be courteous about it, they pushed through the pedestrians to the edge of the sidewalk so they could get a good look. Daiyu glanced at the people nearby, trying to gauge their mood. Most of them looked pretty excited at the thought of glimpsing the prime minister. As soon as the black car pulled into sight, people started murmuring and clapping their hands. A woman bent down to her little girl and pointed at Chenglei. The applause grew louder as the car drew closer.

And then Chenglei was passing in front of them, sitting on a high seat in the back of what looked like a cross between a convertible hearse and a horse carriage with no horses. Daiyu stared, absorbing as many details as she could. Yes, his features were definitely Chinese, but his pale skin betrayed his Caucasian heritage and, even sitting down, he appeared to be taller than most of the Asians she knew. He was a handsome man, with broad cheekbones and heavy eyebrows that drew attention to his dark eyes. His hair was a deep black except for a streak of gray that waved back from the middle of his forehead, giving him a look of distinction. He leaned forward as he sat on his bench, waving back at the crowd as if he was just as thrilled to see them as they were to see him.

Daiyu felt her mild sense of disquiet intensify, forming a coil of worry in her stomach. Chenglei didn't look like a man so terrible that he had to be flung to a different dimension in order to keep a whole world safe.

As the car pulled out of view, Daiyu glanced around at the crowds just now dispersing. People were smiling or talking to friends with great animation, still impressed and a little awed. "Everybody seems to like Chenglei," she observed.

"A lot of people do," Kalen answered.

"What do *you* think about him?"

"I never thought about him much until Ombri and Aurora came," he said. This didn't surprise her. She figured Kalen had probably poured most of his energy into staying alive; he wouldn't have had much time to think about high-level politics. Which was too bad—she would trust his assessment of Chenglei far more than she would trust Ombri's.

Kalen went on, "I've been trying to learn more about him so I understand why they're determined to send him away. So far, the worst thing seems to be the way he's handling the *zaogao* fever epidemic in the northwest territories. Some people say he's not sending enough doctors and supplies to fight the fever. And other people say he's doing everything he can to make sure it doesn't spread. Feng says thousands of people are dying because of him—"

"Who's Feng?"

"He's the son of one of the wealthy families, but he's been disowned. Every few days you can find him in a park or on the street, delivering a speech about what's wrong with the government—particularly Chenglei."

Daiyu smiled a little as she listened to the description. "He's a dissident. I'd love to hear him speak. Where can I find him?"

"I'll ask around. He might be in hiding right now. But even Feng doesn't know how bad Chenglei can be, Ombri says. Aurora says there's no end to the misery he'll bring to Jia. They say he's destroyed whole cultures on other worlds."

And we'll have to take their word for it that such a thing is true, Daiyu thought, *since we can hardly prove it ourselves.* She unconsciously tightened her grip on Kalen's hand as her stomach clenched even harder. "Well," she said. "I'm glad I got a glimpse of him. Now at least I know who I'm dealing with."

They spent another couple of hours wandering around the city before catching a trolley back to Kalen's neighborhood. Daiyu couldn't remember the last time she'd been so at ease with a young man her own age. When she was around the boys at school, she usually felt awkward and unsure of herself; she rarely tried for casual conversation. She knew she had a reputation for being aloof, an impression that was reinforced by her habitually calm demeanor. But she found it easy to talk to Kalen.

They were still talking as they approached the door to his house and caught the scent of something exotic cooking. "Aurora's home," Kalen said as they stepped inside. She let go of his hand for the first time all afternoon.

Daiyu had been half expecting someone as dark as Ombri, but Aurora was almost his exact opposite. She was only slightly taller than Daiyu, porcelain-skinned, blue-eyed, with utterly straight yellow hair that fell almost to her waist. She looked to be about fifty years old, but Daiyu had to wonder. She had gotten the impression that Ombri, at least, had seen a lot of travel; perhaps the servants were as ageless as the gods.

"Here's Daiyu," Kalen said. "She arrived last night."

"Hello, Daiyu," Aurora said, and her voice was low and restful. "I'm so pleased to meet you."

"We haven't seen you for a couple of days," Kalen said.

Aurora returned her attention to the meal she was making. "No, Xiang is keeping me pretty busy," she said. "But that will work to our advantage, I think. She was very excited to hear about Daiyu."

Daiyu was confused. "What about me? Who are you talking about?"

"Xiang. The woman who employs me," Aurora said. She shook some spice into a pot and glanced back at Daiyu. Those blue eyes were truly astonishing. "She is a wealthy, ambitious woman who has no daughters. She has been bemoaning the fact that she is excluded from some of the summer events at the prime minister's residence because they are designed to introduce young women to society."

"Debutante balls!" Daiyu said under her breath. St. Louis had a longstanding tradition called the Veiled Prophet Ball, in which debutantes made their first formal appearances. The History Museum once had mounted an exhibit of Veiled Prophet gowns from decades' worth of dances, and Daiyu had gone three times to see the display.

Aurora smiled at her again. "Here they are called Presentation Balls, and the annual one sponsored by the prime minister is the most glittering event of the season. Xiang has never been able to attend, and she is very disappointed that this year she will be left out again." Aurora scooped what looked like soup from the pot and took a taste. "I wish Ombri would get home. This is ready to eat."

"I'll get the bowls," Kalen said, and started rummaging through the kitchen cabinets.

"What can I do to help?" Daiyu asked, gesturing toward the bubbling pot.

"Nothing. Just sit," Aurora said. She unwrapped a loaf of bread and began slicing it. "So the reason Xiang was excited to learn about you, Daiyu, is that she wants to borrow you."

"What?"

"She wants to pretend you are her niece, take you to the palace, and present you to Chenglei. And I, of course, told her that she could."

Not until Ombri was home and they all sat at the table eating bread and soup and something that seemed like cheese, but wasn't exactly right, did Aurora explain the rest of the plan.

"I told Xiang that I was expecting a visitor from the north-western territories—a poor girl, but full-blooded Han, not a worthless *cangbai* woman like me," Aurora said. "I said you were coming to the city to try to find work. That you had been educated by a rich uncle who lost interest in you when his own daughter bore a child late in life. So you have no prospects and no connections, and you cannot be expected to have the polish of a city woman, but you are genteel. I think this will explain away any oddness in your language or gaps in your knowledge," Aurora added.

"And you want me to pretend Xiang is my aunt so that I can attend the Presentation Ball?"

"Precisely," Ombri replied.

"It's almost three weeks until the ball," Aurora said. "That will give Xiang time to drill you in how to behave in society. And to have clothes made, of course."

Daiyu laid down her oversized spoon. "Wait," she said. "You want me to go *live* with her for a couple of weeks?"

"Perhaps not quite so long," Aurora said. "But you'll certainly have to spend time with her before the ball so that she can coach you in some of the behaviors you will be expected to know."

"You could train me," Daiyu suggested.

Ombri shook his head. "There are subtleties and nuances that you could only learn from a native."

She looked at Kalen for support, and he laughed. "I don't know how to behave at a society dinner."

"You must go live with Xiang, because she is your route to

Chenglei's side," Ombri said firmly. "Once you have banished Chenglei, you will be free to leave Xiang's household and return to your own world."

"Ah, that's something we have to explain very carefully," Aurora said. "Exactly how we want you to send Chenglei home."

# SEVEN

AFTER DINNER THE four of them sat on a brightly colored rug spread over the floor, and Aurora laid a selection of items before her. One was a simple piece of shimmering rose quartz about the size of a robin's egg, polished to a slippery smooth shine. It lay beside a red silk bag with a gold drawstring top. Another was a broad silver bracelet etched with an indecipherable design; it was hinged in the middle, and just now lay open in two connected curves. Next to it was a small scuffed box that looked just big enough to hold the bracelet in its closed position.

Aurora had pulled on thin white cotton gloves that went all the way up to her elbows, and she tossed a similar pair to Daiyu.

"Never touch any of the talismans with your bare hands," Ombri said, his sonorous voice making the prohibition all the more compelling. "They are designed to respond almost instantly to contact with skin. Even if you drop them after only a second or two, the damage will be done. You will already be transported."

"Transported where?"

Aurora pointed at the piece of quartz, and Daiyu picked it up in her gloved hand. For a moment she caught a faint familiar fragrance, as if the stone had been daubed with her father's aftershave or her mother's perfume, but then it faded.

"This piece of quartz is big enough to send you home even if you are nowhere near the gateway," Aurora said. "The talisman was precisely calibrated to send you back to the exact place and time you were when you left Earth. It will be as if not a single minute has passed." She handed the silk bag to Daiyu. "Put the quartz inside the pouch and carry it with you at all times, since you never know when you might need it."

"If ever you feel endangered, take the stone out of the bag and hold it in your bare hand for a moment," Ombri said. "You will almost instantly be home—puzzled, confused, but essentially unchanged."

Daiyu couldn't resist rubbing the smooth quartz through the even smoother fabric. It *did* feel magical, charged with inexplicable energy, although that was probably just the power of suggestion. For a moment, she was horribly tempted to shake the rock into her hand and disappear. She didn't want to go live with Xiang, an utter stranger; she was far from sure that she wanted to be the means of banishing Chenglei from this world. All she really wanted was to go home, to be with familiar people in a familiar place. To forget that Jia even existed.

If, in fact, it did. If, in fact, she was not still dreaming.

It was the first time since breakfast that she had questioned the reality of her new situation. What was even more disturbing was that she had spent very little time all day thinking about her proper world. It seemed—less urgent, perhaps. Less vivid. She had been so content to wander the streets of Shenglang, her fingers interlaced with Kalen's, that she hadn't wasted much energy worrying about the city she had left behind.

What if she became so at ease here in Jia that she forgot there was another life awaiting her in the place where she belonged?

What if she became so comfortable with Aurora and Ombri that she stopped questioning their motives and their explanations?

What if she became so attached to Kalen that she wouldn't want to part with him when it was time to go?

Shouldn't she leave now, while her mind was still relatively clear, while her heart was still disengaged?

Her fingers closed more tightly over the bag. She stared at the golden drawstring.

I'm not ready to leave, she thought. Partly because she was curious. She would like to know if the stories she'd been told were true; how would she ever find out if she didn't let the adventure run its course?

Partly because of Kalen.

Which was ridiculous. She had only known him a day. She wouldn't even remember him once this wild adventure was over. It would be stupid to base any decision on her feelings for a *cangbai* boy.

"All right," she said at last, hoping her voice showed none of her inner strain. "And what about the bracelet?"

Aurora picked it up and snapped it shut around her own arm. It was clear the bracelet was made for a man's thicker wrist, for it was almost big enough to slide down over her gloved fist. "If you touch the silver for more than a second," she said, "you will be sent to *our* world. You will be safe there, and the residents will recognize you as a sojourner who does not belong and who is probably afraid. But most of them will not know where you *do* belong or how to return you there."

Daiyu was alarmed. "Couldn't one of you come after me?"

"We would, of course, try," Ombri said. "But there is a difficulty when you attempt to use a talisman that is not designed for you. It could fling you to a different *time* as well as a different world. We might not know which year, or even which century, you had gone to. It would take us some searching to find you and guide you back."

Daiyu didn't miss the revelation implicit in that remark: He and Aurora could travel backward and forward through time. So could she, apparently, but she didn't have any control over where she might end up.

"Well. Okay. I won't touch the bracelet," she said. "But then how am I going to put it on Chenglei? And why would he allow me to get close enough to do that?"

"At the Presentation Ball," Aurora said, "you will be appropriately gowned. Your costume will include gloves. We will make sure your dress includes a hidden pocket where you will place the bracelet. Every young girl is invited to dance once with the prime minister. During your dance, you will take out the bracelet and place it on Chenglei's wrist. It should be very simple."

None of it sounded simple to Daiyu. "A formal dance? Like a waltz? The only formal dance I know is the Electric Slide."

Aurora did not look discomposed. "I can teach you the basic steps of the *tiaowu*—the dance that continues throughout the ball—but you will have to confess to Xiang that you have not had much practice. I'm sure she will hire an instructor for you. There are certain times during the dance that you should have one hand free so that you can slip the bracelet from your pocket."

"You would do well to practice beforehand," Ombri observed.

"Yes, I imagine I would!" Daiyu exclaimed.

Kalen started laughing. "And then she would do well to practice what she'll say when Chenglei disappears while she's dancing with him."

"*Yes!*" Daiyu responded. "I hadn't even thought about that!"

"I believe your best course would be to simulate shock and hysteria," Ombri said. "There should be little reason to suspect that *you* had any hand in his abrupt departure. I cannot imagine anyone will be observing you closely enough to see you attach the bracelet to his arm."

"And if anyone questions you, or menaces you, merely take out the quartz and send yourself home," Aurora said.

Daiyu took a deep breath. "Okay. I suppose I can see how this would work. Except the part about practicing with the bracelet. If just touching it means spiraling off to a foreign galaxy—well—I don't want to take too many chances."

Aurora nodded. "I had the same thought. I've made a copy from ordinary materials to be found on Jia. You can rehearse with that one without risk." Now she opened the small box to reveal a copper bracelet about the same size as the silver one. "It's perfectly safe to touch this one with your bare hands."

Stripping off her gloves, Daiyu fished the copper band out of the box and practiced snapping it around her left wrist a couple of times. It made a nice satisfying click every time the clasp engaged.

"The protocol of the dance requires you to leave your right hand in your partner's left hand while you promenade," Aurora said. "That means we will sew the pocket in the left side of your dress—and you must learn to handle the bracelet with your left hand."

"That'll be trickier," Daiyu muttered, and tried to fasten the bracelet around her right wrist. She was clumsy enough that the copper band clattered to the floor. "Can't I just brush it against his skin?" she asked.

"We do not want him to sense danger and jerk away before he has been transported," Aurora said. "It is best to take no risks. Plan to secure it around his arm."

"As I said," Ombri commented, "it will be wise to practice. And on someone other than yourself."

Kalen immediately held out his own bare arm. Daiyu tried to

snap the bracelet around his wrist, but she accidentally caught a little skin in the clasp. He smothered a yelp and pulled back.

"Sorry," she said. "Seeming a little less easy all the time."

Kalen laughed back at her. "Even less easy when you're dancing," he teased.

"Do you know how to perform the *tiaowu*?" she retorted. "Because you're the one I want to practice on."

She expected him to say no, but he surprised her. "Yes," he said. "Aurora's been teaching me."

"We have been focusing on this day for a very long time," Aurora explained. "We thought Kalen might make a reasonable partner. Ombri will play music for us whenever you're ready to learn."

Daiyu rose to her feet and everyone else followed suit. "May as well start now," Daiyu said. "The sooner I learn, the sooner I'll be able to go back home."

It turned into a scene of hilarity. Ombri hauled out what looked like a xylophone and used soft mallets to coax music from it. At first Daiyu just stood near the wall and watched Aurora and Kalen tread out the patterns of the *tiaowu*. The moves were very formal, a hand clasped here, a step taken there, a bow, a twirl, a promenade.

"This doesn't look like anything I've seen in cultural videos about China," Daiyu remarked when they took a break. "It's more like something out of a Jane Austen movie."

"The Han culture on Jia has points in common with China, but not everything has translated," Ombri replied.

"And it becomes even more complicated when you add other couples to the dance floor," Aurora said as she motioned Daiyu forward to take her place. "Once you learn the basic steps, Ombri and I will join you, and you'll see how the pattern changes."

"That might not be for a while," Daiyu said. She had slipped the copper bracelet into the pocket of her black pants, and now she stood facing Kalen, arms extended, palm to palm. When the music started, they took their first careful steps, forward, back, to the side. She was concentrating hard, but she stumbled once and missed two key turns. By the time they segued into the part of the dance where he was escorting her in one wide circle around the dance floor, she was so frazzled that she forgot about pulling the bracelet from her pocket to manacle his wrist.

"You lost your opportunity," Kalen said. "That's when you were supposed to fling me back to my own iteration."

"Oops," Daiyu said. "Let's try it again."

She made almost as many mistakes the second time through, and the third, but she was starting to get a sense of the pattern of the dance. It got more interesting when Ombri and Aurora joined them in the middle of the room, both of them humming the music as they danced.

"Well, I finally understand that little turn after the promenade," Daiyu observed when they were done. "Let's do it once more with all four of us."

This time as she paraded down the middle of the room, her

right hand on Kalen's arm as they followed Ombri and Aurora through a sequence of steps, Daiyu managed to free the bracelet from her pocket. The music swooped to a peak, sending a signal to the dancers, and Kalen swiveled in Daiyu's direction. Daiyu snapped the bracelet on his wrist.

Instantly he collapsed to the floor, gasping and writhing. Daiyu shrieked and dropped beside him, crying out his name. Ombri flew across the room as if to fetch an antidote. Aurora came to her knees and tried to grab hold of Kalen's flailing hands.

"Kalen!" Aurora said urgently. "Kalen, can you hear me?"

"You said the copper was harmless!" Daiyu cried.

Abruptly Kalen sat up, laughing, and pushed his hair back. "I was joking," he said cheerfully. "I figured there'd be some kind of uproar when Chenglei disappeared, so—"

Aurora sagged back on her heels and stared at him. Daiyu shoved him on the shoulder. "You practically gave me a heart attack," she said.

He grinned unrepentantly. "Well, I think you ought to prepare yourself for the idea that something pretty dramatic is going to happen," he said.

Ombri had slowly crossed the room again and now he stood looking down at the three of them, his dark face even more serious than usual. "In fact, Kalen is correct," he said. "Daiyu should brace herself for chaos. Well done, Kalen, if somewhat— unnerving."

"I suppose we should try that again," Daiyu said a little doubtfully.

"I don't know how many more tries I have left in me," Aurora said dryly, but she let Ombri pull her to her feet. "One or two more, I suppose."

The four of them completed the dance three more times. Once Daiyu dropped the bracelet—a very bad outcome, all of them agreed—but twice she managed to get it around Kalen's wrist and then brace herself for whatever lunacy he would try next. The first time he shouted for guards to come arrest her. The second time he simply grabbed her in a bear hug and hung on.

"If I'm going to another dimension, you're coming with me," he said.

She broke free and then turned to stare at Ombri. "That wouldn't happen, would it?" she demanded.

"I doubt it," he said. "The talisman should work so quickly that he should have no time to react."

"But if he's holding my hand at that moment and pulls me along with him—"

"We'll come for you," Aurora promised. "As quickly as we can."

"Take out the quartz," Kalen said. "If he drags you with him. Just pull it out and let it send you home immediately."

She was getting flustered. "But what if I'm so confused by ending up in another dimension that I can't remember what I'm supposed to do—"

"Write yourself a note," Kalen suggested. "Put it in the bag. 'Shake this stone into the palm of your hand—and hold on tight.'"

Daiyu put her fingers to her temples. "Sometimes I'm really

not sure I can do this," she said. "I'm not sure I want to."

"Obviously, we should stop for the night," Aurora said. "We can practice more tomorrow. Xiang has commitments the rest of this week—it will be a few days before I take you to her house."

Suddenly Daiyu was exhausted and ready to seek her bed. But before she could claim first dibs on the bathroom, the night was filled with a rich, mournful, metallic clangor.

"What in the world—?" Daiyu exclaimed, turning jumpily toward the door.

Kalen reassured her with a hand on her arm. "It's just the river bell," he said. "Telling everyone the water will be held back tomorrow. Stonepickers should be at the banks in the morning."

"So you'll go to work?" she asked him.

He shook his head. "I'll stay and keep you company."

"I don't think you can afford to lose too many days of wages for me."

"Aurora and I can take care of household expenses," Ombri said. "There is no need to worry about funds."

"So don't worry," Kalen said, smiling at her.

She smiled back. "You know what? I want to come with you."

"*Really?*" he said. He looked delighted.

"Just tell me how to dress," she said. "And I'll be ready in the morning."

EIGHT

THE RIVERBED WAS a muddy mess, and before she'd taken three steps into it, Daiyu was grateful for the knee-high pair of old boots that Kalen had lent her. He had his right arm extended protectively, ready to catch her if she fell, but he was looking down, studying the swirls the currents had left behind.

"See that?" he said when they were about fifty yards from the bank. "Looks like there was a little groove in the bottom of the riverbed, and a whole pile of stones collected in the middle. Let's start there."

There were maybe five hundred other people fanning out to take up positions in the dammed river—male, female, old, young, *heiren, cangbai,* Han. Most of them wore thick, high rubber boots and carried a variety of sacks and tools, but a few waded out barefoot and crouched near the mud line, sorting through the debris with their hands.

"So, what are we looking for?" Daiyu wanted to know.

Kalen dredged a wire net through the top layer of mud and

shook it till most of the soil filtered out. Left behind were about a dozen rocks of all sizes and composition.

"A *qiji* can't form in the presence of certain minerals, so you can leave behind anything that's got streaks of black or red in it," he said picking out three or four stones, showing them to her, and tossing them away. "But anything that's this shade of gray or rose—that could be a *qiji*. Save those."

She looked doubtfully at the rocks remaining in his wire mesh. That still left a lot of possibilities. "Where shall I start?" she asked.

He pointed at a slick of mud a few feet away. "There's some buildup right over there. See what you find."

A little reluctantly, she took a few steps from his side. She had been nervous about walking this far out into the mud, but she hadn't wanted to be left behind on the riverbank. Here on Jia, she didn't actually feel right—she didn't actually feel safe—unless she was near Kalen.

Once she made it to the small tumble of debris that Kalen had indicated, she scooped up her first collection of stones with the long-handled sieve. Of the ten rocks she shook free of the mud, four were black and one was veined with blurry copper. But the rest were a soft, chipped grayish rose, and she dumped them in the shapeless sack she wore on a strap over her shoulder.

This could be a really long day.

She got a rhythm down in the next half hour—bend, scoop, shake, sort, bend again. In addition to stones, she brought up bits of broken glass, fish bones, unidentifiable scraps of metal, what looked like animal teeth, twigs and clumps of bark, the

occasional live worm. Twice when she sorted through her collection of debris, she picked up ordinary gray rocks and felt a
tingle against her fingertips. By this time, Kalen was too far
away for her to shout out a question, so she tossed those stones
in the sack just in case.

By noon she was famished and thirsty, even though she had
brought a handful of crackers and a full water bottle to see
her through the morning. She was just about to tramp back to
Kalen to ask how much longer they would be working when
the air was filled with the silver riffle of dozens of tiny bells.

"Daiyu!" Kalen was calling before she'd even registered
what the pretty noise might mean. "They're going to raise the
gates! Out of the river!"

"Eek!" she squealed, and tried to fight her way faster through
the heavy mud. Kalen laughed and caught up with her, putting
a hand under her elbow.

"They give you time to get out before they lift the gates,"
he assured her.

"It might take me longer than they think to get through the
mud," she said breathlessly.

"How'd you do?" he said.

"I don't have any idea! I picked up a lot of rocks, though."

"Hand me your bag. I'll carry it for you."

"I can carry it myself," she said indignantly. But she didn't
protest too much when he simply reached over and lifted it
from her shoulder, settling the strap across his chest.

"Not very heavy," he teased. "You must have thrown away
a lot more rocks than you kept."

"I thought I was supposed to."

"Never know what you might have left behind."

They were almost at the riverbank when Daiyu stepped in a particularly slimy patch and pitched to her knees. Kalen was beside her instantly, one hand on her arm. "Oops—are you all right?" he asked. She could tell he was trying not to laugh.

She brought her left hand up in one smooth motion and clicked the copper bracelet around his wrist. "I'm fine," she said sweetly.

He stared at her in disbelief a moment before he burst into laughter. Then he stood up and yanked her to her feet, still laughing, and towed her back to solid ground so fast that she was practically stumbling behind him. They climbed out of the mud and a few feet up the stony slope, then Kalen dropped his burdens and turned back to face the river.

"You ought to see them send the water back in," he said.

They settled beside each other on the incline. Kalen gave her his last strip of dried meat, and Daiyu washed it down with her final swallow of water. The small bells were still trilling out their aria of peril. It hadn't been too hot that morning, but now the sun was beating down, and the humidity in the air was taking on an extra malevolence. Daiyu wiped her forehead with her sleeve and felt herself leave a smear of mud behind.

Kalen pointed toward the bridge. "Watch," he said.

And then, as if raised in tandem by precision-trained teams, the three huge river gates began rising. As the barriers slowly ascended, water first began seeping out, then gurgling out, then pouring through in a great frothy frenzy, leaping and joyous as a fluid pack of hunting dogs. The sound built from a mild rumble, like a hundred faucets turned at full blast, to a whooshing roar as the greatest part of the pent-up water came gushing through. And then the noise became quieter, calmer, as the river found its level and the water slowly returned to normal.

"Wow," Daiyu said.

"I know. I thought you'd like that," he said.

"Now can we get something else to eat?"

They returned to the house for the noon meal and found Ombri before them, vague about how he had spent his morning. Aurora would be at Xiang's until late, he informed them, but they could practice the *tiaowu* without her that night.

"First I want to sort through Daiyu's stones and take them in for scanning," Kalen said.

"We brought home *bags* of rocks, but I don't know if any of mine are *qiji* stones," Daiyu said. "Why do some of them feel funny?"

She had the attention of both men. "Feel funny—in what way?" Ombri asked.

She wrinkled her nose. "They thrum. Like there's a really slight power current running through them."

Kalen was looking at Ombri, but Ombri was still watching Daiyu. "Most people can't feel that," the black man said. "I'm surprised you can."

"You know what she's talking about?" Kalen demanded.

Ombri nodded. "A *qiji* has a specific cellular makeup that vibrates at a slightly different level than most of the solid materials on Jia," he said. "I can feel the difference. So can Daiyu, apparently."

"Oooooh, so those were *qiji* stones?" she said, reaching for her bag. "Let me see if I can find them again!"

Daiyu dumped her bag out on the floor and then settled herself on the rug beside the loose stones. Kalen and Ombri sat across from her. She picked through every rock, culling out the ones that sent a faint skitter across her fingertips.

"These two," she said, handing them over to Ombri.

His fingers closed over them and he nodded emphatically. "Oh, yes. Those are full of tremors."

Kalen took them from Ombri's palm, furrowing his brow in concentration, then he sighed. "They just feel ordinary to me."

Ombri gestured at Kalen's bag. "Let's see if she can find any treasures in the stones you brought back."

She sorted more quickly through Kalen's haul. "Only one, I think," she said.

Ombri took the stone from her hand and nodded. "Quite remarkable," he said.

"Still," Daiyu said thoughtfully. "It's not much of a time savings. If I was a stonepicker, I'd still have to spend half the day in the river, touching every rock I found."

"You could sell your services to other stonepickers in the neighborhood," Kalen said. "They wouldn't have to go to the scanners to get the rocks appraised. They could bargain directly with the merchants and make more money off of each *qiji*. Once the merchants learned to trust you, of course."

"And dozens of stonepickers would be lifted out of poverty," Daiyu said. Not for nothing had she listened to her father's lectures on microfinance. "Almost makes me wish I was going to be staying here for a while."

Kalen smiled at her. "I was wishing that already."

She smiled back. "Hand me that big rock. I want to check something."

The minute he offered it to her, balanced on his open palm, she slapped the copper bracelet around his wrist. Ombri's approving "Very good!" was lost in Daiyu's squeal as Kalen dove from his knees and wrestled her to the floor.

"Any iteration I go to, you'll follow me there!" he cried.

"As soon as he releases you, pull out your quartz talisman," Ombri advised. "Or whatever you have chosen to simulate the talisman while you are practicing."

She slipped free of Kalen's hold and rolled to a sitting position. "I haven't. Picked a stone to practice with, I mean. I guess I could just use one of these."

But Kalen was already pulling something out of his own pocket. "I found this in the river today," he said a little diffidently. "I thought it was pretty, so I kept it."

She took the rock from his hand. It was about the size of an egg yolk, although very irregularly shaped, and smooth from long tumbling in the river. The color was a milky caramel veined with darker lines of orange and inset with a nugget of opaque blue. "Oh, I like this," she said. "Thank you, Kalen."

Kalen jumped to his feet. "Time to go sell the *qiji* stones," he said. He carefully placed the three confirmed *qijis* into his bag and then added a handful of ordinary rocks. When he caught Daiyu's expression of surprise, he said, "It would look very suspicious if I showed up with only gems. No one in Shenglang can separate them out by touch alone. The scanners would think I had stolen them."

"That makes sense," she said. "Can I come with you?"

"I'd be glad if you did."

They took a trolley down to the river, north of the red gate, where there was a cluster of industrial sheds that Daiyu supposed held the scanning equipment. Outside each one, lines of stonepickers were already waiting for their bounty to be assessed, and they picked the shed with the shortest line. Soon it was their turn to step inside the testing station, which was little more than a room, a couple of workbenches—and some pretty sophisticated-looking machinery attached to the workbenches. The air inside was stifling and a little acrid; the four men who were operating the equipment and handing out money looked sweaty and bad tempered.

"Next," one of them called out. Kalen stepped forward and poured the contents of his bag onto the black cloth that covered a section of one of the benches. The technician activated the machine and a startlingly bright light played over the stones. Three of them glowed an opalescent pink under the scope's hard stare. The others remained obdurately dull.

"Three," the technician said, scooping them up and transferring them to a scale situated at his right hand. "Six ounces," he added. The man working with him recorded the information and pulled a handful of coins out of a drawer. Moments later, Daiyu and Kalen were back out in the fresh air.

"I feel rich," he said. "I should buy us all a special dinner."

But Daiyu had been in Shenglang long enough to appreciate the precarious nature of Kalen's economic status. "You should save your money," she scolded. "Anytime you get a windfall, you should put part of it away."

"But I want to celebrate," he said. "And I want to thank you. You found *two* of the *qiji* stones!"

"You can buy something small and inexpensive," she decided. "Dessert for tonight's dinner, maybe."

He grinned. "All right," he said. "I know something you'll like."

It was clear that whatever else might not translate between Jia and Earth, chocolate had certainly crossed iterations. Daiyu was willing to believe it had originated in the very first dimension and been faithfully copied ever since.

Aurora was still at Xiang's, so Daiyu and Kalen and Ombri ate dinner without her, topping off the meal with the chocolate confection Kalen had bought. Then Daiyu and Kalen practiced the *tiaowu* over and over, while Ombri tapped out a musical accompaniment. Daiyu closed her mind to her ongoing questions about whether she really should be planning to send Chenglei away and concentrated merely on learning the skills she needed to master. By the end of the evening, she was completely suc-cessful in slipping the bracelet on Kalen's arm during one phase of the dance or another. She had also perfected the art of freeing her practice stone from a little pouch and squeezing it in her palm, even when Kalen was shouting at her or tickling her or dragging her across the floor.

"Bracelet in my left pocket, talisman in my right pocket. That's what seems to work," Daiyu said when they finally called it quits. "We'll have to make sure I have pockets on both sides in *all* my clothes."

"Aurora will take care of that for you," Ombri promised. He put away his musical instrument and yawned. "A long day for me," he said, then disappeared into his own room without another word.

Kalen lingered. Daiyu thought he looked a little troubled. "But you have to remember to write yourself a note," he said. "In case you really do get pulled to another dimension. In case you really do forget who you are."

She glanced around. "Is there something to write with? I'll do it now."

He produced materials that were close enough to paper and pencil that she could understand them, though the paper was rough and the lead of the pencil was grainy. She tore off a piece of paper small enough to fit inside the pouch, and she carefully lettered a few words onto the scrap.

"'Everything's fine,'" she read back to Kalen. "'Just take hold of the stone and don't let go.'"

"That doesn't tell you much," he objected.

"I just want to be reassured and told what to do," she said. "What's the point of a long explanation that I won't believe anyway? 'You've been transported to an alternate universe, but this piece of quartz holds the key to returning home safely.' If I really *am* back in Ombri's world, things will be so confusing that I don't want anything complicated."

"I suppose it might be even more confusing if you found that message once you were already home," he said. "If you didn't remember anything about this trip, you wouldn't know why you needed to be transported."

She laughed. "Well, maybe I'll remember more than Ombri thinks. He didn't know I'd be able to read the *qiji* stones. Maybe he'll be wrong about this."

She turned toward her own bedroom door, but an odd expression on Kalen's face stopped her. He was watching her closely, toying with one of his earrings and looking a little wistful. "What?" she said.

"Will you want to remember?" he said. "Or will you be glad to go home and forget us all?"

She paused with her hand on her doorframe. "Of course I'll want to remember," she said. "The idea of losing any of my memories is terrifying to me when I think about all the ways that could happen—if I have a concussion, if I have a brain tumor, if I fall into dementia when I get old. If I'm *here*, if this is *real*, I want to hold on to it forever."

"It's so strange for me to think that I'll remember you for the rest of my life and you'll forget me as soon as you go back home," he said.

She started to respond but found that she didn't have a good answer. Instead she just looked at him for a long time, taking in the details of his thin face, his wide mouth, the slightly rueful expression in his brown eyes. In just two days, he had turned himself into a true friend; he had become, unlike Ombri and Aurora, someone she completely trusted.

Actually, he had become that the day he rescued her at the red gate.

"I think I'll remember you," she said softly. "I think Ombri is wrong."

There was a rattle at the door and Aurora stepped in, all blond hair and smiling face. "Oh, good, I was afraid you'd all be asleep by now," she said. "Daiyu, we have to get your things ready. Xiang wants you to join her tomorrow morning."

# NINE

THE NIGHT HAD been virtually sleepless, so Daiyu was exhausted, but extreme nervousness kept her wide awake the following morning as she prepared to leave. Ombri had departed early on some mysterious errand, but Aurora and Kalen stepped out of the house behind Daiyu. Kalen was carrying a small suitcase filled with an assortment of Aurora's castoffs, although Aurora had assured Daiyu that she'd never have to wear anything they'd assembled.

"Xiang will have you in custom-made clothes before the day is out," Aurora predicted. "She will not want you to shame her by appearing in public wearing anything as awful as what you've got on right now."

Daiyu glanced down at her gold shirt and black pants, the outfit she'd been wearing when she walked through the Arch. She had the silver bracelet in her left pocket, the quartz stone in her right, just to accustom herself to the feel of their weight. "I don't think I look so bad," she said.

"She favors a much more elaborate style of dress. And so will you, while you're with her."

Daiyu was not entirely certain she trusted Aurora, but she was anxious at the idea of going to Xiang's house with no one else she knew nearby. "You'll be at Xiang's, won't you?" she asked hopefully. "Every day?"

"Most likely," Aurora said. "But Xiang will want you to very quickly forget that you and I were ever friends. I'm a servant and a *cangbai*. It will be better if you never seem to notice me—unless you have an order to give me."

Daiyu looked at Kalen. "And you'll come visit me?"

"Daiyu," Aurora said sharply. "While you are with Xiang, you will not be permitted to mingle with the lower classes. You must not think you can continue your friendship with Kalen."

Daiyu ignored her, keeping her gaze on Kalen. "I can't bear it if this is the last time I am ever to see you," she said.

He smiled, but his expression was wistful. "Aurora's right, though. People like Mistress Xiang do not even realize people like me exist."

Daiyu shrugged and turned back toward the door. "Fine. Then I'm not going to Xiang's. I'm not staying on Jia if I can't see Kalen."

Out of the corner of her eye, she could see a sleek black car turn the corner and head their way. No other vehicle like this had come to the neighborhood since Daiyu had been in residence. Surely this car had been sent by Xiang.

"Daiyu—yes—very well," Aurora said urgently. "We will

find a way for you to meet with Kalen. Please do not take this moment to destroy all our careful planning."

Daiyu inhaled a deep breath and faced the street again, just as the car purred to a stop. The Han driver who stepped out seemed to be trying not to sneer as he glanced around. "I have come for the girl Daiyu," he said in a cold voice.

"This is Daiyu. I will accompany her to Mistress Xiang's," Aurora answered.

The driver nodded. "You are expected," he said. He didn't even glance in Kalen's direction.

Wordlessly, Kalen strapped the luggage onto the back of the car. The driver helped Aurora into the passenger compartment, an unroofed seating area behind the driver's bench. Daiyu watched Kalen with a growing sensation of despair. She could not even hug him or take his hand to say good-bye; this unfriendly employee of Mistress Xiang's seemed like just the type to report such transgressions. She could not make him swear he would keep Aurora's promise and find a way to see her while she lived in Xiang's house. She probably shouldn't even speak to him one last time.

But she did. She ignored the driver's outstretched hand and trained her fierce gaze on Kalen. "I will not forget your many kindnesses," Daiyu said. "I will not forget any of it."

He didn't speak, but his eyes met hers, and in his expression she read both sadness and resolve. He nodded once, very briefly, and she knew it was an answer to the unspoken question on her own face: *Will I see you again?* Then he turned away.

She took the driver's hand and stepped into the car, settling herself beside Aurora, who gave her a quick look of exaspera-tion. The driver put the car in motion; within three minutes they had turned two corners. Daiyu had to suppress a clutch of terror at the thought that Kalen was now irretrievably out of sight.

She took a deep breath and tried to focus on the trip. Soon enough they were winding through streets that she had never explored with Kalen—wide avenues lined with massive trees that shaded mansions crowded together on the bustling street. They had left most vehicular traffic behind as soon as they en-tered this district, which was clearly where the wealthy lived. The driver had followed such twisting streets that Daiyu was having a hard time placing where they might be in relation to St. Louis, but she knew there was no neighborhood like this in the same space back home. Maybe these houses stood along what would be Jefferson or 20th, home to the big skyscrapers that housed financial companies. In both iterations that would mean that these neighborhoods enjoyed a concentration of money.

"I usually walk this distance or take the trolley," Aurora murmured to Daiyu. "This is much nicer, don't you think?"

Daiyu nodded without answering.

A minute later, the car stopped in front of one of the most impressive houses in the district. It was three stories high and built mostly of white stone, with red pagoda-shaped accents over the main door and a few of the bigger windows. The house was surrounded by an inviting and well-tended garden, which in turn was enclosed by a latticed wooden fence that ran around the entire property. The front walkway was accessed through a round moon gate. The whole aspect was so serene that Daiyu felt a little of her trepidation fade.

The driver jumped out, grabbed her bag, and offered her a hand out of the car. "Mistress Xiang awaits," he said in an important voice. "I will take you to her."

Xiang was terrifying.

She was a tiny woman, almost lost in an enormous room overdecorated with gold furnishings, gold statuettes, red wall hangings, and scattered pieces of jade and enamel. She sat stiffly in a plush chair covered with gold cushions, her black hair and black clothing irresistibly putting Daiyu in mind of a spider at the heart of a particularly gorgeous web. She looked old enough to be Daiyu's grandmother, with deep lines etched into her face, and eyes so dark it was impossible to find a pupil. Those eyes were boring into Daiyu the minute the driver led her across the threshold.

"Daiyu has arrived," he announced.

"Leave her with me," Xiang said in a voice made raspy with age and perhaps whatever the local version of alcohol and cigarettes might be.

The driver bowed and stepped back, then Aurora did the same. There was the soft sound of the door closing, and Daiyu was left alone with Xiang.

Daiyu stayed near the door, trying to appear self-possessed

without looking too sure of herself. She had to act as if she knew she was better than the servants but not nearly as good as Xiang. She tipped her head down slightly but did not drop her gaze, and she and Xiang studied each other for a few moments.

"Come closer," the old woman finally said. "Sit by me." She unfurled her hands to gesture at an ornate footstool situated beside her chair. Her fingers ended in impossibly long fingernails painted the brightest red.

Daiyu complied, folding her hands in her lap and continuing to watch Xiang. She kept her expression absolutely empty—hard to do when her heart was pounding.

"Tell me how old you are," Xiang commanded.

"Seventeen."

"Describe your parents."

"My mother is a farm worker in one of the northwest provinces," Daiyu replied. Aurora had fashioned a sketchy history for her, assuring her that Xiang wouldn't want many details. "My father was a laborer in a manufacturing plant. He died when I was a little girl."

Xiang waved one of those red-tipped hands to indicate her lack of interest. "Han, both of them?"

"Full-blooded. Yes."

"I suppose you have no education."

"A little. I can read—" At least, she could as long as she was wearing her translator ring. "And do math. And—"

"I see you have not been educated in the art of conversation," Xiang interrupted.

Daiyu was silent.

"Still, no one expects young girls to speak, and they won't listen if you do," the old woman continued. "They will look at your face, and your face is good." Unexpectedly, Xiang put out her hand and used those red talons to lift Daiyu's chin. "The skin is exquisite. The lips are too large, but the eyes are perfectly acceptable."

This did not seem to require an answer either.

"I have no interest in adopting you," were the next surprising words out of Xiang's mouth. "Put that thought out of your mind this instant."

"It was never my hope, Mistress."

"But if you present yourself well in front of my friends, and if you please me, I will be generous. I will pour enough money into your hands to allow you to return to your wretched province and buy any husband you desire."

Daiyu lifted her chin and Xiang's hand fell away. "I didn't know that men could be purchased, Mistress."

Xiang's laugh had little humor in it. "Everything can be purchased," she said. "Not everything is worth the price. Men very rarely are." She tilted her small head and pursed her lips, which accentuated all the wrinkles in her face. "I believe I will purchase you," she added. "Do not disappoint me."

Now Daiyu allowed the slightest bit of frost to come to her voice. "I am not in the habit of disappointing anyone," she said.

Xiang smiled, a somewhat chilling expression. "Then you will be my most beloved niece."

✻

As Aurora had predicted, Xiang was unwilling to tolerate Daiyu's unfashionable attire for an instant. The dressmaker was summoned before Daiyu was even shown to her room. The thin, fidgety *cangbai* woman promised she would have an assortment of acceptable outfits available by nightfall, and she would instantly begin work on formal clothing for social events. As soon as the woman bowed herself from the room, Xiang tilted her head again and surveyed Daiyu out of narrowed eyes.

"The hair is very plain," she said. "And yet, simplicity is an affectation that is popular this year. We might do well to leave it."

"I would rather not cut it, if you please," Daiyu said, trying not to show alarm. How strange it would be to arrive back in St. Louis with a new hairstyle she could not remember getting!

"Stand up. Good. You are short enough to wear heels—or are you too clumsy to walk in them?"

"I manage all right if they're not too high."

"Unbutton your shirt. Show me your bosom." When Daiyu did not comply, Xiang snorted. "Very well, show me however much of your skin you are comfortable displaying. Yes, you will be able to wear the new fashions. The necklines will look very good on you. I will lend you some of my jewels—I have just the necklace for you to wear at the Presentation Ball. Are your ears pierced?"

Daiyu pushed back her hair to show off her gold hoops. "Yes."

"Good. You can wear my earrings as well. You will have to take off that ring, of course."

Daiyu balled her hands into fists. "I won't," she said calmly.

At first Xiang was so surprised at being refused that she didn't even look angry, and then her face darkened. "And why not?"

"Because it is my mother's, and it is the only thing of value that she owns, and she gave it to me to tell me that I am the thing she values most of all," Daiyu said. *Even though Xiang will not respect your family, like all Han, she respects the notion of heritage,* Aurora had told her. *Whenever you cannot explain your behavior, rationalize it through family custom. It will not please her, but she will accept it.* "I will not take it off."

"Very well," Xiang snapped. "But you must wear it under your gloves at formal events."

Daiyu nodded. "Mistress, I will."

"Can you dance?" Xiang asked next. "Do you know how to behave at a dinner table? Do you know how to address a man of wealth?"

Daiyu took a deep breath. "I have little experience in any of these matters," she said. "But I am willing to learn."

"Yes, I see we have much work to accomplish before the ball," Xiang said. "Let us waste no time beginning."

✳

If Daiyu had had anyone to talk to, she would have described the next three days as a crash course in charm school. It seemed like every minute was passed in some kind of instruction or beautification ritual. The house was filled with specialists imported to make Daiyu over into the perfect Han debutante. The dressmaker measured every dimension of her body; a stylist tried different combinations of hair and makeup and accessories. A dancing instructor brought in an entire classroom of students to allow Daiyu to practice the *tiaowu* in a simulated ballroom. All the practice with Kalen had paid off; Daiyu found it easier than she'd expected to execute the steps with an acceptable level of grace.

But she missed performing the dance with Kalen. She missed his smile of encouragement when she did well, his murmurs of explanation when she stumbled, his inventive antics every time she slapped the bracelet on his wrist. She had known him such a short time; how could his absence weigh so heavily on her heart?

Xiang would have been horrified to know how many of Daiyu's thoughts were given over to a *cangbai* workingman—although, admittedly, it was hard to think of anyone else when Xiang was nearby. During those three days, the old woman lectured Daiyu endlessly on social etiquette, usually while they sat at a series of extraordinary meals. They ate four times a day, gorging themselves on lavish spreads—braided breads, spicy meats, fruits cut into fantastical patterns, vegetables so delicately fried they were only a kiss away from raw. Chocolate finished up every meal, accompanied by the local version of tea.

If she hadn't spent so much energy learning to dance, Daiyu was sure she would have gained ten pounds.

"When you are seated beside an older man, you do not speak to him until he has addressed you," Xiang said late on that third day. "You may speak first to an older woman or a woman your own age, and it is *expected* that you be the one to greet a man who is your age or younger. It would be very rude of him to address you first."

"What if I can't tell his age?"

Xiang looked at her with narrow disapproval. "You should be able to," was all she said.

At dinner parties, she should not eat anything until the host had had at least three bites. The guests in attendance would always number some multiple of nine. At the ball, she could not dance with anyone who had not been introduced to her by Xiang herself. She must refuse every invitation twice, accepting only the third time it was extended. She was to call herself Xiang's niece but say very little about her supposed blood relations.

"If anyone presses you for details about your family, just say, 'It is better that I not speak of my mother.'"

"And your sister's husband—my father?"

Xiang waved her hand and made a dismissive sound. "Even better not to speak of *him*."

"When will I get to meet the prime minister?" Daiyu asked. She had just been told that she could not speak to him at all except to answer his direct questions, so it seemed reasonable to ask.

"You will be presented to him at the ball, but you might meet him before then," Xiang said in a considering voice. "I might take you to a breakfast the day after tomorrow. I would like to see how well you behave in such a setting among some of my friends."

"I will do my best, Mistress. And the prime minister will be there?"

"Yes," Xiang replied. "He is scheduled to attend."

TEN

"BREAKFAST" WAS A misnomer, Daiyu thought two days later as she and Xiang left for the event shortly after noon. They'd already eaten one meal, and Daiyu was pretty sure Xiang had found time for another snack while Daiyu was having ropes of gold braid woven into her hair.

She actually welcomed the driver's assistance as they climbed into the car, since her stiffly pressed and heavily embroidered clothing made it hard to bend her knees and elbows. The air outside was thick with humidity and hot as any July day in St. Louis, which made her devoutly hope that they didn't have to travel far or her carefully assembled outfit would be accented by streaks of sweat. She was grateful to see a stretched canvas cloth providing a roof over the open vehicle, but it couldn't compare to air-conditioning running at full blast.

Xiang frowned at Daiyu for the entire ten minutes of the ride. "I wonder if I was too eager," she mused aloud. "I wonder if this is too soon."

"I will try to behave appropriately, Mistress."

"Just keep your eyes lowered and say as little as possible."

The car pulled up before a house that was as grand as Xiang's, joining a long line of similar cars depositing an elegantly clad congregation on the street. Daiyu kept her head modestly tilted down but tried to take in as much as she could. Friends met each other with exclamations and embraces; acquaintances were more reserved, extending one or both palms to press against the other person's. No one came up to hug Xiang, Daiyu noticed, though everyone nodded at her and quite a few lifted their palms for her to touch as she and Daiyu walked by.

Everyone stared at Daiyu with frank interest and then turned to whisper something to whomever was standing closest.

They were among the first to step inside, and Daiyu looked around quickly. This house was sunnier than Xiang's and a little less cluttered; some kind of flowering plant brightened the front hall and showered sweetness through the air. Her immediate first impression was of an atrium, and the impression didn't fade as a servant led them through long, open hallways festooned with more greenery and filled with more light. The sun beating through the glass might cook her alive, she thought, but the visual impression was one of airy beauty.

A woman hurried forward to meet them, her hands outstretched, her face alight with pleasure. She was about Xiang's age and Daiyu's height, dressed all in a royal blue that was spattered with bits of silver.

"Xiang!" she exclaimed, and was bold enough to give the

other woman a hug. "You have come after all! And, look, you have brought your niece. What a pretty girl!"

"She might not be entirely worthless," Xiang said. "I thought I would see how well she performs here among friends."

"I am Mei," the other woman said, turning to address Daiyu, her hand outstretched. Daiyu pressed her hand to Mei's and quickly dropped it. "What is your name?"

"Daiyu, Mistress."

"How long have you been in the city, Daiyu?"

"Only a few days."

Mei seemed to be listening closely. "Her accent is strange," she said to Xiang. "But not unpleasant. I assume you chose her ensemble? A magnificent job, as always. Your taste is reliably exquisite."

Xiang waved a dismissive hand. "This is just something we were able to find in the closets. I assure you, she will be much better attired at the Presentation Ball."

On these words the rest of the guests began to filter in, still laughing and talking among themselves, still eyeing Daiyu with undisguised curiosity. About a third of the guests were older women, she noticed now—women about Xiang's age and with the same air of affluence and arrogance. She supposed these were the women who wielded the most power in Shenglang, the ones she would have to be careful not to offend. Daiyu kept her expression pleasant, offering sweet smiles when any of these women spoke to her and thanking them quietly for any kindness they displayed.

The balance of the company was a mix of men and women

of varying ages, though there were few older men. The young men all clumped together, greeting one another with rude familiarity and laughing easily, seeming to take little notice of anyone else in the room. But Daiyu, watching covertly, saw them scanning the ranks of the pretty young women, who mostly stood passively beside their mothers. Now and then, when one of these girls caught a young man's eye, he nodded a greeting or flashed a smile. Several of the young men watched Daiyu with an open appraisal. She supposed strangers might be novelties in this rarefied society—or maybe what was rare was Xiang's sponsorship of a poor relation.

Xiang kept Daiyu close to her side and only introduced her to a few people, glaring so meaningfully at Daiyu that she had little incentive to say much. Still, she could tell the reaction to her was mostly positive, and Xiang started to relax a little.

"Shall we sit down to eat?" Mei said after there had been about twenty minutes of this aimless chatter.

"Where's Chenglei?" an older woman asked.

"He has been detained, but he will be here as soon as he can," Mei promised. "He told us not to wait."

The whole group moved into a sunny dining room in a glassed-in conservatory. Xiang, Daiyu, Mei, and six others sat at a table in the center of the room. Daiyu was placed between Xiang and a man who might be in his fifties—certainly old enough that she knew to respect the prohibition against initiating conversation. He had no interest in talking to her, at any rate; he sat with his back half turned to her and spoke with

great intensity to the couple on his left. Something about im-
migrants and insufficient laws. She didn't catch it all and she
didn't really care.

Xiang didn't speak to her either, so Daiyu concentrated on
her meal, taking small portions and watching Mei whenever
she wasn't sure how to handle a glass or an eating implement.
The food was more highly spiced than the dishes she'd had at
Xiang's and she didn't like it as much, but all around her she
heard people complimenting the taste, the texture, the creative
combinations.

The breakfast plates had been cleared away and servants
were bringing in trays of the inevitable chocolate, when there
was a murmur of excitement and Daiyu glanced up to see
Chenglei striding in. He smiled generally at the room, nodded
directly at Mei, but then did a curious thing. He stopped at the
very first table—the one nearest the door, the one where even
Daiyu could tell the least important guests were relegated—
and paused to exchange a few words with the people sitting
there. They beamed up at him, extending their hands for him
to press, and a few came to their feet to greet him. He spoke to
everyone at the table, even if briefly, before moving on to the
next group at the adjoining table. Everyone in the first group
was left smiling at his attention.

Mei leaned forward to address Xiang. "Such a handsome
man! That perfect streak in his hair!" she murmured, though
everyone at the table could hear her. "I sometimes think, if I
were not so much older—"

It was clearly a joke, and everyone laughed lightly, except the man next to Daiyu, who frowned. "He is brilliant, which matters much more than his beauty," he said.

"Part of his brilliance is that he knows how to exploit his beauty," Xiang said dryly.

"I will concede that he has both, and I admire him for each," Mei replied.

Chenglei continued to work his way around the room, still smiling, still pressing palm to palm. Mei had motioned a servant over and ordered a clean plate to be brought to her table for the prime minister. A plain-featured woman who had said almost nothing during the meal rose to her feet and excused herself, quietly stepping out of the room. Daiyu was fascinated. She remembered that Xiang had told her the number of guests at an event must always be divisible by nine. Had there been extra members of Mei's household dressed and ready to fill any open places at the tables? For instance, if Xiang and Daiyu had not arrived, might there have been another young girl and perhaps a tired old man who would have been invited to partake of the breakfast in their places?

It was nearly half an hour before Chenglei made it to their table, and then he did not immediately take a seat, but instead made the circuit to greet everyone. Mei and Xiang were on their feet, and so was the unpleasant man, so Daiyu stood too.

She found that her heart was beating fast and her breath was quick and shallow. She had been imported to Jia specifically to meet this man, and now perhaps she would learn why Ombri and Aurora thought he was so dreadful. She had the silver bracelet in her left pocket, the quartz stone in her right, but she wasn't wearing gloves, and this didn't seem like the venue for causing someone to vanish mysteriously. Chenglei had finished bantering with Mei, and now he took another step closer to Daiyu.

"Xiang! How good to see you!" Chenglei exclaimed. He bent down to kiss Xiang on the cheek, and she responded with the faintest blush and an expression of supreme satisfaction. "You look to be in extraordinarily good health," he continued. "Or perhaps it is just your ageless beauty that takes my breath away every time I see you."

At the fulsome compliment, she gave an almost coquettish smile. "I am old, prime minister, but vain as any woman. I shall choose to believe you even though I know you lie."

He laughed. "But that is all any politician can ask for, Mistress!"

Xiang gestured at Daiyu, who kept her gaze determinedly on her shoes. "I know you have heard me talk many times of my sister, who unfortunately lives far away from me. It is a sad thing to be separated from family! But she has kindly sent me her daughter to keep me company this summer. May I introduce you? Daiyu, this is Prime Minister Chenglei, the most intelligent man in all of Shenglang."

Chenglei loosed an exclamation of pleasure and held up both of his hands, palms out, toward Daiyu. "But what a pretty girl she is!" he said. "How long will she be staying with you?"

"For the summer at least, and longer if all goes well," Xiang replied.

Daiyu lifted her hands to press them against Chenglei's. His fingers were longer than hers by a full inch, and his skin was pleasantly warm. She could feel him peering down at her. "Tell me, Daiyu," he said, "are you enjoying your stay in Shenglang?"

He had addressed her directly; she must respond. She looked up, hoping her expression seemed shy, and found him smiling down at her. Mei was right. That streak of gray in his dark hair added the perfect complement to his basic good looks. Not only that, his smile was peculiarly attractive. Warm and intimate, it invited her to smile back or to whisper a secret.

"Very much," she said.

"What parts of the city have you seen?"

"Mostly Xiang's house. It is magnificent!"

"What, you haven't been to the aviary yet?" When she shook her head, he said, "Oh, you must go. It is my favorite place in the city."

That was not a question, so she did not reply. He still had not dropped his hands. In fact, he seemed to be leaning forward a little, so that the pressure of his touch increased. His smile became teasing. "And certainly you will be coming to the palace soon, will you not?"

"I hope so, Prime Minister."

"For the Presentation Ball, at the very least! I suppose you and Xiang are spending all of your time poring over dress designs and hairstyles so that you will be able to outshine all the other young girls who are making their appearance that night."

She couldn't help but giggle. It wasn't the actual words he

said, it was the way he delivered them, in such a friendly, personal, and amused fashion, as if they shared a long history of private jokes and idle conversation. "I just want to make sure I do not shame Mistress Xiang," she said.

"In what possible way? Come, tell me."

"I have only recently learned the *tiaowu*," she admitted. "Sometimes I still get the steps wrong."

"You won't get them wrong when you are paired with *me*," he said. "I am a very good dancer. My partners always look graceful." He paused. "You *will* dance with me, won't you? I will be so disappointed if you say no."

Since every girl presented at the ball was to be partnered by Chenglei—and he knew it—the question was ridiculous. Yet she felt a little flutter of excitement at his words. She was charmed by his eagerness.

"Prime Minister, you would honor me immensely if you would invite me to dance with you," she said. "How excited my mother would be to hear that you had led me in the *tiaowu*!"

"Then your mother will be thrilled to receive the very first letter you send her after the ball," he said with a little chuckle. He finally lowered his hands and Daiyu dropped her arms to her sides. "For you will have much to tell her! I suddenly find I cannot wait for the Presentation Ball."

Xiang appeared to be positively elated as they rode home a short while later. "That could hardly have gone better!" she exclaimed, waving a decorative fan in front of her face, since the car's awning wasn't enough to turn back the late-afternoon heat. "You behaved just as you should—you did not embarrass me at all—and Mei's son could hardly take his eyes off of you all meal."

"Mei's son? Which one was he?"

"The young man in the green jacket embroidered with suns."

"Oh. I didn't get a chance to talk to him, but he looked very nice."

Xiang snorted. "He's wealthy, which is more to the point. I had not given any thought to trying to make an alliance for you, but if that's the way things appear to be heading—hmmm. I will have to consider that."

An alliance? As in a *marriage*? What a horrible thought! Surely Daiyu would not be on Jia long enough for any kind of courtship to progress too far. "He might be angry when he discovers I am not really your niece," Daiyu ventured.

Xiang glared at her. "And how will he discover it? Unless you are foolish enough to tell him."

"But—if your sister ever comes to Shenglang—or your true niece does—"

Xiang waved a hand as if to consign those unfortunate relatives to oblivion. "They will not come," she said. She lapsed into thought again.

"The prime minister seemed very gracious," Daiyu said after a moment.

"Oh, Chenglei is the worst kind of flirt," Xiang said in a complacent tone, sounding like an indulgent aunt who secretly approved of her nephew's wild excesses. "He can make women *and* men fall in love with him. It is all the same to him, as long as people admire him. I told him once that if he had not ascended to office, he would be the perfect courtesan. He laughed and said that a courtesan had even more power than a politician, and that if he ever tired of his present job, that was the one he would pursue."

"I suppose that everybody likes him," Daiyu said.

"Well, of course they do!" Xiang exclaimed. "Didn't you?"

"Yes, Mistress," she replied.

The rather frightening thing was that her words were true.

Aurora slipped into Daiyu's room that night while she was getting ready for bed, as she had almost every night that Daiyu had spent in Xiang's house. Before she had arrived at Xiang's, Daiyu had expected that it would be easy to find time every day to exchange a few words with Aurora, who had explained her position in the household as *assistant to the mistress of the wardrobe*. That had not sounded like a job that would take a great deal of time.

That was, of course, before Daiyu had seen the extent of Xiang's wardrobe. And her own.

"How was your breakfast at Mei's house?" Aurora asked in

a hushed tone. She was not supposed to be in Daiyu's room, but they had prepared their cover story if she was caught. Daiyu would say she had found a tear in one of her shirts and was too embarrassed to tell Xiang she had ripped it, so she had begged the *cangbai* servant to come to her room in stealth. They both stood near the door that led to Daiyu's closet—which was actually a chamber bigger than her bedroom back on Earth.

"I was nervous the whole time," Daiyu admitted. "But Xiang seemed pleased with me afterward, so I guess I did all right."

Aurora smiled. "If she didn't berate you for your clumsiness and stupidity, you must have been outstanding."

"Chenglei was there," Daiyu said abruptly.

Aurora grew very still. "Did he speak to you?"

"He spoke to everyone in the room, including me." She hesitated and then said, "He was nothing like what I expected."

"How did he seem to you?"

"Gallant. Intelligent. Charismatic." She met Aurora's eyes. She knew her own expression was suspicious. "He did not strike me as a man who was *evil*."

"I have always thought true evil had a seductive charm," Aurora said quietly. "It is very easy to shun someone who is deliberately cruel, and everyone loathes a man who is brutal and vicious. Such people have a hard time winning followers. But an individual who is gracious, who is attractive, who smiles and flatters and praises—that is a person who can lead whole nations to disaster. Who would not want to follow such a man or woman? Everyone is drawn to beauty and wit."

Daiyu was far from convinced and made no attempt to hide that fact. "But there are plenty of people who are attractive and courteous who are *not* horrible," she argued. "There's a man at my father's church who's so good-looking, you'd think he was a television actor. But he runs the soup kitchen and he volunteers at the prison, teaching law classes. So you can't just say beautiful people are bad."

"I didn't say that," Aurora said. "I said evil is seductive. It's two different things."

"I suppose I'll get a chance to gauge him a little better when we dance at the Presentation Ball," Daiyu said.

Aurora watched her narrowly for a moment. "I suppose you will."

Daiyu changed the subject. "How's Kalen?" she asked, as she had asked every night. "Have you thought of a way that we can see each other?"

"Daiyu—"

"I heard the bronze bell ring tonight," Daiyu went on. "So I know he will be at the river tomorrow. Maybe I can convince Xiang that I need to buy something at the shops down by the Zhongbu."

"And will you also convince her that you need to go by yourself, so that no servants see you go wading into the mud, seeking out *cangbai* boys?" Aurora asked in a sharp voice.

Daiyu lifted her chin defiantly. "You promised me I would be able to see Kalen again," she said. She left the implied threat unspoken. *If you don't keep your promise, I won't stay at Xiang's.*

Aurora studied her a moment in silence. "He has taken a job," she said at last, almost reluctantly, "at the aviary. He helps clean the grounds."

"The aviary!" Daiyu exclaimed. "Chenglei mentioned it to me. I bet Xiang would let me go there."

Aurora shrugged. Her blue eyes were troubled. "Perhaps she would."

There was a sound in the hall, most likely one of the servants walking by. Aurora and Daiyu both fell silent, listening, until the faint noise receded.

"Time for me to go," Aurora said.

"Tell Kalen I'll come see him at the aviary," Daiyu said.

"I'll tell him you'll *try*," she responded. "Be careful, Daiyu."

She slipped out into the hallway so quietly that even Daiyu could not hear her footsteps moving away. Daiyu thought, *I'll be careful after I've had a chance to see Kalen.*

 # ELEVEN

XIANG WAS AMENABLE to the idea of Daiyu touring one of
the city's well-known attractions, possibly because of the way
Daiyu phrased her request.

"Yesterday the prime minister asked me if I had seen the aviary, and I was ashamed to say that I had not," Daiyu said in a
mournful voice over breakfast. "What if he asks me again at the
Presentation Ball? What shall I tell him then?"

"You shall tell him you have visited the grounds and enjoyed
them very much," Xiang said, tapping her long red fingernails
on the tabletop. "That is a most excellent idea. I myself cannot
abide the place, for there are bird droppings everywhere, and
it is hot, and all sorts of people may be found there. But you
might enjoy it."

"When can I go?"

Xiang considered. "Tomorrow afternoon. You have no appointments with dressmakers or dancing instructors, so you

may take a few hours to go. I am expected at the council, so I will not accompany you."

Daiyu tried not to let her excitement show on her face. "May I go by myself?"

Xiang looked undecided, but eventually shook her head. "No. I will have one of the servants go with you. Perhaps I should ask Mei if her son would like to escort you—but no, it is too soon. Perhaps in a few days."

That was a complication Daiyu didn't need, but she merely nodded her head. "Yes, Mistress. Thank you, Mistress. I will be happy to go tomorrow."

Daiyu only wanted to visit the aviary for a chance to see Kalen, so she was surprised by her own reaction to its grandeur and gorgeousness.

The whole expedition was unexpectedly perfect. Aurora had managed to be selected as the servant who would accompany Xiang's niece to the bird sanctuary, and she nodded almost imperceptibly when Daiyu asked her an imploring question with her eyes. *Did you tell Kalen? Will he be there?* The driver was in an expansive mood, and he actually pointed out a few city landmarks they passed on their way. As always, Daiyu tried to figure out where they might be if Shenglang was really St. Louis, but within a few turns, she was hopelessly lost. They were going east and south, she thought; other than that, she had no idea.

The aviary was huge—a latticework iron cage at least the size of a city block. From the street, all she could see through the black grillwork was plant life, giant trees brushing the top of the structure, great leafy vines twining around every individual rod so densely that it was almost impossible to see in. Daiyu stood before the entrance, mouth gaping, staring at the clustered greenery. She saw a flash of feathered red near the pointed apex.

"I've never seen anything like this," she said to Aurora in a low voice. The driver had asked when he should come back for them, and Daiyu had said, "Two hours from now," but she was wondering if she should have said, "Tomorrow." It might take her that long to walk around the inside of this place.

"It is most impressive," Aurora agreed with a smile. "Even more so inside."

Indeed, once they were through the gate, Daiyu stared even harder. The aviary was full of lush vegetation that took up most of the available space from the ground right up to the top of the iron cage. At the lowest level, the soil was covered in thick grass and the occasional patch of flowering shrubbery. In the middle level, short trees spread their stubby branches, heavy with summer green leaves; and towering above the whole space, giant oaks and elms sent their reaching limbs poking through the metal restraints of the grill. Ropy vines tied all the levels together, twining around trunks, dropping down from overhanging branches, bursting into erratic blossom at the most unexpected junctures.

Birds were everywhere.

Some gathered on the branches, chattering and calling; some swooped from that lush green ceiling toward invisible prey below. Others hopped along the ground, pecking at nuts or insects. A few clung to the tree trunks, tapping their beaks against the bark. A few, as large as peacocks, strutted across the lawn and uttered incomprehensible cries of disdain.

Every bird in the aviary was red, some a deep vermilion, some a speckled white and crimson, a few with black markings along their wings and tail feathers. Daiyu only recognized two or three species that looked vaguely similar to the birds she knew back home—those might be woodpeckers, those scarlet tanagers, and cardinals were everywhere—but most of them looked unfamiliar and exotic.

"What an amazing place," Daiyu said, turning to Aurora with her eyes wide open.

Aurora handed her a silk parasol. "You'll want to use this as we walk around. Otherwise you'll come home with bird droppings in your hair and on your lovely blouse."

Indeed, the smell of avian excrement was pretty strong, though not intense enough to be truly unpleasant, and the whole narrow walkway that wound through the interior was covered with white and gray spatters. On the other hand, the thick greenery kept the temperature inside the aviary noticeably cooler than the air outside, though the aviary was just as humid. Daiyu could already feel her carefully styled hair start to loosen and frizz.

"Why are all the birds red?" she asked, snapping the parasol into place over her head.

"The story is that red was the favorite color of the wife of the man who built this place nearly a century ago. So he collected red birds from all the corners of the world and had them installed here. Some of the species here are extinct in other parts of the world. Zoologists from all over Jia come to study them."

"I can see why," Daiyu said, and began strolling forward.

The stone path meandered around some of the giant trees and past a variety of fountains and shallow pools filled with birds dipping into the water and shaking off their feathers. A flock of tiny creatures skittered by at eye height, so small that Daiyu at first thought they were butterflies. Now and then she felt a small *splat* on the top of her parasol and was increasingly grateful that Aurora had brought it along.

Scattered in strategic places along the path were stone and wooden benches, many of them occupied by bird-watchers with viewing glasses or students with sketchpads. Not far away, a young man with a bucket was scrubbing the bird droppings off a black wrought-iron bench. Daiyu imagined that he faced an unending task in this place. At their approach, the worker looked up and grinned. It was Kalen.

Daiyu had to choke down her squeal of delight, but she absolutely could not contain her smile. She was so glad to see him that she wanted to run down the path and throw her arms around his neck, but of course she couldn't, not in front of witnesses. None of the people nearby looked affluent enough to be friends of Xiang's, but too much was at stake for Daiyu to be stupid.

"Aurora," she said in as stately a voice as she could

manage. "Let us sit for a time on that bench that has just been cleaned."

"Yes, young mistress," Aurora replied.

Kalen, too, was exercising self-control. After that first grin, he schooled himself to look solemn and deferential. He bowed when he saw them approach and extended his arms as if to present the bench to them. "Would you like to sit for a while?" he asked. "I could hold the young lady's parasol to protect her head."

"She will sit," Aurora said. "I will continue my walk."

And so, seconds later, Daiyu and Kalen were alone. Well, if you discounted the young girl sitting ten feet away, apparently engrossed in her easel and paints, and the couples ambling past, and the mothers with their young children spilling off the pathway into the untamed bushes. Kalen stood respectfully behind the bench, holding the parasol at a deliberately low angle. It would be hard for anyone walking by to see Daiyu's face. Of course, she couldn't see Kalen's face either, and she wanted to—she wanted to hang over the back of the bench and gaze up at him while she told him everything she'd seen and everything she'd done since she left for Xiang's. But she had to sit here and appear elegant and bored and proper.

"Tell me what you've been doing," she said, her voice warm even as she tried to keep her expression cool. "Tell me everything."

"My life is the same as it always is," he said. "Quieter now, with you gone."

"Did you pick stones the other day? I heard the bell ring."

"Yes, I was at the river all morning. But I only came home with one *qiji*."

"Well, that's better than none!"

She heard the smile in his voice. "That's what I thought."

"Aurora told me you took the job here. Does that mean you'll stop being a stonepicker?"

"No, I can do both. Gabe's been working here for the last couple of months and he helped me get hired."

"Were you worried about money?" Daiyu asked softly. She thought about all the food that went to waste in one day at Xiang's. Enough to feed Kalen for a week.

There was a slight sound, as if he'd shrugged. He transferred the parasol to his other hand, never lifting it away from her face. "Everyone worries about money."

"Maybe you could sell your earrings," she suggested, "if you ever get too desperate."

He laughed softly. "They're just made of cheap metal, so they wouldn't even fetch the price of a meal. But I like having a second job. When Ombri and Aurora leave—"

She twisted around to look at him. "When are they leaving?"

He gave her a lopsided smile. She thought his face looked thinner than before. "Once you send Chenglei away, they won't have any reason to stay in Jia."

For some reason, that had never occurred to her. "But then what will happen to you? Will you have to give up the house?"

He made a circular motion with his free hand, indicating

she should face forward again. Unwilling, she obeyed. "I don't know yet," he said. "We haven't talked about it. It doesn't matter."

"Well, of course it does! I hate to think of you sleeping out-side in a tent once cold weather comes—"

"You won't be thinking of me at all when cold weather comes," he said lightly. "Not if you're back in your own itera-tion by then."

The words made them both fall silent again. Daiyu's rush of pleasure in the meeting instantly dissipated; she actually felt sick to her stomach. She clasped her hands together hard.

"I'm sorry," Kalen said. "I shouldn't have said that. It's just that I think about it a lot."

"It's so unfair," she said in a subdued voice. "Ombri and Aurora descend on you and draw you into this escapade and change everything in your life. And then they disappear and everything they brought with them disappears, and you're left with a story you can't tell anyone and memories that no one else shares. I am in despair just knowing that all of this will evaporate the minute I'm back home. I can't *stand* it, thinking I won't remember you. But it might be just as bad to remember all of it and know you can never have any of it back again."

"I don't mind," he said. "I mean—I *do* mind, knowing that I'll never see any of you again—but I'd rather have had the adventure than not. I'd rather know the people and lose them than never have them in my life at all."

"It's so hard," she said, her voice very low.

He changed the subject, his voice determinedly cheerful.

"So what's it like at Xiang's house? As frightening as you expected?"

She managed a light laugh. "Just about! Xiang is a bitter little spider in this golden web, and I always have the idea that she's plotting things all the time, some of them not very nice. She seems to like me, though. At any rate, she doesn't scream at me or call me names. And once or twice she's said things that make it sound like she's considering keeping me here past the ball. As if I really *were* her niece and she was thinking of adopting me."

Kalen laughed. "There's a thought! You could stay in Shenglang. Then you wouldn't have to worry about me being lonely after all."

Daiyu laughed. "I like the idea of staying in Shenglang with *you,* but I don't think I could stand to keep living with Xiang," she said. Belatedly, she added, "Besides, I couldn't leave my parents like that! They'd be so worried about me and I'd miss them too much."

As she said the words, it occurred to her with a sort of buried horror that she hadn't missed her parents at all in the last couple of days. In fact, today she hadn't even thought of them until that very moment. What was wrong with her? Was Shenglang putting such a spell on her that she was slowly but surely forgetting her former life, her *true* life? Or was the mere act of passing through iterations too difficult for the brain to absorb? She had been warned that her mind would not be able to retain memories of Shenglang once she returned to her own time and place. Maybe she could not retain memories of

St. Louis if she was in Shenglang too long. The thought was terrifying.

"Daiyu?" Kalen said, his voice concerned. "What is it? What did I say?"

"Kalen," she whispered, "I think I'm forgetting things."

"What things? I can help you remember, if they happened in Shenglang."

"No—my family—my life in St. Louis. It seems so faint and so far away. As if *this* is the world that's real, and *that's* the dream, that's the place that doesn't really exist. Kalen, what happens if I forget them? What happens if I don't remember where I really belong?"

"Do you remember it now?" he asked gently. "Your true life?"

"Yes—I think so. But how do I know? What if I've forgotten things already?"

His voice was low, unruffled, soothing. "I'm sure you haven't. Nothing important, anyway. Tell me about it. Describe your mother and father to me. Tell me about your house."

As always, his words, his very presence, chased away some of her fear. She took a deep breath. "My father is this tall, thin, happy guy. He accepts everybody. He trusts everybody. He never holds grudges. He tried to be a banker, but he didn't know how to be a corporate man, so he started buying and rehabbing houses. He likes to work with his hands. No matter what you need, if you ask my dad for help, he'll give it to you. His eyes are as blue as Aurora's."

"I think I'd like him," Kalen said.

"Oh, and he'd like you. My mom—she's the practical one. She can always figure things out, everything from reading a map to budgeting for groceries. She sort of holds my dad to the Earth, you know? If she's around, you know that nothing can go so wrong that she can't fix it. And she *understands* things. Like why you want a certain dress or why you like a certain boy. No matter what you need to tell her, she'll listen."

"You don't have any brothers or sisters?"

She shook her head. "They adopted me from China." She knew as soon as she said the phrase that it would make no sense to him. She rubbed her fingers over the dragon ring and tried again. "They're not Han," she said. "Where I come from, most of the Han people live on the other side of the world. It's the *cangbai* folk who pretty much run my country. My parents are *cangbai*, like you."

"Is that strange?"

"They're my parents and they love me," she said. "It doesn't feel strange at all."

"Where do you live?" he prompted. "What does your house look like?"

So she told him about the tumbledown property in Soulard that, by the end of the year, would be restored to a quirky elegance, and then gave him details about some of the other houses they had lived in. She described the backless red dress she had worn last year to a cousin's wedding, the item of clothing she loved most in the world. She named her best friends, listed her favorite books, and would have outlined the plots of her favorite movies if they'd had time. But she could see Aurora pacing slowly toward them down the walkway, and she knew they had already stayed longer than Xiang would have liked.

"What color do you like best?" Kalen asked, handing her the parasol as she came to her feet.

She risked turning around to look at him so he could see her smile and, maybe, some of her relief. So that she could see *his* smile, which flashed instantly in response. "It changes," she said. "*That* I don't have to worry about forgetting."

"You don't have to worry about forgetting any of it," he said. "I'll remember."

TWELVE

DAIYU HOPED TO return to the aviary often to see Kalen, but it was soon clear there would be no chance to do so in the next few days, for Xiang had filled their schedules with activities. There were still dancing lessons to get through most days, still dressmaker fittings to endure, but now Xiang was adding more social events to their calendars. There was another breakfast—which Chenglei did not attend—and a formal dinner so somber and precisely orchestrated that Daiyu was afraid all night that she would hold an elbow wrong and be disgraced forever. She scarcely said a word and ate only the smallest bites of the sumptuous food, but apparently she did nothing unforgivable, because Xiang took her to another dinner a few nights later.

During this time, only two events really stood out to Daiyu as significant. One because it gave her another chance to observe Chenglei, the other because it showed her what her life on Shenglang could be like if she stayed—not as Kalen's friend, but as the niece of one of the richest women in the city.

"Wear your prettiest blouse today," Xiang ordered her one morning over breakfast. "The purple one with the gold embroidery. Mei is coming for lunch. It will be very casual, of course, but she will be inspecting you. You want to look your best but not as if you were trying."

Daiyu hid a smile. Any high-school girl completely understood that imperative. "Yes, Mistress."

So she changed into the new purple blouse, wearing it over the omnipresent black pants—though both top and trousers were of incredibly fine material and so perfectly made that they turned her ordinary figure into an exquisite hourglass. It had been fairly easy to learn how to use the cosmetics available to her, so she applied what passed for rouge, mascara, and lip gloss. Xiang had carelessly lent her a whole case full of jewelry, but for a "casual" meal, Daiyu would keep her gold hoops. She appraised herself in the polished chrome square and thought she looked pretty good.

Daiyu was surprised, but Xiang obviously was not, when Mei arrived with her son in tow. "I hope you don't mind," Mei said after kissing Xiang on the cheek. "He told me he had very important plans today but they were canceled, and I said, 'You have not shown any respect to my old friend Xiang in many months. Why don't you take me to her house?' He will not stay for the meal, of course, I would not be so rude as to bring along an uninvited guest—"

"I would not be so rude as to turn aside a young man who has kindly escorted his mother out on a summer day!" Xiang replied. "I am sure those lazy servants have prepared plenty of food. One should always be prepared to show hospitality to friends."

"Daiyu, have you met my son Quan?" Mei asked, drawing him forward. "He is my youngest and a very good man."

Daiyu finally lifted her eyes to get a good look at Quan. He was about average height and solidly built, with his black hair cut very short and eyes of a peculiar light gray. He wore tiny silver hoops in both ears, and two silver rings on his left hand. His expression was friendly enough—slightly embarrassed and slightly amused to be part of his mother's machinations, but not truly uncomfortable—and his gaze was direct. He was wearing all black, embroidered with cobalt blue stars. Like her own, a studiedly casual look. Apparently, only Daiyu had been unaware that this meeting would occur.

She guessed that he was at least five years older than she was, so it was his place to initiate the conversation, which he did immediately. "Hello, Daiyu," he said, extending his palm, briefly touching hers, then letting his arm fall. "I saw you at my mother's breakfast, I think."

"Yes, and I saw you," she said, then winced at the inanity of her reply.

"Oh! There were so many people there! No time to get to know each other," Xiang said. "This is much better for real friends to talk. Quan, I am so glad you can join us."

They moved to a dining room that Daiyu had not been in before. This was a much bigger space, obviously designed to accommodate large numbers of guests, though today it was divided into a more intimate configuration by the placement of several painted screens. The rest of the décor was similarly opulent—velvet chairs, fussy wall sconces, an arboretum of plants, and half a dozen small jade statues on pedestals scattered around the room.

The rectangular table had been set with three places, but servants were even now ostentatiously laying a fourth place—to make it *very* clear that Quan had not been expected. Another servant came in, bowed to Xiang, and unobtrusively removed a black jade figurine of a bearded man.

Daiyu widened her eyes and did a quick count. Now there were five statues and four live people in the room. Nine individuals to sit at the meal. She tilted her head down and did her best to keep from smiling.

"Please, everybody, sit," Xiang said, waving her hand. "Mei, you must try this chair! I just bought it and I cannot decide. Do you think it is comfortable enough to keep? Is it perhaps too bright in color? I need someone who has good taste to advise me."

This little charade, of course, meant that Mei would be granted the best seat at the table. Daiyu hung back as Xiang carelessly directed Quan to his place—"Why don't you sit there?"—then took her own chair. The empty spot belonged to Daiyu. She had been unable to decide if it would be better to be seated next to Quan, where she would be forced to speak to him, or across from him, where he might have ample opportunity to stare at her. It looked like the matriarchs wanted them to talk. Still keeping her eyes modestly lowered, she slipped into the seat beside him.

At first, there was no opportunity for conversation. Course after course was brought to the table, and all anyone remarked on between bites was the deliciousness of the food. Even by Xiang's gourmet standards, Daiyu had to agree, the meal was outstanding.

Not until they were sipping tea and nibbling on a chocolate confection did the foursome have a chance to resolve into couples. "Xiang! Did you hear what that awful Lanfen said to me?" Mei demanded.

"Tell me," Xiang replied, her black eyes already alight with malice. "Though I can believe that she would say anything."

The older women turned their shoulders toward the other two and leaned forward to exchange low-voiced gossip. Of course, they would be able to audit anything Quan and Daiyu might find to talk about, but it was clear they were urging the younger two to try to make conversation.

Daiyu knew better than to speak first. She blew on her tea to cool it and took another sip. Part of her was fighting down a disastrous desire to giggle. That Xiang would truly be matchmaking for her false niece! That Mei's son might actually show an interest in her! It was so calamitous it could only be funny.

"I understand you are a visitor to Shenglang," Quan said at last.

She was not going to make this easy for him. Maybe he would decide she was rude and tell his mother he was not interested in pursuing her. "Yes."

"Where do you normally live?"

"With my parents in the northwestern provinces."

"It is much better in Shenglang, don't you think?"

"*Much* better," she replied.

There was a little silence.

"I have traveled to other parts of the world," Quan announced.

For a moment Daiyu was startled. Most of the inhabitants of Jia she had encountered so far seemed to believe Shenglang was the only part of this planet that actually mattered. She had started to think there *were* no other continents or cities. "Really? Where did you go?"

He reeled off a few names and when, just to keep the conversation from becoming impossibly awkward, she asked a few questions, he willingly responded with expanded detail. From what she could piece together, he had been to the parts of Jia that corresponded to Russia and China, and he would like to go to Europe. His mother, it seemed, had an interest in foreign trade, and Quan was of a commercial bent.

"My sisters only care about spending money," he said, his voice scornful. "But I like to make it."

"I might like to spend money if I had it," Daiyu said wistfully. "But I've always been forced to be very frugal."

She thought he might be disgusted at the reminder that she was poor, but instead he seemed pleased to learn she knew how to economize. He nodded approvingly. "It's good to be careful with money," he said. "We are lucky we have a prime minister who understands taxes and revenue."

Ah, finally a topic that she cared about. "I met the prime minister at your mother's breakfast," she said. "He seemed like a very intelligent man."

Quan grew animated. "Brilliant! He can analyze any situation and discover the solution. He can bring together warring factions and get consensus on issues that have divided the city for generations."

Daiyu was so surprised, she actually looked up at him. His gray eyes were full of admiration. "Really? What kind of issues?"

"The river, for one," Quan said. "Perhaps you have had an opportunity to learn how we mine for *qiji* stones?"

Daiyu nodded. Oh, yes.

"My mother owns some of the companies that test and buy *qiji* gems," he said with some satisfaction. "She makes a great deal of money from them. So do many of the other wealthy families of Shenglang. But ten years ago, there was a bitter dispute with the cities farther down the river. They claimed that we were mining too many *qiji* stones. Because they, too, dam the river and sort through the stones to find treasure."

That hadn't even occurred to her, but naturally, if the river flowed by analog cities such as Memphis and New Orleans, the residents of those towns would also want to pull wealth from the water.

"It was very ugly," Quan continued. "Southern cities were making pacts with northern cities to send more workers upstream to mine all the *qiji* stones before they could make it to Shenglang. There was talk here of permanently damming and rerouting the Zhongbu River. It was a bad time."

"How did the prime minister find a solution?" Daiyu asked.

"First, he called together representatives from all the major cities for a conference and he simply spoke to them. He has a very calming way about him—people listen to him," Quan said.

Daiyu nodded. She had observed for herself his hypnotic charm.

"Then he persuaded everyone to abide by a schedule in which each city takes its turn damming the river to search for stones. It is fair for everyone, and no one feels as if they are being cheated out of any wealth. Some of the smaller cities even cooperate with each other to share scanning equipment, which is very expensive. And Chenglei is the one who got everyone to work together."

Daiyu could not help but be impressed—and thoughtful. If, as everyone had told her, Chenglei cared only about the affluent classes, no doubt he had just been trying to ensure that the upper strata of Shenglang society did not squander their energy squabbling over the very resources that made them wealthy. Even so, it sounded like no one had suffered and everyone had benefited from his collaborative approach.

Once again, Chenglei was not behaving in the way she would expect from an out-and-out villain.

"I am glad you told me that story," Daiyu said. "Now I like the prime minister even more."

"My mother says we haven't had such a good man in office in many decades," Quan said. "Of course, I can't remember that far back!"

They both laughed. Daiyu almost asked him some innocuous question about what other activities he liked besides finance and world travel, but she didn't want him to think she was actually interested in him. So she cast her eyes down again and let him try to come up with another topic.

That proved to be unnecessary; the older women apparently had decided the young couple had had long enough to get acquainted. "Look at the time!" Mei exclaimed in a wholly unconvincing tone of voice. "Quan, we have appointments back at the house. We must be going."

After many thanks and compliments, Mei and her son departed. Xiang turned to Daiyu with a sly, triumphant look on her face.

"Mei's son and my niece," she said, and her voice was gloating. "Do you realize how much money that woman possesses? Every mother in the city wants Quan for her daughter. Yet I will be the one to secure him."

For a moment Daiyu had trouble breathing. "I had no thought of marriage when I came to Shenglang, Mistress," she said.

"Call me Aunt," Xiang said.

Aurora refused to be alarmed by the turn Daiyu's life was taking. "We didn't anticipate this, but it's not so terrible," Aurora said as she slipped inside Daiyu's room that night. She actually seemed amused. "In fact, this is good news! It means you will have more opportunities to see Chenglei. If Mei's son is courting you, you will be a highly prized guest."

"The more balls and dinners and breakfasts I attend, the

more likely I am to make a mistake!" Daiyu exclaimed.

"You haven't made any mistakes so far," Aurora said.

Daiyu's next words came out as a challenge. "The more hours I spend with Quan, the less time I will have to slip away and see Kalen."

Aurora pressed her lips together, no doubt to hold back a reply like, *That might not be such a bad thing.* Instead, she said in an even voice, "Don't worry. You will find time for Kalen."

After Aurora left, Daiyu sat for almost an hour before the open window. Her room was on the second floor, overlooking a portion of the garden that was filled with hundreds of perfumed flowers. It didn't seem like it would be that hard to climb out the window, shimmy down an ornamental pillar, and land on the soft soil. Could she find her way through the dark city to the house in the *cangbai* neighborhood where Kalen lay sleeping? Could she catch his attention without waking Aurora and Ombri? Would he wriggle out his own window and walk her slowly back through the deserted streets, listening to her stories about Xiang's matchmaking and Quan's politics, helping her sort through her own confused impressions? Would his very presence calm her jangled mind?

She had so many more things to tell him, things she wanted to store with him so the memories would not be lost. The slogan on her father's favorite T-shirt, the name of her mother's face cream, the actors pictured in the photos she had taped up in her locker at school. She was alarmed when she couldn't remember her computer password or the phone numbers of her three best friends. How soon would the other minor details be lost to her? How quickly would Jia cover her memories like a persistent and opportunistic ivy?

Kalen will remember everything that's truly important to me, she tried to reassure herself. *It won't be so terrible if I forget. Kalen will know.*

THIRTEEN

"ARE YOU INTERESTED in politics?" Quan asked Daiyu two days later.

They were strolling through the conservatory at his mother's house. Ostensibly, Xiang and Daiyu had dropped by Mei's to return a scarf that Xiang had borrowed some weeks ago. They were not going to stay long—"But why don't you put on that green top anyway? Yes, that one"—yet Mei had encouraged Quan to show Daiyu her herb collection. It was a ploy so thin as to be insulting, but Quan and Daiyu had stepped into the thick humid air of the conservatory and dutifully inspected the mint and basil. At any rate, that's what the leaves looked like to Daiyu, but she wasn't much of a gardener.

"I never paid any attention to politics when I lived with my mother," Daiyu said cautiously, not sure how to answer. "Why?"

"Chenglei is addressing the council later today, and I thought you might enjoy hearing him speak. You asked about him the other day."

She didn't want to encourage him, but Daiyu couldn't help but show her excitement at that. "Yes! I would love to hear him. Oh, Quan, how thoughtful of you to include me."

He looked pleased at her enthusiasm. "We must ask Xiang, of course, for she might have something else planned for you."

No plan could compete with the prospect of you spending time at my side, Daiyu thought cynically. "Yes, of course. I hope she will let me go!"

But Xiang, as expected, was quite content to see Daiyu disappear on an expedition with Quan, and Mei looked equally complacent. Xiang said, "You will bring her back to my house, please, before dinner."

"Yes, Mistress," Quan said, bowing. "Thank you for your permission."

A few moments later, Daiyu was surprised to find Quan acting as his own driver in one of those open-air cars that apparently only the rich could afford. "Your mother doesn't keep a chauffeur?" Daiyu asked as she settled beside him on the front bench instead of sitting in the passenger compartment in back. This was a much more pleasant way to travel, she decided at once. A little windy, but with a greatly improved view.

Quan smiled happily and tightened his hands on the wheel. Away from his mother's presence, he was instantly more relaxed and energetic. "She keeps five. I like to drive myself."

She quickly saw why. He was very fast, accelerating around

pedestrians, carts, and other vehicles with a speed that would have been reckless if he hadn't been so very precise. She tried not to gasp when they turned blind corners, but she did hold tightly to her seat and wonder what he might think if she started shrieking at him, *Slow down, you moron, you're risking my life!* She thought he would be so astonished he might never speak to her again.

Something to consider for the future.

When they had whipped down enough streets and skidded around enough obstacles, he abruptly pulled up with a flourish in front of a long, imposing building that simply screamed *government offices.* Daiyu wasn't sure—she thought they might be at the site of the cavernous St. Louis Convention Center. In this iteration, the building was made of a serviceable dull beige stone ornamented at a few entryways with perfunctory pagoda curves, and a banner across the front proclaimed an official welcome.

Quan found an open space in an attended parking lot, then hopped out to help Daiyu from the car.

"We might have to hurry a little," he said, retaining his hold on her hand.

Actually, they were running as they dashed through the shadowy hallways of the building and raced up two steep flights of stairs. The corridors were relatively full of people—aides and clerks, Daiyu supposed, and maybe reporters if Shenglang had any media outlets—and Quan apologized more or less continuously as he towed Daiyu behind him. She was breathless when he led them through a doorway on the third story, and they found themselves on an upper balcony of a large auditorium.

She glanced around quickly to get her bearings. Yes, this looked exactly like what she would expect from a public forum. Below them, on the ground floor, there was a dais where people could deliver speeches. Rows of seats faced the dais, and two balconies ran the full circumference of the auditorium so visitors could watch the entire proceedings.

Two men stood on the dais now, exchanging elaborate insults couched in flowery, formal language. Every seat on the bottom story was filled, about half by men, half by women, everyone Han. The balconies were much emptier, but clusters of visitors sat in the stiff, straight chairs or leaned over the railings to get a better look at the action. Everyone in the first balcony also was Han and looked to be financially comfortable, but there was a varied assemblage here where Daiyu and Quan had come to rest.

"Are you sure we belong up here?" she asked him in a whisper as they went to lean on the balustrade.

He gave her a careless grin. "Too many people I know one level down. Up here, I don't have to talk to anyone."

She grinned back, feeling a moment of genuine liking for him. But her attention was instantly caught by the drama below, as the two feuding speakers ended their presentation, bowed to the audience, and stepped down from opposite sides of the dais. In the silence that followed, it was easy to hear one man's footsteps as he approached the stage, climbed the stairs, and then stood for a moment, merely scanning the audience. Daiyu had the ridiculous thought that he took the time to look at each

individual council member, offering a swift moment of recogni-
tion; certainly it seemed as if he met *her* eyes when his gaze
swept over both upper stories.

After a silence that grew even more still as he waited, Chenglei finally began speaking. "My friends, it is good to be with you
all today," he said, and again Daiyu was instantly captivated by
the intimate warmth of his voice. It was as if he was addressing
each of them separately, telling each of them exactly what they
wanted to hear. "I have listened to the arguments of these fine
men and women, and I have been struck by their words. I have
been impressed by their research, and I have been moved by
their passion. Clearly everyone here in this room today wants
to do what is right and is willing to sacrifice tirelessly to bring
about the best result. I salute you all."

He paused, and once more he sent his gaze around the room.
His eyes briefly touched Daiyu and moved on. "We have a hard
task before us. People in the northwest territories are dying of
zaogao fever. For those of us healthy in Shenglang, what is our
responsibility? Let me tell you a story."

Again, he paused, seeming to collect his thoughts. Daiyu
leaned forward, impatient to hear more. She imagined everyone
in the whole auditorium echoing her movement. Certainly, beside her, Quan did the same.

"As you know, there are prohibitions against people with
zaogao fever traveling from their homes to seek aid. Many
people—including some of you in this council—have railed
against this seemingly inhumane quarantine. You are to be honored for your open hearts and the kindness of your intentions.

Some of you perhaps know others with similarly kind intentions living in the town of Gangshi on the western coast. Gangshi decided to make itself a haven for those poor diseased souls. Its residents opened their city. They opened their gates. They opened their hearts.

"Today we just got word—the entire city of Gangshi is infected. Every adult, every child, Han, *cangbai* or *heiren*. The deaths already have been staggering, but some remain alive—in order, perhaps that their suffering may be sustained. In order that they may look upon themselves, and their decisions, with horror.

"My friends, do you believe every citizen of Gangshi welcomed the sick and the dying? Do you believe that every young mother gazed down at her sleeping son and decided, 'Yes, this is what I will do. I will risk the lives of those I love most for a principle, for a gesture'? Don't you believe that some of the residents voted to hold the quarantine? Do those people deserve to die alongside the good-hearted rebels who invited disaster to cross the line? No—but they are dying anyway.

"Fellow councilors, citizens of Shenglang, my friends. We are rushing aid to every part of the northwest territories. We have funded philanthropic doctors and eager scientists who have set up outposts in these bitter lands, fighting the battle with death, sifting through science for a cure to *zaogao* fever. We are not leaving our comrades, our siblings, our fellow creatures alone to suffer and die. But it is madness to even think of lifting them from their diseased beds and carrying them into our own houses to offer them succor and shelter here. It is suicidal—no!

it is genocidal—to allow them to break quarantine. We suffer to see them suffer—but if we share their lives, we share their deaths. The quarantine must stand until we have found a cure. Or Shenglang will become like Gangshi, a town of walking dead."

His easy, hypnotic voice had grown sterner and more powerful as he spoke, and his final words were delivered in a ringing tone. The minute the last word sounded, all the listeners were on their feet. The auditorium shook with applause and roars of approval. Even the *cangbai* man in the upper balcony was chanting out his agreement; even the old *heiren* woman dressed in ragged clothing was clapping her hands.

Even Daiyu was nodding. Perhaps it was what he said, perhaps it was the way he said it, but everything Chenglei said made sense. She was sure she should be picking apart his speech, finding the error of logic, the vital flaw, but at the moment, she couldn't think clearly. At that moment, she believed Chenglei.

Astonishingly, Xiang had no plans for Daiyu the following day. No appointments with dressmakers or deportment specialists, no accidental meetings with Mei or her son.

"May I go to the aviary, then?" Daiyu asked over their second meal of the day. She posed the question casually, but, under the table, her hands were clasped together so tightly they hurt. She hadn't seen Kalen in days, and she missed him with a pain that was almost physical. She didn't know if she would be able to maintain her meek façade if Xiang refused her now.

But she didn't. "I suppose you may. The driver will take you."

"Thank you, Aunt."

There had been no time to tell Kalen that she would be coming, and she tried not to think about the possibility that he might not be working in the bird house that afternoon. But she had scarcely taken ten steps past the black grillwork gate before he came bounding up to her, a bucket in his hand sloshing water over the sides as he ran.

"Daiyu! Is something wrong?"

She was so happy to see him that she almost threw her arms around him, but she knew better than to do anything so foolish. "No. Yes. I mean, nothing has happened, it's just that I'm so *confused*. And I *missed* you."

He set down his bucket and led her deep into the aviary. They stepped past bushes covered with twittering scarlet birds, past shallow reflecting pools, past the giant trees and the hanging vines all decorated with patches of feathered red. She could hear the muted rumble before they came across the artificial waterfall situated at the heart of the aviary, a cheery tumble of water charging down a stone face about two stories high and feeding into a bubbling pool.

"Back here," Kalen said, and flattened himself against the surface of the stone to edge behind the sheet of water. He disappeared.

Daiyu held her breath and, fully expecting to get drenched, followed him.

Instantly she found herself in a shallow and surreally lit alcove curtained by the rushing water. There was a damp space about three feet wide between the stone wall and the water itself.

"Kalen! What a wonderful place!" Daiyu exclaimed.

He had pulled off his shirt and was spreading it on the ground. His bare chest and arms were wiry, muscled with years of labor, but he was far too thin for someone of his height. "Here. You can sit on that," he said, settling on the ground so she would have all of the fabric for herself. He had to pull his legs up tightly to make sure his feet weren't dangling in the water.

She didn't bother protesting; she knew he would insist. So she dropped beside him, leaned her back against the rock, and locked her arms around her updrawn knees.

"I'm so glad you were here today," she said. "I always feel safe when I'm with you."

"So what happened?" he asked. He prodded her with a finger in her ribs. She grabbed his hand to make him stop and then didn't let go.

"Chenglei," she said.

"You've talked to him again?"

She shook her head. "Heard him deliver a speech. About why the sick people in the northwest need to be quarantined."

"Well, that's always been his position."

"And everything he said sounded so plausible," she said. "I

mean, he could very well be right. If there's some—some—plague in the northwest territories and it moves to Shenglang, it could wipe out half the population. It's not like it hasn't happened before in the history of the world. At least, my world."

Kalen was watching her, his face unreadable. But his hand was still clasped with hers, warm and comforting. "Then why are you confused?"

"Because he's wrong! I know he's wrong! If a civilized society turns its back on its weakest members, then it is no longer a civilized society. And the sick and the dying are the weakest of all. If I learned nothing else from my father, I learned that."

Now Kalen gave her a smile and squeezed her hand. "See?" he said quietly. "You didn't need me to remember *that* for you."

For a moment she was startled, and then she laughed. "You're right. I can practically hear my father saying the words." She shook her head. "But it took me a long time last night to come up with the counterargument. I lay awake for at least three hours, trying to figure it out."

"And that's why you're confused?"

Still leaning against the stone, she turned her head to look at him. "I'm confused because I don't know how he could make it sound right in the first place. How he could make me believe him when I know he's wrong."

"A lot of people believe him," Kalen said. "It's hardly surprising that you did too."

"Aurora says that evil is seductive," Daiyu said, her voice troubled. Aurora also said that Chenglei was evil. Daiyu was far from sure Aurora was right on either count.

Kalen grinned. "Does she? I've always found evil to be flat-out ugly. But maybe she knows a higher class of villain than I do."

Daiyu gave him an absent smile. Her voice, she could tell, was anxious. "But what if Chenglei is not actually a villain? What if he's just mistaken? What if he truly believes that Shenglang is endangered? I might not agree with his conclusions, but that doesn't make him a bad man, just a misguided one."

Kalen didn't answer, just watched her with his calm brown eyes. When she went on, her voice had dropped to a murmur. "What if Aurora and Ombri are wrong? Worse, what if they're lying? What if Chenglei doesn't deserve to be sent away after all?"

She half expected him to berate her for her loss of faith, to state with conviction that Aurora and Ombri were pure-hearted as angels sent from the most benevolent of the gods. But he didn't. "I have come to believe in them, but I can only speak for myself," he said slowly. "And maybe I would have believed in anyone who gave me a place to live and food to eat. Maybe I would believe in Chenglei if he was the one who offered me shelter. Maybe I'm just a simple man."

"Kalen," she whispered, "that doesn't help at all."

He laid his free hand along the side of her face, drawing her toward him until their noses almost touched. "You have to act on whatever it is you believe," he said, his voice very low. "No one can tell you what that is. Not me, not your father, not Aurora or Ombri. Only you."

"I wish you *would* tell me," she replied, still whispering. "You're the only one who makes sense to me."

He closed the distance between them, placing a gentle kiss upon her mouth. Instantly, she was flooded with a sense of well-being, a conviction that everything would be fine. She dropped his hand so she could twine both arms around his neck, and she scooted closer so she could kiss him back. His other arm came up to encircle her waist and his kiss grew a little harder; he shifted positions to draw her deeper into his embrace.

And then abruptly he released her with a muffled exclamation of annoyance. At first she was shocked, and then she started laughing. He had accidentally swept his feet through the waterfall and now he was wet up to his knees.

"I hope nobody was walking by just now and happened to see your feet poking through the water!" she exclaimed.

"Well, that'll teach me to be places I shouldn't be, doing things I shouldn't do," he remarked. He seemed cheerful but a little unsure, as if utterly unable to predict what she might say now.

She laughed a little shakily. She was fully aware of all the reasons it was a bad idea to be kissing Kalen, from Xiang's horror at his unsuitability to the fact that she would be leaving him behind forever in a matter of days. Even so, she felt decidedly pleased with herself; she knew the heat in her cheeks was part embarrassment and part delight. "Then it seems unfair that you're the only one who got drenched, since I shouldn't have been here doing that either," she said.

"I don't think I'll be mentioning it to Ombri," he said.

"I don't think I'll be telling Xiang."

He smiled, but quickly turned serious. She wished he would

take her hand again, but he didn't. "I wonder if it might do you good to hear Feng talk about Chenglei."

"Who's—oh, the dissident you told me about? I'd like that."

"I'll see if he's got anything planned. It's been a while since I've heard him, so maybe he's still in hiding. They say that Chenglei hates him."

"Every political party needs the righteous anger of the loyal opposition to keep it honest," Daiyu said.

Kalen laughed at her. "Is that your father talking again?"

"No, that's Isabel. My boss." Daiyu paused, for she hadn't thought about Isabel in days. "If you let Aurora know where he'll be, I'll try to get free to go hear him."

He hesitated. "Sometimes Feng speaks at fairly disreputable places. Will you be afraid or uncomfortable?"

"Not if you're with me," she said honestly.

He nodded. "We'll meet here and then slip away."

"Aurora won't like it," Daiyu said. "She doesn't want me to do anything to risk Xiang's displeasure."

"I'll find a way to give Aurora a message so that she won't realize what we're planning," Kalen said.

They smiled at each other in perfect complicity. For the most part Daiyu was a docile and obedient daughter, but she had learned years ago that there were times the adults in her life didn't need to be apprised of all her plans.

"I suppose I'd better go," she said. "But it was so good to finally see you again! And to talk face-to-face without having to pretend!"

His smile deepened. "It *was* good," he said meaningfully, and she blushed again. She scrambled to her feet and shook out his shirt, which was now both wrinkled and a little mudstained, before handing it back.

"I hope your shoes and pants dry," she said. "Sorry you got wet."

He shrugged and pushed her gently toward the opening where they had squeezed in. But right before she flattened herself against the stone, he stopped her with a hand on her shoulder. When she looked up, he gave her one more brief kiss.

"In case I never have another chance," he said.

She looked up at him for a moment. "I hope you do," she said.

Out from behind the tumbling water, back on the formal pathways that led through the aviary, Daiyu opened her parasol and strolled toward the gate. She moved as if she was in no great hurry, pausing every once in a while to admire one of the streaks of bright red that painted the humid air. She glanced back only once, to see Kalen on his knees, scrubbing a stone bench. He did not even look up as she stepped through the gate and back to the car where the driver sat waiting.

FOURTEEN

THE FOLLOWING DAYS were devoted entirely to getting ready for the Presentation Ball, which was only four days away. *How could it be so soon?* Daiyu thought, as something like dread washed over her. She knew that the minute she snapped the bracelet on Chenglei's wrist, her time in Shenglang was effectively over. Oh, she might be able to stay another day or two, curious to see how the city changed once Chenglei was gone, but there was no reason for her to linger.

One reason, of course.

Every time she thought about leaving Kalen behind, she had a moment when she actually could not breathe. It was bad enough knowing she would never see him again—never have a chance to watch his face light up when he caught sight of her— never tuck her hand in his and feel, for as long as she held on to him, that she was safe and the world was good. But knowing that once she left Jia, she would leave behind all memories of Kalen, made her absolutely frantic. She *could not* forget his shy smile and his easy way of speaking. She *could not* forget those magical kisses behind the shimmering wall of translucent water. Surely Kalen's face had been imprinted on her heart, a shape and a memory that she would carry with her no matter what dimension she called home.

To distract herself from her constant anxiety over Kalen, she tried to throw herself wholeheartedly into preparations for the ball. She submitted uncomplainingly to the final round of dress fittings; she sniffed dozens of perfumes as she and Xiang worked together to find Daiyu's perfect scent. She exclaimed in unfeigned wonder as Xiang spread the contents of her jewelry box on a table in her ornate parlor.

"*Aunt!* What beautiful gems you have! I've never seen anything like these!"

"No, and you never will again, though Mei thinks her own jewels are worth as much as mine," Xiang replied, preening a little. With her long lacquered nails, she picked through the necklaces, the earrings, the pins, the rings, the bracelets. "When we chose the fabric for your dress, I had thought it might look best with pearls and sapphires, but now I am wondering. I believe *qiji* stones would go with it even better. What do you think?"

And she picked up a short strand of exquisite pink gems thickly clustered on a slim gold chain.

Daiyu could only stare.

There had to be a hundred *qiji* stones on this necklace, so many it would take a stonepicker months to mine them from the river. That was shocking enough all by itself, but Daiyu also was amazed to finally see what a polished *qiji* looked like—and to realize that she recognized it. It was a *qiji* that the old woman had handed her back at Fair Saint Louis; it was a *qiji* that had pulled her through the Arch into this iteration. She had been enthralled with the very first one she had seen, and she'd had no idea what it was.

"My dress is—is blue," she stammered.

"Yes, but the accents are not," Xiang said. Very true; the neckline and the last quarter of the sleeves were heavily embroidered in pink and rose and coral. "Just think how this color would draw out those shades!"

"I would love to wear something as beautiful as this necklace," Daiyu said honestly. Xiang still held it out in her extended hand, so Daiyu gently touched the glowing pink gems. An electric tingle ran up her fingertips, magnified by the number of stones.

"And the earrings," Xiang said. "And the bracelet. Here. Try them on."

It was like wearing a collar that hummed and buzzed around her throat; the earrings jangled against her cheeks, and her wrist was alive with sparkles. Even against the ordinary dull beige of Daiyu's shirt, the gems glowed with a scarcely banked fire. She gazed at herself in the chrome mirror, astonished that the *qiji* gems weren't throwing out visible flares.

"Oh, if I could take something like this home with me," Daiyu said with a sigh. "Even one *qiji*. I would remember my days in Shenglang for the rest of my life."

Xiang didn't seem offended by the covetous note in Daiyu's voice; she actually seemed pleased at Daiyu's reaction. "Well, as to that, who knows how long it will be before you go home," she said in her usual calculating way. "You might choose to stay. You might choose to marry. You never know what could happen."

Daiyu nodded silently and continued to watch herself in the chrome, turning this way and that to see how the pink of the shimmering stones threw a subtle color into her cheeks. Xiang, of course, was imagining Daiyu married to Quan instead of returning to her dreary parental home in the disease-stricken northwest; but Daiyu was wondering what it would be like to live with Kalen in Shenglang instead of returning to St. Louis where she belonged.

Two days before the Presentation Ball, Aurora brought her a note from Kalen. "He drew this for you because he thought you might want to remember the stonepickers once you'd gone home," Aurora said, smiling a little. "But he's not much of an artist."

Daiyu took the picture from her and laughed out loud. It was obvious he had tried to sketch in the dam, the bell tower, the red gate, a pedestrian bridge, and the stonepickers themselves, bent double over the muddy riverbed as they dropped items into their shoulder bags. But the perspectives were sadly off and a number of erasures had worn the paper through in spots.

"I don't suppose I would have done any better," Daiyu said. She gave Aurora a straight look, somewhat challenging. "Can I see him before I go to the ball?"

Aurora assumed the speculative and tense expression she usually wore these days when Daiyu mentioned Kalen, as if she was always wondering how Daiyu's fondness for the *cang-bai* boy could bring this whole delicate mission crashing down. "Unless Xiang permits you to visit the aviary again, I am not sure how."

"Then afterward?" Daiyu said. "Once the ball is over? And Chenglei is—is gone? Can I see him then?"

"Before you return to your home?" Aurora said. "Yes, I'm sure we can arrange that."

Daiyu nodded, as if that satisfied her. "Good. Make sure you thank him for sending me this picture."

"I will."

The minute Aurora left, Daiyu examined the paper intently, looking for a hidden message. Not until she turned it over did she see the careless words scrawled on the back and crossed out, as if this page had been used as scrap paper before it had been turned into an artist's canvas. There was a column of numbers added up, a list that might have been a reminder about groceries, and then two words: TOMORROW AFTERNOON.

Daiyu carefully folded the paper and tucked it inside the red silk pouch that held the rose quartz stone. She never went anywhere without the quartz in her pocket; if she suddenly had to depart for her home iteration, she didn't want to risk leaving this precious memento behind.

❋

Xiang was not enthusiastic about Daiyu's plan to visit the avi-ary one more time, but Daiyu allowed herself to show a little agitation over breakfast. "I keep thinking about how important tomorrow is—and what I must say and must not say—and it makes me very nervous," she said, casting her eyes down and biting her lip. "I find the birds and the garden very soothing."

Xiang hunched an impatient shoulder. "Fine. You would do better to lie in your room and sleep, but go let birds dump their excrement on your head, I don't mind. But I need Aurora's help. You must go alone."

"Thank you, Aunt. You are very good to me."

Xiang made an annoyed sound and turned away.

Kalen was hovering just inside the front gate at the aviary. She could not run to him and fling her arms around his neck, as she wanted to do; instead, she nodded at him coolly and walked on by, and he fell in step behind her. The driver had told Daiyu he would wait out front with the car until she was ready to go home again, so she and Kalen had to exit by the back entrance. Even once they were outside, she could not take his hand as they negotiated the crowded streets. She had worn the plainest of the clothes that Xiang had given her, but even so, Daiyu was dressed like the daughter of a wealthy family. Beside her, Kalen looked more than ordinarily unkempt. It would be bad enough if someone saw them together, but she could always claim she was paying a *cangbai* laborer to perform some task for her. Less easy to use that excuse if she was clinging to his hand, smiling in a wide and foolish manner, appearing to be half in love with the boy.

Or wholly in love.

"I've missed you," she said when they were far enough from the aviary that it seemed safe to talk. "I thought about you a couple of nights ago when I heard the river bell. Did you find any *qiji* stones when you went out?"

"Two," he said. "Small ones, though."

He sounded indifferent, but she was instantly concerned. "Are you worried about running out of money?" she asked.

He shrugged. "I'll be all right."

"But—"

He looked down at her with an odd, sweet smile. "There are other things that worry me more right now."

He didn't say it, but he didn't have to. "I know," she said softly. "Sometimes I can't think about anything else but what happens when I go back to St. Louis."

"Well," he said, "you haven't left yet."

They were some distance from the aviary before Kalen finally hailed a trolley, having let at least three others pass by. This one was more battered than most, its wooden seats worn and stained, its motor loud and doleful. The clientele was exceptionally grungy. Daiyu was even more conscious of her expensive, finely embroidered shirt, her silk trousers. Most of the other riders ignored her, but one older *heiren* woman watched her for the next ten minutes with a look of sullen resentment.

"This is our stop," Kalen said, and they hopped off in a truly disreputable part of town. Daiyu couldn't even guess where it might correspond to any part of St. Louis. It was worse than Kalen's neighborhood, where the residents at least tried to maintain what amenities were still in place. Here, there were almost no whole buildings standing; the shells of wood and brick structures made an erratic skyline against the glaring sun. In some spots, weeds and shrubbery partially obscured the rubble of fallen houses. Other lots were completely barren, littered with trash and glittering piles of glass.

Yet children ran playing through the streets, and women paused in their endless tasks to share news and heartache. Campsites set up among the shattered foundations and fabric hanging from the ruined windows proved that vagrants and squatters called even this desperate vicinity home.

"Are you afraid?" Kalen asked her.

She shook her head. "I wish I was wearing something else," she said. "A shirt like this just mocks their lives."

"Turn it inside out," he suggested. They ducked behind the half wall of a fallen house and he stood with his back to her to offer added protection from curious eyes. The embroidery was scratchy against her skin but she felt a little less conspicuous as they moved forward again. Casually Kalen took her hand, and casually she allowed him to keep it.

Another five minutes' walking took them to an intersection where four large buildings apparently had once stood; even their hulking ruins were impressive, gray and heavy and throwing long silhouettes of welcome shade. A small crowd had started to congregate in those patches of shadow. Daiyu could hear a voice proclaiming excited, angry sentences before she got close enough to see the speaker or make out the words. She noticed that the crowd was made up of more men than women, more *cangbai* and *heiren* than Han, but it was still a pretty broad mix.

She edged around the back of the crowd, Kalen a reassuring shape beside her, until she could get a good look at the speaker. He was standing on a chair, and his head and shoulders were visible above the mob. His face was long and a little narrow, framed by neglected shoulder-length black hair. He had the build of a muscular man, but the gauntness of someone who had missed a lot of meals for a long time. While they watched, he raised his hand above his head in a hard fist and spoke with passion.

"That's Feng," Kalen murmured in Daiyu's ear. She nodded and listened.

"Bad enough that he has quarantined the northwest provinces, effectively condemning every living soul above the Maiwei River to death," Feng was shouting. "Bad enough that he has made it a felony offense to help an individual infected with *zaogao* fever. If your mother is dying, you cannot go to her! If your sister is sick, you cannot fetch her! If your father is starving, you cannot cross the Maiwei and bring him food. *But no one else can either!* He has closed the roads, he has cut off the supplies. Everyone in the territory will die!"

Appalled, Daiyu stared up at Kalen. "Is that true?"

He shrugged. "I don't know."

"How does *he* know?"

He shook his head and shrugged again, his expression sad.

Feng was bending down to pass out stacks of paper to the people in the front of the crowd. "Look, these are copies of the official order that was sent out a week ago, signed by Chenglei himself, to stop all aid at the Maiwei River. The last shipments of food and medicine went out eight days ago. Nothing has been sent across the border since."

The crowd began to shift and murmur, growing more disturbed. The papers were scrutinized and handed around. One copy made its way to the back row with surprising swiftness, and Kalen plucked it from someone's hand. He bent down so he and Daiyu could study it together. It was a bad reproduction of what looked like an official document, decorated with a river-and-dragon device that Daiyu guessed was the city seal of Shenglang. The wording was complex, and she had a much harder time translating written than spoken language, but it indeed appeared to be an order to terminate supply shipments to the northwest provinces.

It was impossible to tell if the document was authentic.

Deeply troubled, Daiyu looked up and began listening to the rest of Feng's speech. "Did you know that Yazhou has passed a resolution to send relief to the northwest territories?" he demanded. "We are the richest country in the entire world, we have the most sophisticated medicine, and yet foreigners are crossing the entire *ocean* so they can take care of our people! These sick and starving people are not *cangbai* or *heiren*—these are not the people Chenglei *despises*. These are Han! People with whom he shares a bloodline! And yet he will let them die because it is too much trouble to keep them alive.

"If he does not care about the sick and suffering of the outer coasts, who will he choose to ignore next? Who else will die because he is selfish or careless? Will he decide that the *heiren* are too impure to live? Will he decree that they all must die? Will he place restrictions on the *cangbai*—deny them access to money and property?"

"I never yet saw a *cangbai* with a coin to his name!" someone from the crowd called, and many listeners laughed. The sound had an uneasy relief to it; clearly Feng's rhetoric was making them all uncomfortable. And yet, Daiyu noticed, no one was leaving. Instead, more people were arriving every minute. Some of them were not the disenfranchised and poor who called this district home. A few looked like well-to-do merchants and young adults with some university education. Individuals Chenglei would not want to alienate.

"Yes!" Feng called back. "We have long lived in an unjust society where a man might sometimes be ashamed to call him-self Han! But until Chenglei took up the prime minister's title, a *heiren* man could earn a decent living. A *cangbai* woman could own a house and run a business. But Chenglei has proposed the Purity Property Law—"

"It didn't pass!" someone else yelled.

"And do you think that's the end of the matter?" Feng de-manded. "Do you think Chenglei will not revise that law and submit it again under another name? Chenglei wants one thing and one thing only—prosperity for a handful of Han families who control the power and wealth of Shenglang. Everyone else may be a slave, or everyone else may be a corpse—he doesn't care. As long as he achieves his ends."

"Why does it matter to you?" a *cangbai* woman cried out.

She was standing a few feet away from Daiyu, rocking a baby against her shoulder. "You're one of them! A Han boy with a bank account."

The crowd laughed and Feng laughed with them. He pushed his hair back from his thin face with an impatient hand. "Chenglei hates me more than he hates any of you," Feng said. "Because I speak the truth, and men like Chenglei are always afraid of the truth. He would kill me if he could. He would send me to the northwest provinces to die of fever."

Someone else shouted another question, but Daiyu didn't hear it. Kalen's hand had come up to grip her arm, and suddenly he was hauling her away from the assembled people. She started to protest, but then she heard it too—the sound of a dozen vehicles racing too fast over the broken roadways, headed in their direction.

"Chenglei's personal guards," Kalen whispered, urging her to move faster.

"Kalen," she breathed. They began to run.

# FIFTEEN

OFFICIAL-LOOKING VEHICLES arrived from two different directions, tires squealing and car doors slamming. There was a noise that was halfway between a horn and a whistle, but far more shrill, and the sound of people screaming. Another car came swerving up the very road that they were running down. Kalen jerked Daiyu into the dubious shelter of a ruined building and began wading through the upended stones and pools of disintegrated mortar. She could hear the car screech to a stop; heavy footsteps hit the broken pavement and skidded on the unstable rubble. The guards were coming after them.

Kalen yanked her out through a window that had almost evolved into a door and, ducking low to avoid being seen, pulled her behind him to an adjoining building that was in similarly bad shape.

"If we get separated," he murmured in her ear once they were inside the tumbled walls, "take this road. Turn left when you get to the big street with all the trees. The number sixteen trolley will take you back to the aviary."

"Why would we get separated?" she whispered back.

He put a finger to his lips and they paused to listen. A short distance away, from the direction of the crowd, Daiyu could hear more screaming and the sounds of heavy objects striking something soft. She thought the guards were beating the mob with cudgels or clubs.

"Kalen," she whispered, but he just shook his head. Silently, he urged her toward the high sill of a window that might once have overlooked a half landing. With his help, she swung herself up and over the crumbled ledge. She thought she saw the shadows of two men enter the building on the other side just as she dropped to the ground outside. Kalen scrambled out seconds after her.

A shout from inside the ruined structure—they had been seen. Hard boots hit buried stones as the men headed toward the easier exits left by the ruined walls. Kalen shoved Daiyu forcefully in the back.

"*Run!*" he cried.

The guards were coming around the building now, mouths open in ugly yells, nightsticks raised. "Kalen!" she said frantically. "Kalen, I can't leave you—"

"I can't stand it if anything happens to you," he said. He kissed her hard on the mouth and then pushed her toward the street again. Turning his back on her, he charged toward the oncoming guards with an inarticulate cry. Sobbing, she did as he had told her, stumbling across the broken fields of masonry, hearing behind her the fading sounds of blows and shouts.

They wouldn't kill him, surely they wouldn't kill him. It was civil disobedience, it was disturbing the peace, it was a minor infraction. In St. Louis, he might be wrestled to the ground and handcuffed and maybe thrown in jail for the night, but what did she know about the laws in Shenglang? Maybe he would be beaten bloody, maybe he would be left to die, and she wouldn't *know,* she couldn't go to him later and find out, and by midnight the next day she might very well be back in her own time with no memory of Kalen's existence at all.

Shuddering with sobs, she halted, hesitated, and almost went back. At that moment, she didn't care if she horrified Xiang by getting beaten or jeopardized her mission on Jia by getting arrested. She didn't spare a thought for Aurora or Ombri or Chenglei. She wanted to go back—she *would* have gone back—except she didn't want to make things worse for Kalen. A blow to her body would be a blow to his heart. He would sacrifice himself trying to save her. She could not endanger him any more than she already had.

She forced herself forward again, crying even harder. Blinded by tears, she fell down twice, scraping her left hand raw and leaving smears of dirt on her trousers and her shirt.

Her shirt. Inside out still to make her less noticeable. She could not possibly return to the aviary with her clothes in such disarray. She wiped her hands across her eyes and looked around. By now, she was on the fringes of this ragged part of town; she was almost to the respectable neighborhoods of Shenglang.

There were more people on the streets, and the buildings here were whole, if not particularly well-maintained. She slipped behind one of them, not greatly caring at that moment if anyone saw her stark naked, and rearranged her clothes. Her hair was no doubt a mess and her face probably was streaked and blotchy, but maybe she could calm herself to a more suitable state while she rode the trolley.

What was happening to Kalen?

Daiyu bit back another sob and hurried on her way. Here was the broad, tree-lined boulevard that Kalen had told her to look for. She turned left, somehow convinced she was headed toward the river. Two trolleys passed by, neither of them bearing the number she wanted. Her adrenaline rush was ebbing, and suddenly she was so tired she didn't know if she could continue another step. She was seriously considering collapsing to the sidewalk when she was startled by a vehicle pulling up so close to her that she actually jumped away from it in alarm.

"Daiyu!" It was Quan, staring at her in astonishment as he cut the motor and swung out of the car. "Daiyu, what happened to you? Has someone assaulted you? Here, climb in! Let me take you home."

He darted around the side of the car and laid a hand on her shoulder. She staggered under the pressure, and he caught her with both hands, gazing down at her with his gray eyes. "Daiyu," he said in a wondering voice, "what have you been doing?"

Her hands clutched his forearms as she stared up at him. She had been so focused on getting to safety that she had not bothered to come up with a good lie. "I . . ." she said, "I fell down."

He did not release her, did not lift her up into the car, just continued to watch her. "What were you doing," he said slowly, "here on the north side?"

He made *the north side* sound like the pit of hell. She was willing to bet that all sorts of illicit commerce happened in this part of town and that Quan was suddenly wondering if Daiyu was addicted to drugs or some other unsavory excitement. The so-traditional Quan would be disgusted to think she was drawn to such pursuits, Daiyu thought. But he had caught her in extraordinarily compromising circumstances. Only partial truth would do—very partial.

"I got lost," she said, letting her eyes fill with tears again. "I was disobedient! I begged my aunt Xiang to allow me to go to the aviary, telling her it would calm my anxious mind, but I was lying to her because I wanted to get out of the house. I am a country girl! I am not used to being so bound and restricted, and I wanted to see more of the city. So I snuck out of the aviary, and I got on a trolley, and I rode around the city. But after I got off and walked a while, I couldn't remember how to get back, and I went the wrong way, and I was so afraid! Those *houses*! Have you seen them? They're falling down! But people are living in them anyway. Someone asked me for money and I said I didn't have any, and then someone else asked me, and I started to run away, and then I fell down, and I—I—oh, my aunt Xiang will never forgive me."

Now she allowed herself to cry in earnest. "She won't take

me to the Presentation Ball! She'll say I'm no good, like my mother, that I don't deserve good luck and beautiful things. I just wanted to see the city, and now I'm ruined. She'll send me away tonight!"

Just for a second, Quan hesitated, but when Daiyu turned her head, trying to hide her face, he drew her in for an awkward hug. "No, she won't, she'll never know," he said. "I'll tell her you have been with me all afternoon."

"And she'll think you have been beating me with your fists," Daiyu wailed into his shoulder. "I must look like I have been savaged in the streets."

He laughed softly. "We can take care of that. We'll find a place where you can straighten your hair and wipe your face and get something to eat. You will look perfectly fine by the time I take you home."

Daiyu allowed herself to be comforted; she pulled back to stare at him with red-rimmed but hopeful eyes. "But I left the driver at the aviary," she said. "He has been waiting all this time."

"We will first tell the driver that you have come into my possession," Quan said, and the way he said *possession* would have given Daiyu pause if her circumstances had not been so dire. "You will see. I can make all of this unpleasantness go away."

She smiled at him through her tears, trying to make her expression melt with gratitude. "Thank you, Quan," she said. "You are the kindest man. I am so glad you found me."

He helped her into the car and climbed over her to start the engine, and soon he was racing through the streets with the reckless speed she remembered. She squealed, which made him laugh, and she laughed back at him. In ten minutes, they were at the aviary, dismissing the driver; five minutes later, they were walking into a small, casual café. Quan ordered for both of them while she disappeared into the bathroom to clean up. When she returned to the table, she thanked him shyly, flirting a little from under her lowered lashes.

All this time she was trying to hold back an urgent, untamable terror. All this time she was finding it hard to breathe, hard to think, hard to do anything but succumb to hysteria. All this time she was thinking, *What has happened to Kalen?*

Xiang was not at all displeased to learn that Daiyu had spent the afternoon with Quan. She tapped two of those long red fingernails against Daiyu's cheek, staring up at the taller girl with her dark eyes brightened by excitement.

"So the bird cage is not so interesting after all," the old woman said, her face crinkled into a smile of satisfaction. "I am glad to hear it."

"No, I—I did not go there to meet him," Daiyu said, knowing Xiang would not believe her denial. She had balled up her left hand, which was scraped from her fall, and hidden it against her black trousers. Good thing she would be wearing gloves tomorrow night. "I promise you, Aunt."

"Well, you would have done better to stay home and soak your feet in oil all afternoon, but you have not done so badly," Xiang said, dropping her hand, but still smiling. "I suppose he asked you for nine dances?"

"Yes, but I told him I could only grant him three." This particular ritual of courtship Xiang had drilled in her head so often that she had made the proper response without even thinking about it.

Xiang nodded. "Excellent. This is turning out even better than I hoped."

Daiyu wondered how quickly Xiang would revise that opinion once Daiyu vanished into the night.

She was so worried about Kalen that she could hardly get through dinner; her stomach nearly revolted when she tried to eat. "I am nervous about tomorrow evening," she said when Xiang demanded what was wrong with her.

"Well, do not show your nervousness to the prime minister," Xiang snapped. "He does not like cowering girls."

Daiyu lowered her eyes and toyed with the food on her plate. "Yes, Aunt."

Once she was in her room, she could do nothing but pace and stare out the window as she waited for Aurora's visit. Over and over again in her mind, she replayed those last few minutes—the guards charging at Kalen with their weapons raised, Kalen fearlessly running to meet them. She heard the sounds of fists hitting flesh and boots hitting bone. And she had run away, she had left him there—

She practically pounced on Aurora when the blond woman finally slipped through the door. "How's Kalen? Did you talk to him? Is he all right?"

Aurora shut the door firmly and stared at Daiyu. "Why should anything be wrong with Kalen?"

Daiyu strangled a sob. "I was with him this afternoon—and some of Chenglei's guards attacked us—and I ran away—Aurora, he told me to! I wouldn't have left him, but he pushed me aside—"

Aurora's face was a study in apprehension. She glanced at the door, as if afraid spies hovered on the other side, then pulled Daiyu all the way across the room.

"Quietly," she said. "Tell me what happened."

Daiyu stumbled through the narrative, clumsy with the words as she saw the darkening expression on Aurora's face. "And I don't know what happened to him," she finished up. "You have to tell me! You must go to the house to find out, then come back here to let me know."

"I can't do that!" Aurora exclaimed, her voice soft but her anger unmistakable. "Daiyu, you have risked everything! If any of those guards had caught you—if Xiang were to find out where you had been—"

"I know, I know, I'm very sorry," Daiyu said hastily. "Xiang would throw me out of the house and I would have no chance to get close to Chenglei—"

"Worse than that! We could be exposed! If you were arrested and searched, the bracelet would be found, and Chenglei would instantly know what it was! He would realize that Ombri and

I were here looking for him, and he would put up so many safe-guards that we would never get close to him again. We have always been prepared for the possibility you could fail, but as long as you are not discovered, there is no great harm done. It would take more time, but we would find another sojourner and try again. But if he knows we are on Jia, if he knows we are trying to send him back—he will seal himself off so effectively, we will never get another chance."

"I'm sorry. I truly am," Daiyu said, but she could tell her voice sounded impatient, not contrite. "But, please. You have to let me know what happened to Kalen."

"I can't return here once I have left for the day. You know that. I do not have so privileged a place."

Daiyu almost glowered at her. "Aurora, I almost didn't come back to Xiang's house because I was so worried about Kalen. If you don't let me know what has happened to him, I swear I will leave here tonight to find out for myself—and I won't be permitted back inside either."

Aurora pressed her lips together. "Fine. Ombri or I will re-turn and leave a message of some sort. A red scarf in the yard will mean that Kalen is hurt. A green scarf will mean that he is perfectly whole. I will braid them together if he is hurt but his injuries are not severe. We will leave one of the scarves in the garden below your window."

Daiyu nodded. "And if he—if he is dead?"

"He's not dead," Aurora said sharply.

"If he is?"

"A black scarf. But he is not dead."

"All right. Then go home. And come back as fast as you can."

Daiyu had one hand on Aurora's arm, pushing her toward the door, but Aurora did not budge. For such a delicate woman, she was surprisingly solid. "Don't stay awake all night fretting over this," Aurora said. "You must be at your best tomorrow. You must be rested and beautiful and charming and quick-witted. Everything we have schemed for succeeds or fails to-morrow night."

"I know," Daiyu said. "I will go to bed as soon as I see the scarf in the garden. As soon as I know if Kalen is all right."

There was a long pause, while each of them had the same thought. Daiyu added in a whisper, "Don't lie to me, Aurora. Don't tell me he is alive if he is dead, just so I do my part."

Aurora's hair seemed to brighten in indignation. "That is something Chenglei would do, so I would not," the blond wom-an said. "Whatever the truth is, I will give it to you. And in return, you must give us your best effort."

"I will," Daiyu said. "Now go, please, and quickly return."

The next hour passed so slowly it was as if each minute were being etched in glass to be preserved for all posterity. Daiyu paced around her room, stopped long enough to brush out her hair and get herself ready for bed, and then took up the pac-ing again. Every five or ten minutes she paused at the window and stared out into the fenced yard, hoping to see a signal left behind by Aurora or Ombri. She had a feeling that even if she stood there and watched for the rest of the night, she would not actually catch a glimpse of either servant of the gods creeping into the garden. She didn't know why, but she believed they could make themselves invisible, if they chose; they could prob-ably teleport or walk through walls or fly. Just because they hadn't showed such powers to Daiyu didn't mean they didn't possess them.

It was well past midnight when she paused in her agitated circling to gaze out the window again. And there it was—a braided shawl of red and green, seemingly blown into the gar-den by a careless breeze. The colors would have been difficult to see except that Aurora had thoughtfully left the scarf within the circle of light that a street lamp threw into the yard. Red and green intertwined. Kalen was injured, but not critically.

Even as Daiyu felt a profound relief course through her mus-cles, leaving them jittery and loose, she wondered if Aurora was telling the truth. Aurora must have realized that any other flag would have sent Daiyu fleeing into the night, despite her promise—the news that Kalen was gravely wounded, the news that he was dead. Even a green scarf, the harbinger of good news, would have caused Daiyu to run from the house, because she had witnessed enough of Kalen's beating to know that this signal would have been false.

Somehow Aurora had known to leave behind the only token that would make Daiyu keep her place.

SIXTEEN

XIANG STOOD BEFORE Daiyu and studied her like a preda-
tory bird examining a potential meal. "Stand taller," she commanded. "Throw your shoulders back—show off your bosom.
Let me see you walk across the floor."

Had she been doing this all over again, Daiyu thought, she
would have spent more time practicing how to move in the
ridiculously high heels that Xiang had commissioned to match
the blue dress. She was surprised the shoes didn't actually hurt,
for they made her rather large feet look slim and graceful. But
they were so perfectly constructed that they were quite comfortable except for the fact that she was sure she would fall off
of them.

"Keep your eyes lowered until you have been addressed,"
Xiang went on with her instructions, which had been repeated
so many times already that Daiyu knew them by heart. "Never
take your gloves off while you are dancing."

That last injunction, at least, Daiyu was absolutely certain to obey. She clasped her hands together before her, and the blue cotton of the gloves was a perfect match for the dyed silk of her dress.

It was possibly the most beautiful item of clothing she'd ever owned, though it looked nothing like any dress she had ever worn. The top was made of layers of thick silk so heavy there was very little drape from the shoulders to the hips, though it had been cut so that it pinched in subtly at the waist. The sleeves were very straight and came all the way to her wrists; the square neckline was deep enough to show off the upper curve of her breasts. The saturated cornflower blue of the fabric was accented at the neckline and wrists with a wide border of brilliant embroidery in shades of pink and coral. Her black skirt—tight at the waist and falling all the way to the tops of those high-heeled shoes—flaunted a matching border at the hem.

Qiji gems glowed at her throat, her wrist, her ears, and her fingers, and tingled insistently against her skin. The dragon ring was a cool, familiar shape under the folds of the right-hand glove.

Her hair had been braided with so many ribbons that someone might have to look twice to be certain she wasn't wearing a tapestry on her head.

"Come closer to me," Xiang commanded. "Let me see when I can smell your perfume. Stop. There." Xiang sniffed the air. "Yes. Perfect. Not a drop more."

"No, Aunt."

Xiang tilted her head and gave Daiyu one final survey. "I

believe we are ready," she said. "I don't think we have forgotten a thing."

Daiyu rested her hands flat against her skirt. Through the fabric of the gloves and the silk of the dress, she could feel the silver bracelet in her left pocket, the quartz stone in her right.

She had not forgotten anything either.

Xiang said, "Then it is time to go."

Daiyu had not expected to sleep at all the previous night, but in fact the combined effects of panic, terror, and relief had put her out almost as soon as she finally sought her bed. She had still been asleep in the morning when Aurora came in with Xiang's own personal dresser to help Daiyu begin the long process of getting ready. As soon as she was awake and coherent, Daiyu sent Aurora a sharp look of inquiry, and the other woman nodded. *Kalen is fine.*

Still, Daiyu hadn't been entirely reassured until Aurora slipped her a note—which she had instantly realized could not have been faked. "I'm bruised and a little bloody, but no broken bones," Kalen had written. "Don't worry. Do what you're supposed to do. If you remember, think of me every time you see a waterfall."

He was safe, then. He was not dead. Daiyu would do what she had come to Jia to do, and then she would be gone.

If she could bring herself to leave Kalen behind.

For their ride to the prime minister's palace, Xiang's car had been closed up. A shell of glass and a metal roof replaced the usual open-air awning, keeping the passengers safe from any breezes but intensifying the smells of perfume, cosmetics, starch, and hair oils. It was nearly eight in the evening, but here in the heart of summer, night had not yet fallen, and the temperature inside the closed vehicle was stifling.

Daiyu made no comment. She merely sat on the seat across from Xiang, hands folded in her lap, eyes cast down. Although she did not look up to make sure, she was certain that Xiang would approve her meek demeanor.

She was less certain that Xiang would approve of her plan to hurl Chenglei to another dimension.

The outing with Kalen had decided her. Feng's words had been convincing; the tales of rescinded supplies and starving families had touched Daiyu's heart. Chenglei could not be left here to wreak incalculable damage. He must be sent home where he could be contained by people who knew how to punish evil.

All Daiyu needed was one dance. . . .

When the driver turned onto a wide, rolling boulevard that seemed to stretch north and south, Daiyu started paying attention to their route. Soon the road was clogged with hundreds of cars, all configured in the formal "closed" style of Xiang's. Daiyu peered through the glass to try to see the occupants of the other vehicles, catching only a glimpse of silk here, a flash of jewels there.

"Don't be rude," Xiang said.

Daiyu subsided back onto her seat. "Are they all going to the ball?"

"If they are people of any substance, yes."

Finally, their car pulled up in a graceful, curved driveway in front of a grand house. Daiyu let a servant help her down while she stared up at the building, making no attempt to hide her curiosity. It was as big as the convention center in downtown St. Louis, but more deliberately elegant, a five-story structure of white stone, black marble, and painted red accents. The roof-line quirked up at all corners in that familiar pagoda-style architecture; she thought there was a cupola perched on the very top of the building. She followed Xiang past two fountains alive with colorful fish, past perfectly kept stands of topiary, and into a huge hallway where a crowd had already assembled. Daiyu tried to keep her eyes modestly lowered, but she could not help sweeping her gaze from side to side, trying to get a sense of the size of the room, the art, the décor. She received mostly an impression of high walls, red velvet curtains, and gold statuary. The carpet beneath her feet showed a pattern of dragons interspersed with suns and stars.

Slowly the throng emptied into an even grander room with a ceiling so far above them it must have risen through all five stories to crowd against that cupola on the roof. Daiyu risked one quick glance up and then had to forcibly restrain herself from staring at the intricate painting on the ceiling. The walls showed an alternating pattern of red velvet curtains and panels of woodwork painted in impossibly detailed scenes. The floor featured inlaid marble patterns that mimicked the dragon-and-star motif of the outer room.

Suddenly Daiyu straightened and looked around again, her eyes too wide for maidenly modesty. Could it be—? They had seemed to travel west and north to arrive there; she was sure the river was several miles due east if she stepped out the front door and kept walking. The prime minister's house stood on the same site as the Fox Theatre, an unparalleled spot of opulence and beauty.

It made Daiyu feel a little less nervous to be someplace that reminded her of home.

Nothing else about the evening felt remotely familiar.

Despite all of Xiang's instruction beforehand, Daiyu did not understand the protocols that governed the evening. By rules mysterious to her, everyone else seemed to know where in the room to stand, when to sit, whether or not to speak. If there was food, Daiyu never saw it. There was music, but it was odd and not, to her ear, particularly melodic—some percussive beats overlaid with a wandering woodwind. Ombri's exercises on his keyboard had been more tuneful than this. Daiyu just stood close to Xiang, saying nothing and moving not a step unless Xiang indicated that she should. It was clear this was going to be a long night.

When a gong sounded repeatedly, Xiang linked her arm with Daiyu's and led her to a short line that was forming in the middle of the room. A quick scan led Daiyu to believe that all the young women and their mothers—or aunts—were queuing up to be presented formally to the prime minister. Maybe she wouldn't have to wait till the dance after all. Maybe she could offer him a little something extra during her presentation. . . .

But Xiang had hold of her left arm, and unless that changed soon, it would be difficult to slip the bracelet from her pocket. Not only that, the presentations were clearly the focal point of the evening, and everyone standing on the sidelines was closely watching each introduction. If Daiyu magically made Chenglei disappear right now, everyone in Shenglang would see it happen.

She had time to consider her options; the line moved slowly. But when it was her turn to be introduced, her choices evaporated. Xiang had clasped Daiyu's left hand in both of hers, and with a flourish, she transferred that hand to Chenglei. He pressed it between both of his and inclined his head.

"Prime Minister, may I present to you my niece, Daiyu, my sister's daughter," Xiang said, her voice a little louder than it needed to be so that everyone nearby could hear the next boastful sentence. "Of course, you have met her already."

Chenglei smiled down at Daiyu with every evidence of pleasure. She had forgotten how very handsome he was; she had forgotten how appealing his smile could be. He did not release her hand, and she could feel the warmth of his palms even through her glove. "I have met her indeed, and I enjoyed our conversation very much," he said. "Xiang, I compliment you on your good taste in sponsoring such a niece. She is very pretty, and I discern some intelligence in the brilliance of her eyes."

"Thank you, Prime Minister," Xiang said.

"As I recall, Daiyu, when we last met you had just arrived in Shenglang," he said. "Tell me, have you had an opportunity to see more of our city?"

"Indeed I have, Prime Minister," she said, keeping her voice soft and shy. "I remembered that you said the aviary was your favorite place, and I have been there three times."

"And did you enjoy it?"

"Very much! The birds were breathtaking and the spirit of the place was peaceful."

"I am gratified to learn that an old man like me can still advise a young woman on activities she will find pleasing."

"You are hardly old, Prime Minister," Xiang said.

"It is when I am surrounded by such youth and beauty that I most feel my age!" he replied with a certain rueful charm.

Xiang smiled. "It is when I am surrounded by youth that I most revel in my intelligence," she said slyly.

Chenglei laughed and finally dropped Daiyu's hand. She brushed at the pocket of her skirt, but it was clear she would have no chance to pull out the bracelet; this interview was over. Chenglei said, "Xiang, your intelligence is never for a moment in doubt."

She gave him a regal nod. "Prime Minister." And then she took hold of Daiyu's arm and pulled her away, and the next young woman stepped forward with her mother.

Daiyu would have to wait until the *tiaowu*.

✳

Another hour went by before the dancing began. After Cheng-lei made it through the presentation line, there was a little excitement in the corners of the room: Four fountains sprang to life, bubbling with colorful liquids. The guests exclaimed aloud in pleasure and began making their way to one corner or another.

"We must visit all the fountains and sip from each one," Xiang directed, pushing Daiyu subtly toward the one where a cranberry-colored concoction sprayed from a chrome nozzle into a gleaming black marble base. "They represent health, prosperity, luck, and long life."

Daiyu was thirsty, so she was grateful for the chance to drink something, though they were only allowed to dip minuscule cups into each fountain and take tiny sips. The cranberry liquid, red for health, had a sharp and bitter taste, but left her mouth feeling refreshed. Prosperity was conferred by a syrupy green brew that was much too sweet for Daiyu's liking. Long life was symbolized by rich flowing cocoa, and Daiyu noticed that many people had second and third helpings at this fountain, since the flavor was so delicious. But it was at the citrus-flavored fountain of lemon-colored water that Daiyu refilled her cup again and again. She felt like she was going to need all the luck this world could provide.

She and Xiang were still standing by the lemon fountain when the music changed from the drums-and-oboe duet to something a little livelier. This was more like what Daiyu would consider dance music. At the same time, the whole mass of people pressed toward the outer walls to leave the central portion of the room open. Quickly enough, couples began streaming back onto the floor and arranging themselves into the pattern of the *tiaowu*. Daiyu had a brief, dizzying moment remembering the first time she had tried out those steps in the small house that Aurora and Ombri owned. Her palms had been pressed to Kalen's, and as always, that light contact had reassured her, made her feel protected and secure. She could do anything if Kalen was there to help her through. . . .

She could *not* think about Kalen—not here, not tonight. She stared fiercely out onto the dance floor, forcing herself to see what was in front of her and not what her wistful heart insisted on remembering.

Xiang was still giving instructions, so Daiyu concentrated on listening to her voice. "Remember, when Quan asks you to dance, you must refuse twice. You only say yes the third time," Xiang said.

"I remember, Aunt," Daiyu replied.

She had not seen Quan within this whole crush of people, but apparently he had been tracking them, for Xiang had scarcely finished speaking when he materialized at her elbow. Daiyu was glad to see him; his presence would help her keep thoughts of Kalen at bay.

"Mistress Xiang, may I be permitted to partner your niece in a dance?" he asked.

"It is acceptable to me, but you must ask her," Xiang replied.

Quan turned to Daiyu. "You are the most beautiful girl in the room. Please, Daiyu, will you dance with me?"

Daiyu kept her eyes lowered as she said, "Oh, young master Quan, surely there are other girls here who are more deserving of such an honor."

"It is I who would be honored if you considered me deserving of your time. Will you dance with me?"

"I am certain I would shame you with my clumsiness."

"I am certain you will humble me with your grace." He held his hand out. "Will you dance with me?"

She laid her gloved palm on his arm. "Thank you for extending me the kindness of your attention. Yes, I will."

By the end of the dance, Daiyu was completely in control of herself again, completely back in the present moment. She had to be, to make it through the *tiaowu* without a mistake. It was very formalized; every step was precisely calculated. One thing she had learned from the rehearsals at Xiang's was that the music rarely changed, and no dance had a beginning or an end. Couples merely slipped into and out of the pattern as they wished, although it was expected that they would stay on the dance floor about twenty minutes before removing to the sidelines again. Daiyu found that she had been trained so well that the steps came to her almost naturally now. Her only real worry was falling off the ridiculously high shoes.

"Are you entirely recovered from your adventures yesterday?" Quan asked her when the movement of the dance brought them face-to-face.

For a moment, her composure slipped. She had not entirely recovered from her fear for Kalen, but that was not a part of the adventure she could discuss with Quan. She bowed her head and felt some of her hair ribbons brush against her cheeks. "I am, thanks to your kind concern."

"And was your aunt angry with you when you returned to her house?"

Daiyu's left hand hovered near her pocket. She focused on imagining how, if Quan were Chenglei, she would whip out the bracelet and snap it on his wrist. "On the contrary, she was delighted to know that I had spent my day in your company. She thinks you are a handsome and interesting young man."

"Only Xiang thinks that?" he said in a teasing voice.

She smiled. "I think you are a kind young man, which is better than *interesting* any day."

"And are you enjoying the Presentation Ball?"

"It is a little overwhelming," she confessed. "I am afraid I will make a mistake or behave foolishly, and everyone will stare." *Or I will cause your prime minister to disappear, and everyone will scream.*

"I think you are behaving charmingly, and if anyone stares, it is because you are so lovely."

"Thank you, Quan," she said. "You *are* a kind man."

They stayed on the dance floor for only the proper twenty minutes before Quan returned her to Xiang. The old woman already had another suitor lined up, a young man whom Daiyu vaguely remembered seeing at Mei's breakfast. When he asked Daiyu to be his partner, she refused twice before gracefully accepting, though she really wanted to accept him on his very first offer. She wanted to postpone for as long as possible her inevitable dance with the prime minister.

She was terrified to dance with Chenglei. What if she fumbled, what if she failed?

What if she succeeded?

Would she create such an uproar that she would instantly have to use her own talisman to return to her home iteration, or would she be able to stay in Shenglang long enough to say her good-byes?

Surely, surely, she would have at least one more chance to see Kalen. She made a promise to herself: Even if she was discovered, even if she was in danger, she would not unwrap and seize her piece of quartz. Not in this ballroom, not tonight. She would not return to Earth before she had spent one final hour with Kalen. . . .

But even once she had made that decision, she dreaded the moment the prime minister took her hand.

Covertly, while she completed this dance with her current young man and then a second dance with Quan, she observed Chenglei. He was almost always on the floor, paired with one of the young debutantes, though he didn't have time to give each partner a full twenty minutes of his attention. The girls always had their eyes chastely cast down, but Daiyu could usually see them trying to hide their smiles. The prime minister was clearly lavishing on them the same warmth that Daiyu had found so appealing. Chenglei seemed to be having a marvelous time. His handsome face was lit with a wide smile; his dark eyes were bright with approval of everything he saw. He might be a terrible leader and a terrible man, but he had the supreme gift of charm.

She lost track of Chenglei during her third dance with Quan. Quan requested a fourth dance, as he had to—and she refused, as she had to. He asked, "If I cannot dance with you, is there something else I can do to show my admiration?"

"I am very thirsty," Daiyu replied.

"Then I will fetch you something to drink from one of the fountains," he replied at once. "Which flavor do you prefer?"

"The flavor of luck," she said.

"I will instantly return," he said, and departed.

Smiling, Daiyu turned back to her aunt and found Chenglei at Xiang's side. Her heart bounded in her chest; all the air was sucked from her lungs.

"Niece," Xiang said, "the prime minister has come to claim his dance with you. Be a good girl and do not force him to beg for this favor."

This was Xiang's way of reminding her that the traditional rule of three solicitations would be suspended in this case. "Indeed, Aunt, I will always behave as you direct me." Her inability to breathe made Daiyu's voice even softer than custom dictated.

"Come, then, give me your hand," Chenglei said, holding out his own. Daiyu laid her right hand in his and let him lead her back onto the dance floor.

It was time for Chenglei—and Daiyu—to go home.

# SEVENTEEN

SOME OF DAIYU'S anxiety eased as they slipped into the familiar rhythms of the dance. She had practiced, she could do this; she knew not only the steps of the *tiaowu* but the trick of securing the bracelet on her partner's arm. The time for thinking was past. Now she must be guided by instinct and memory.

"Young Daiyu, you dance with a great deal of grace," Chenglei observed after they had stepped through the first few measures of the pattern. "I seem to recall that you were nervous about performing well."

That was something she had said to him back at Mei's more than two weeks ago. Why would he retain such a useless bit of conversation? "I am glad the prime minister is pleased with my ability," she said. "But I am embarrassed that he remembers anything I said when it was so ridiculous."

"I am trying to remember the whole of our conversation, with limited success!" he said, humorously dismayed. "So you will kindly have to remind me. You are Xiang's niece, of course. Where does your mother live?"

"In the northwest territories."

He peered down at her, instantly concerned. "Oh, Daiyu," he said in a hushed and sympathetic voice. "Is she in one of the infected cities?"

Cursing herself for not having expected this question, Daiyu bit her lip and shook her head. "No, Prime Minister. Perhaps a year ago she moved south of the Maiwei River to be with my uncle, my father's brother. She remains in very good health, but of course she is sad about all of her friends who are quite sick."

Chenglei sighed mournfully. The movement of the dance turned them; now he held her left hand in his. "This is the cause that has concerned me most during my time in office," he said. "The illness raging through the northwest territories. At night when I should be sleeping, I pore over reports from the scientists who are desperate to find a cure. Here on our conti-nent, we have had no breakthroughs, but there are doctors in Yazhou who are making splendid progress in finding drugs that may halt the disease."

"Yazhou?" she said, startled. Feng had mentioned supplies being shipped across the ocean from what was essentially Asia. "They are trying to find a cure for *zaogao* fever?"

"Indeed they are. I like to think they are inspired by a hu-manitarian fervor, but I suspect they are afraid that any illness we spawn here may leap the water and infect their own coun-tries. We have tried to contain it, you know, but every day we learn of a new outbreak somewhere. I do fear for the health of this whole country—and for the entire world. We must find the cure, and very soon."

She hardly knew what to think. "I admire you for your commitment, Prime Minister."

"Well, not everyone does!" he said. "There is a man in town named Feng—perhaps you have not been here long enough to hear his name—he despises me and everything I stand for. He claims to be a pure man of justice, while I am a wicked man of influence, but the truth is, he hates me because he was among a group of young men who were ruined shortly after I came to office. There was a scandal—too sordid for the ears of young girls. Now his only ambition is to see me discredited. I would not care at all except that people are starting to listen to him. And even then I would not care except that if people begin to distrust me, I cannot do my job. I cannot fund the research being done at home, I cannot forge alliances with the governments in Yazhou. Everything stalls and more people die. This is the bitterest reality of my term so far."

The movement of the dance separated them at just that moment. Daiyu was suddenly palm-to-palm with an older gentleman who was completely bald and absolutely expressionless. What he might see on her own face she could scarcely imagine. She felt dizzy and utterly confounded. If the room had tilted and they were now dancing on the painted ceiling, she could hardly have been more confused. Could Chenglei be telling the truth? Was Feng merely a disgraced aristocrat trying to get revenge?

Were Aurora and Ombri simply interdimensional bounty hunters who had their own agenda?

How could she possibly know?

The music offered up its signal and Daiyu turned away from her new partner and back toward Chenglei. He took her right hand in his and they promenaded in a stately fashion down the center of the room. Now, by sheer force of habit, her left hand crept to the pocket of her skirt. Through the smooth cotton of her glove, she could feel the hard contours of the bracelet. In twenty seconds, maybe less, Chenglei would swing her around to face him as he reached out to take hold of her other hand. This was the time; this was the moment she had trained for.

"Please forgive me," he said in a very low voice. He sounded utterly sincere. "I should not have talked of such distressing topics on such a light-hearted occasion. I should have spoken only of your braided hair and your sparkling jewels and the grace of your dance. I am sorry I have ruined the ball for you."

He sounded so despondent that her denial was instant and genuine. "No, Prime Minister, you have ruined nothing for me! I have been thinking to myself how honored I am that a man so gifted would take the time to speak of such extraordinarily important subjects to a woman as insignificant as me."

"You do not seem insignificant in the least," he said.

The music cued him and he pulled her around to face him. Daiyu offered up her left hand, open and empty. He circled her once and began the promenade again, back in the other direction. Her left hand would now remain safely within his for the duration of the *tiaowu*.

"What does your aunt have planned for you for the rest of your visit?" he asked.

"I am not sure," Daiyu answered, a little at random. Part of her was thinking, *I have failed! This is disastrous!* And part of her was thinking, *I could not pronounce judgment on him. I have done the right thing.* One tiny corner of her mind was holding a celebration. *I do not have to leave Kalen just yet.* Every part of her was shivering with an adrenaline rush, as if she had narrowly avoided being crushed by a falling boulder. "She has many social engagements."

"Every year, over the midsummer holiday, I invite a couple of friends to stay at the palace with me for a few days," Chenglei said. "Perhaps you and your aunt would like to be among my guests this year."

Daiyu could think of nothing Xiang would like better—it did not take much knowledge of Shenglang society to guess that this must be the most prized invitation of the season—but she knew better than to make a promise on the older woman's behalf. "You must ask my aunt, but if I have any influence with her, we will be there," Daiyu replied. "I am so honored at such an invitation! I can scarcely speak my delight!"

"Come, then. Let us ask her right now," Chenglei said, gracefully extricating them from the press of dancers. He still kept her left hand in his, as if he knew it would handle the weapon that could send him to oblivion. But he needn't have bothered, Daiyu thought. She had changed her mind; she had deliberately let opportunity pass her by. Chenglei was in no danger from her now.

Quan—who was starting to seem just a little *too* faithful—was standing with Xiang when Daiyu and Chenglei made their way back to her. In his hand Quan held a much larger glass filled with the lemony mixture. Daiyu sipped from it while Chenglei made his proposition to Xiang and Xiang instantly accepted, with only the barest attempt to disguise her gleeful satisfaction. Daiyu didn't bother to listen to them talk, didn't bother to make conversation with Quan beyond thanking him for the drink. She merely took another swallow and wondered just exactly what kind of luck she had bargained for.

Daiyu slept late the next morning, or at least that was what she hoped Aurora would believe. As soon as she had gotten to her room the previous night, she had locked her door and she had not opened it when Aurora knocked quietly on the wood. She did not open it that morning, either, when the knock came again. She just stood in the center of the room, her hands at her throat, her heart in turmoil.

She didn't know what she had done; she didn't know what she should do.

She needed desperately to talk to Kalen.

He would not be at the aviary today; he would be at the river. While Daiyu was sipping lemonade punch at the ball, she had heard the great bronze bell toll out its call for workers.

But she knew how to find him on the river. . . .

"Aunt, may I go to the aviary this morning?" she asked Xiang when she joined the old woman for the second meal of the morning. She was hungry, since she had skipped the first one.

Xiang looked smug, clearly believing that any trip to the bird house was cover for an assignation with Quan. But Daiyu knew that Quan would be out of the city for two days, running errands for Mei. There was no risk that he would come to the house and expose Daiyu's deception.

"I suppose you may," Xiang said. "You do not need to bring one of the servants. I think you know your way around the city well enough by now."

"Thank you, Aunt."

"But we have much work to do in the next two weeks to prepare your wardrobe for the summer holiday! You will want to look your best for the festivities. The dressmaker will be here tomorrow morning. Do not make any other plans."

"Yes, Aunt. Thank you."

By now Daiyu was an old hand at arriving at the aviary with some pomp and exiting in stealth. Once she was back out on the crowded street, she had to ask several people before she found someone who could tell her what trolley to take to the river, but in fact the journey wasn't long at all.

She jumped off as soon as she saw the red gate and made her way across the yin-yang patterns of rock that bordered the riverfront. It was only about an hour before noon, and stone-pickers were already starting to climb out of the Zhongbu, bags over their shoulders, boots making a creaking, squishy sound as they trudged through the mud. But there were still several hundred people bent over the riverbed, sorting through rocks, snatching up the occasional treasure. Daiyu cast back and forth along the bank, trying to pick Kalen out from the dozens who looked just like him from a distance. It would be so easy to miss him. Did she have time to go to the house? Would she be able to get free again tomorrow, after the dressmaker left, perhaps? Could she trust Aurora to take a message?

She wouldn't have to—there he was, lanky and loose limbed, strolling out of the sucking mud as if it did not tug on him at all. She ran toward him, arms outstretched, so impatient she almost dipped her fine shoes in the wet riverbed. He looked up when she called his name, and his face broke into a delighted smile. From both sides of the river, high-pitched chimes began to send their fluttery, urgent message. It was as if his smile had triggered the music, as if the sight of his face had filled her head with silver excitement.

He slung the bag more securely over his shoulder and caught both her hands before he was completely out of the river. "What are you doing here?" he demanded, taking the last noisy steps out of the mud and onto the bank. "Did something happen?"

She was examining his face, bruised around the eye and cut around the lip but not permanently disfigured. "How badly were you hurt?" she demanded in turn.

Other stonepickers brushed by them as they trudged out of the river, and Daiyu heard the sibilant sound of the first threads of water seeping under the gates. "Not so badly," he said. "Come on, we can't just stand here. Someone might notice you."

"I can't stay very long."

"You shouldn't be here at all."

It was as if they couldn't settle into the rhythm of a proper conversation. There was too much to say, there was no privacy, everything was too important. "I have to talk to you," she said.

He nodded and glanced around as if looking for a place of safety, then his face lit with a grin. "The bell tower," he said. "Gabe's just leaving. He's got a girl now, so he doesn't stick around long once he's sent the signal."

Casually they headed toward the tower and casually Kalen tried the lock on the gate to the stairs—which, as Gabe had told them, was broken. Daiyu was so determined to talk to Kalen that even the perilous spiral staircase did not slow her down for longer than it took to inhale a deep breath and begin climbing. She didn't look down, didn't let herself think about how high she was above the ground. Kalen was right behind her, his hand just below hers on the railing, ready to catch her if she slipped.

She didn't, and finally, *finally,* they were alone together on the narrow catwalk at the top of the tower. Daiyu turned immediately into Kalen's arms and, needing no other invitation, he bent down and kissed her thoroughly. She thought he tasted like rainwater and sunlight and the indefinable fizz of *qiji* stones.

When she broke the kiss, for a moment she leaned her head against his chest and shut her eyes. "I was so afraid they would kill you," she whispered. "I couldn't bear to leave you, and yet I did. And I almost didn't believe Aurora when she told me you would be all right."

"Oh, I've been beaten up a time or two in my life," he said, his voice soothing. One of his arms was still wrapped securely around her waist; his free hand was stroking her hair. "It takes more than a few ugly guards to do me any damage."

Her voice muffled against his shirt, she said, "I didn't put the bracelet on Chenglei at the dance."

His hand didn't falter. "I know you didn't. The world would be a much different place today if you had."

"I suppose Aurora and Ombri are very angry with me."

Now his hand stilled. "They just assumed something went wrong with the plan. That you didn't have a chance to slip the bracelet on his arm."

"I could have," she whispered, "but I didn't."

"Why not?"

She burrowed her head deeper into his shirt, catching the familiar scent of his skin even under the odor of mud and fish and river stink. She didn't know how to answer.

"Daiyu? Why didn't you?" The hand that had been patting her head came around to tilt up her chin. "I hope it wasn't because of me."

She let him lift her head and she stared up at him in hopeless confusion. "Maybe it was—maybe that was a part of it," she said. "But I think even more it was just that I can't be sure. How can I do such a dreadful thing to someone else when I'm not positive he is guilty as charged? It would haunt me the rest of my life."

He attempted a smile. "The rest of your stay in Shenglang. Not so long."

"I think I'd remember some of it," she whispered. "I think part of me would remember I had done something wrong. I wouldn't know what, but I'd know it was dreadful. And it would eat away at me. Forever. Kalen, I can't do it."

He nodded and dropped his hand, drawing her head back

to rest against his chest. "You can't fight battles that you don't believe in," he said. "You can't be a soldier in somebody else's war."

"Maybe some people can," she said, "but I can't."

They were quiet a moment, standing intertwined on the narrow catwalk. Finally Kalen stirred and lifted his head, which had come to rest on the top of hers. "So what do you do now?" he said. "How soon do you go home?"

She pulled back a little, enough to see his face. "I think I have to stay for the next two weeks," she said. "Chenglei invited Xiang and me to come to his house for the summer holiday, and Xiang is so excited. I think I have to give her that much—it will be such a blow to her when I suddenly disappear."

Kalen grinned. "She's become fond of you?"

Daiyu made an inelegant sound. "I don't think she's fond of anyone. But she's enjoying the benefits of having an eligible young woman in the house. We're using her, after all, and I feel bad about that, too. So I want to do this one thing for her before I go."

"I wonder what Aurora and Ombri will do next to try to get rid of Chenglei," Kalen said.

"Maybe they'll find someone else to carry out their quest," Daiyu said. "Some other sojourner who finds the choice much simpler than I did." She reached into her pocket and drew out the silver bracelet, carefully wrapped in multiple layers of silk. "Give this back to them. Tell them I can't do it."

Kalen took it gingerly and stowed it in an outer compartment of his bag of rocks. "They'll be disappointed," he said. "But I think they'll understand."

She was immeasurably relieved once she had handed the bracelet over. She felt lighter by pounds, not ounces; she felt as if she had suddenly been cured of a bitter, suffocating consumption. She smiled at him. "So! How did you do today? Find any *qiji* stones?"

"*You* would know," he said. "Here, let me show you what I kept."

He carefully set the bag down between them and they both knelt on the narrow walkway. Daiyu rummaged through the stones he had rescued from the river, her fingers settling on each rough surface and moving on. "Oh! There's one!" she said, pulling it out. "A big one, too. Look at that, Kalen! That's worth two stones any day."

He grinned. "I almost threw it back because it seemed too good to be true. Really? That's a *qiji*? I'm rich!"

"You almost threw it back!" she repeated, and her voice filled with mock horror. "You foolish boy! Are you always so careless with items of value?"

"No," he said, abruptly sober. "I know what matters. And I never throw those things away. I hold on to them as long as I can."

As he spoke, he dropped the *qiji* into his bag and came to his feet, drawing Daiyu up beside him. She stared at him, suddenly as serious as he was. "These days are precious," she said. "I don't want to throw them away either."

"I don't want them to end," he said.

She studied his face for a moment, trying to memorize it. Trying to file that memory away in a place that wouldn't be erased by a trip through the gateway. "At least we know they won't end right away," she said. "At least I won't leave Sheng-lang for two more weeks."

"Maybe you could stay longer," he suggested. "A month."

"I have a life to get back to," she said. Even if it was harder every day to remember that life.

"But if it doesn't matter how long you're gone," he said in a low voice. "If you will return to your world just an instant after you left it—then it doesn't matter how long you're in Shenglang. You could stay a year. You could stay twenty years. And then go home."

She took a deep, hard breath, because that hadn't occurred to her. Live an entire lifetime in Shenglang—marry—have children—grow old. And then when she had finally had her fill, when she had saturated her soul with memories of Kalen, she would pull out the rose quartz talisman and go back to her own world, her proper place. She would live two consecutive lifetimes, though she would only remember one, unless fragments and glimpses of the first one, the impossible one, glittered up from her subconscious now and then. She would become one of those odd, impassioned people who claimed to have been reincarnated, who claimed to have lived through exotic pasts that even now shaped them and haunted their dreams.

The thought made her shiver. Maybe every one of those lunatics was absolutely accurate—maybe all of them were sojourners who had slipped accidentally or by design through some gateway into another world and time. Maybe their patchy memories were of alternate iterations as foreign and familiar as Shenglang.

Maybe Daiyu would remember enough of her time with Kalen to comfort her bereft soul. There was a hope to hold on to.

"I can't," she said, whispering again. "I'm afraid that even if I stay till the holiday I won't want to return. If I stay a year, I won't remember I have another place to return *to*. I'd never go home, and sooner or later, I have to think, time would start going forward again on Earth without me. I love you, Kalen, but it would break my parents' hearts if I never came home to them. The longer I stay here, the more it will break *my* heart to go."

"Well, that's something for me to remember when my own heart is aching," he breathed against her mouth. He had put his arms around her again, leaning over the bag of stones to take her in an embrace. "That you said you loved me."

She had both arms wrapped around his body as tightly as they would go. "And I'll remember you," she said. "I know I will. I can't possibly forget anything as precious as this."

EIGHTEEN

THE NEXT TWO weeks passed in a blur of dressmakers' appointments, cobblers' visits, highly public outings with Quan, highly secret trysts with Kalen, and meals too numerous to count. Xiang took every opportunity to lecture Daiyu on things she needed to know to be the perfect guest, and the two of them shopped for days to find just the right gift to present to their host. It must not be too expensive, for the prime minister was not supposed to accept costly items from his constituents, but it must not look shabby, either. It was Daiyu who suggested they give him an exotic plant ornamented with a replica of one of the red birds so plentiful at the aviary. Xiang commissioned the foremost artisan of the city to create a tiny creature out of silk, feathers, and enamel. It looked exquisite against the deep green of the leaves and the black jade of the vase.

"Every part of this gift will remind the prime minister of his conversations with you!" Xiang exclaimed. "A most excellent present!"

They were to be at Chenglei's residence for three days—
two and a half, really, since they and his other guests would
depart once they had consumed an intimate breakfast the morning after the holiday celebration. It had taken some carefully
casual questioning on Daiyu's part to get a sense of what to
expect of the holiday itself. She had been in Shenglang almost
five weeks now, so it should be roughly the middle of August—
the hottest part of the summer, at least in St. Louis—and this
event appeared to be an acknowledgment of that. Outdoor cel-
ebrations would take place all over the city, especially at night;
official and unofficial fireworks displays would burst overhead
until dawn. Clothing appeared to be one of the more interesting
aspects of this particular holiday, since people dressed for the
heat in thin fabrics and sleeveless ensembles.

"Girls who do not care about their reputations will sometimes take off their clothing altogether, or at least their shirts,
when the young men exhort them," Xiang had told Daiyu with
a sniff. "It is very unbecoming."

Sounded like the average Mardi Gras celebration to Daiyu,
and she hid a grin. "I would never do anything so disgraceful,
Aunt," she said.

She had no incentive to do so; she loved the dress Xiang
had commissioned for her. It was a slim black sheath that fell
from her shoulders to her ankles in the simplest of lines. It was
embellished with thousands of pearls sewn on in the shapes of
suns and quarter moons, and a border of pearls set off the high
round neck and both armholes.

It featured hidden pockets on both sides, but she didn't need them. She had given away the silver bracelet, of course, and she only bothered to carry the quartz talisman every few days, whenever she remembered. She had lost that edge of paranoia, the conviction that she might suddenly have to escape from Shenglang. She would go home, of course—very soon, right after the festival—but it would be a planned journey, not an abrupt and disorienting departure.

She had not seen Aurora again. At times she wondered if Xiang had dismissed the *cangbai* woman or if Aurora just had nothing to say to Daiyu. She was sorry if Aurora was angry with her, but she would not have been able to apologize. She supposed it was just as well that the other woman kept her distance.

The day before Daiyu and Xiang left to take up their brief residence at the prime minister's house, Daiyu had two very different meetings with two very different men.

She was at the aviary, of course, for both. The one with Kalen was short and unsatisfying, for the bird house was too crowded for them to attempt to sneak away to the waterfall. So she sat on one of the freshly scrubbed benches and Kalen stood behind her, holding her parasol.

"How will you celebrate the holiday?" she asked him. She often found herself greedy for the most minute details of his life, and sometimes she asked him questions about wholly insignificant matters. *What did you eat for breakfast today? Where did you get that shirt?*

"There are usually parties on all the streets in my neighborhood," he said, and she could hear the grin in his voice. "Plenty to drink, a few fireworks, and lots of pretty girls in very skimpy clothing."

"Don't you go telling girls to take off their shirts for you," she said sternly. "Xiang told me what happens in some parts of town."

"I'll behave if you will," he said. "No showing yourself off to Chenglei and his friends."

The idea made her laugh. "I will be *very* proper. Anyhow, the way this dress is made, I'd practically have to be naked if I wanted to show off my chest."

"I wouldn't mind that so much," he said, still smiling, "if I was the one you were showing it off to."

"*Kalen!*" But she was laughing. "Am I asking *you* to strip your clothes off?"

"Well, you might ask," he suggested, "and see what I do."

Now she was blushing, though she was still laughing. "This hardly seems the place."

"Maybe before you go," he said. "Once you come back from Chenglei's."

There was a sweet thought. There was an incentive to disappear from Xiang's mansion the minute the holiday was over. But . . . "Somehow I don't think Aurora and Ombri are going to want me hanging around the house too long once I leave Xiang's," she said.

"We won't have to stay in the house," he said. "It's summer, and I know where we can buy a tent. We can pitch it in a vacant lot between a couple of buildings. You can stay as long as you like."

"Maybe we could borrow some blankets from Aurora and Ombri," she said. "I don't mind sleeping on the ground."

"We'd get our water from the public faucets," he said. "Make our meals over an open fire. It's a pretty good life as long as the weather's nice."

"And with two of us working the river, we'll be able to earn money twice as fast," she said, getting deeper into the spirit of the fantasy. "I can tell a *qiji* the minute I touch it. Maybe we can make money *four* times as fast."

"Maybe we can save enough to buy a house of our own."

"It doesn't have to be very big," she said.

"Just enough room for the two of us."

"And then one day we'll decide to have a baby. . . ."

The words conjured up a vision so real, so desirable, that she almost gasped—and then, when she realized it would never come true, she almost whimpered. Kalen had fallen silent; she thought that he, too, was struggling with a sudden sense of powerful loss. She felt his hand brush the back of her neck, a touch of reassurance so light that no one in the aviary would be likely to mark it. It took all her control not to twist around on the bench and reach out for his embrace.

"I'd pick that life, if I was staying in Shenglang," she said, her voice almost a whisper. "I hope you'll find someone else who can live it with you."

"It doesn't seem likely that I will," he said quietly.

She didn't know how to answer. She couldn't bear the thought that he would be alone the rest of his life—but she hated imagining him sharing *her* tent, *her* small house, with some brisk, cheerful *cangbai* girl. Her only comfort, and it was bitter, was knowing that she would not remember enough of this adventure to be jealous of any girl who might capture Kalen's heart.

"Well," she said, "I suppose neither of us can be sure what the rest of our lives will hold."

"I suppose not," he said, and she could tell he was attempting to lighten his voice. "I never would have guessed that *this* part of it would hold *you*."

Quan met her at the aviary's front gate. That last exchange with Kalen had shaken her; it was an effort to summon a smile for Quan. Fortunately, she didn't have to talk much at first. The instant Daiyu had settled herself on the front seat of his car, he took off down the crowded streets, dodging around trolleys and terrifying unwary passersby. Between the wind and the noise of traffic and the shouts of angry pedestrians, there was no chance to make conversation.

By the time they stopped at a fancy café, she had somewhat recovered her poise, though she had to work at it to present her usual expression of serene good nature. Quan ordered frozen chocolate drinks for both of them, and Daiyu was pretty sure that the ice for these beverages cost more than the ingredients. She should have been appalled at the expense and the casual way Quan covered it, but she was hot, thirsty, and more than a little sad. She took the first few sips and closed her eyes to savor the cool, rich sweetness. Nothing had ever tasted so good.

Quan chatted easily about how he had spent his week and how much he was looking forward to the summer holiday at Chenglei's. Only a handful of honored guests would spend the holiday at the prime minister's house, but dozens would be invited for the festivities that night.

"When will you arrive for the celebration?" Daiyu asked.

"A little before nightfall. Everyone waits till dark, of course, to set off the fireworks."

"Xiang is so excited," Daiyu said. "It's as if she's never been on holiday before."

"Never as an overnight guest," Quan said. "This is her proudest moment. The fact that Chenglei likes you has done a great deal to boost her social credit. She has already made two business deals that have eluded her for the past year."

Daiyu was disquieted by the words. What would happen to Xiang's social credit once Daiyu mysteriously disappeared? Of course Xiang could always say Daiyu had been called back suddenly to her mother's side, but even so, it would look very strange. And if Xiang herself didn't know what had become of Daiyu, she would worry. She might think Daiyu had been murdered or kidnapped—she might raise an outcry or contact the authorities—

"What's wrong?" Quan asked.

Her perturbation must have showed on her face. "Oh—I was just thinking how strange it will be to go back home after the exciting time I have had here in Shenglang."

Quan looked surprised. "Are you going home? Back to the northwest territories?"

Daiyu nodded, wishing she had found some other topic to turn the conversation. "I think I must. And perhaps soon. My mother did not send me here to become a permanent burden on my aunt, you know."

Quan studied her soberly. "I think perhaps she did," he said. "Though I am convinced Xiang does not think of you as a bur- den. I am convinced Xiang expects you to stay in Shenglang, perhaps to make your home with her forever."

"That would be kind of her," Daiyu murmured. She could see where this conversation was going and she wasn't sure how to stop it. It had been painful, but so very sweet, to sit with Kalen and pretend they had a future together; she was not sure how to get through that same discussion with Quan.

He took a deep breath. "I too am growing accustomed to the idea that you will be in Shenglang always," he said. "The city would seem very dull to me now if it were missing your beauti- ful eyes and your captivating laugh."

She kept her eyes lowered and her laugh in abeyance. "As in- deed I would find Shenglang to be quite empty if you were not in it," she said. "You have been such a good friend to me."

There was a short pause. She knew—from Xiang's constant tutelage—that young men did not propose marriage directly to young women, but worked through their mothers and aunts to make agreeable arrangements. But what if he spoke to Mei tonight and Mei came running to Xiang's house as fast as her feet would carry her? Daiyu could only guess, but it seemed like the summer holiday would be a propitious time to announce a betrothal. Surely there must be some way to stave this off. She could not in good conscience accept a man's proposal when, in a matter of days, she planned to abandon his city forever.

She could not say she was willing to marry him—not even in pretense, not even knowing the words were lies—when she was in love with another man.

She looked up, smiling with false brightness. "Let us not talk of serious things until after the holiday!" she said. "Let us just be merry and lighthearted for a few more days. After the summer festival, who knows what will have changed."

He inclined his head. "Who knows, indeed. As always, you are wise, Daiyu."

If only that were true. "As always, you are gracious, Quan."

She turned her attention back to her frozen chocolate concoction only to find that all the ice had melted. She pushed it aside—she wasn't sure she could swallow another drop.

They arrived at the prime minister's house in time for the second morning meal of the day, which they ate outside on a shaded veranda that overlooked the lush green lawns behind the mansion. Daiyu counted three fountains and such a variety of plant life that the property could have doubled as a botanical garden. Servants were busy setting up tents and tables for the next day's festivities, and it was pleasant to sit under an awning on a hot day, sipping cool drinks and watching competent people work on interesting tasks.

Chenglei's other guests were two couples who each had one daughter, so, as was proper, a total of nine people sat together for this agreeable meal. Daiyu had met one of the girls at the Presentation Ball and the other one at Mei's, though she had had no conversation with any of the parents. In fact, she didn't have much conversation with any of them on this occasion, either, since the three girls were expected to be merely decorative while the older adults carried on a lively discussion about the current political situation in Yazhou. Daiyu would have been bored if she hadn't been so replete with food that she was content to merely sit and look over the lawns. She saw one of the other girls impatiently ball her hands into fists and then slowly force her fingers to relax, and she grinned to herself. Not every Han girl was as meek as she appeared. This one would probably grow up to be as strong-willed and outspoken as Xiang herself.

In the afternoon, the housekeeper gave them a tour of the house, which Xiang particularly enjoyed, and they played board games in one of the plush parlors. When most of the others disappeared to nap or check their holiday outfits one last time, Daiyu escaped outside to stroll through the lawns and inspect the decorations more closely. There would be plenty of fragrant potted plants and strings of brightly colored paper lanterns, she saw, as well as dozens of little wrought-iron tables and chairs scattered across the yard. She guessed that food and drinks would be served under the gaily striped tents, and perhaps fireworks would be shot off from that structure that laborers were building near the back edge of the property.

"Are you looking forward to the celebration, Daiyu?" a man asked. She turned swiftly to find that Chenglei had approached her silently while she was staring at the scaffolding, trying to gauge how big the stage would be when it was completed.

She smiled and bowed her head. "We don't have anything quite like this back home," she said truthfully.

"Have you ever been to a celebration in Yazhou?" he asked.

In Asia. She shook her head. "No, Prime Minister," she said. "I've never traveled outside of the continent."

He turned and began pacing slowly back toward the house, and she fell in step beside him. "Oh, you should go sometime," he said. "Shenglang is the center of the world, as we all know, but Yazhou is a marvelous place, full of ancient secrets and a brooding beauty. Not everyone appreciates it, but I suspect in your soul a capacity for wonder. A willingness to look beyond the ordinary and the familiar to embrace the extraordinary and the strange."

She shivered a little when he said the words, which were truer than he had any right to understand. "Thank you, Prime Minister," she said, her voice subdued. "No one has ever paid me a compliment quite like that before."

"I traveled in Yazhou for years before I came to Shenglang," he said. "You would be astonished at the items I brought back with me—plates and dishes made of gold, statues carved of jade in every color, masks made of feathers, jewels that put a *qiji* to shame. All of them from vanished civilizations so old we cannot remember when they existed and we can only guess at what they believed. When my days seem overlong and my problems insurmountable, I hold one of these old artifacts in my hand and I realize how small a part I play in the ongoing story of the world."

Was it his voice? Was it his words? He inspired in her a desire to study those lost societies, to dig through layers of rock and silt to find those antique treasures. "I would love to see such jewels and such statues," she said earnestly.

"Would you? Come to my office tomorrow morning and I will present them to you one by one. I think you will be amazed and delighted. I would show them to you now," he added, smiling ruefully, "but as you see, I am being summoned for some far less enjoyable duty."

Indeed, they had arrived at the house by now and found a servant waiting at the doorway with a sheaf of papers in one hand and a portfolio in the other. "I will not keep the prime minister from his important tasks," Daiyu said, bowing her head and stopping at the door. "But tomorrow I would be happier than he knows if he would grant me the privilege of viewing his foreign treasures."

"Then it is an appointment," he said. "I look forward to the chance to show them off to someone who will love them as much as I do."

Neither of them mentioned the assignation over dinner that night, at which the nine of them sat down to a meal so lavish it made Xiang's ordinary feasts look like food that might be served at Kalen's table. However, Daiyu did tell Xiang that night before they parted to go to their separate, luxurious bedrooms.

"This is very good," Xiang said, her dark eyes bright with satisfaction. "He likes you. He did not ask Lanfen's daughter to come to his office and look over his treasures. I will not boast, of course, but you might find a way to let it fall that you have seen some of Chenglei's most cherished artifacts. In a very guileless manner, of course."

Daiyu hid a smile. "Of course, Aunt."

Xiang then launched into yet another lecture about how to behave during the celebration. Daiyu barely listened; she had heard these particular instructions too many times to count. Plus, she was distracted by the low, cascading tones of the big river bells calling the stonepickers to come to work in the morning. Chenglei's house was far enough from the waterfront that the bells were barely audible, and Daiyu was washed with an unreasonable sense of panic. As if she was too far away from Kalen—as if she would not hear him if he called her name. She clenched her hands tightly to her sides and strained to hear every last stroke of the bells until the final note faded into the night.

 NINETEEN

CHENGLEI'S OFFICE WAS a long, high-ceilinged room that overlooked the back lawns and ran half the width of the third story.
It could be accessed from two hallways feeding from two different stairways, and each doorway was blocked by a heavy
red-velvet curtain held back by a golden rope. The extended
bank of windows took up one entire wall, but the other long
wall was covered with art and artifacts. Chenglei started his
presentation by taking Daiyu on a little tour.

"I love this cloisonné mask for its soft colors and intricate
detail, but I do not believe it was ever worn, even in a ritual
ceremony," he said as they paused to admire one item. "It looks
too small, don't you think? Unless our ancestors from Yazhou
were much tinier than we are today."

"Perhaps it was a child's mask?" Daiyu suggested.

"That is what some scholars have considered. But it seems
very heavy for a child, don't you think?"

"What was the purpose?"

"Ah! No one knows. Unfortunately, that is the case for many of these items."

They moved on to study a dragon about the size of Daiyu's forearm, carved of apple-green jade and accented with gold on its eyes, its tongue, its talons, and its tail. "Can you believe it? That item is more than a thousand years old," Chenglei marveled. "What artisan took up his tools to liberate this creature from insensate stone? Who was he? A craftsman who produced masterpieces for emperors? A student who practiced his skills late into the night? Was he arrogant enough to believe that his work would last for centuries or humble enough to hope that he could sell his figurine to buy another meal for his wife and starving daughter?"

His words filled Daiyu's head with images of Han artists industriously bent over workbenches, their eyes intent, their expressions enraptured. "Will anything you or I create last long enough to make people wonder about us ten centuries from now?" she asked in turn.

He turned to her, delighted. "Precisely! What mark will we make on our world? What good will we do, what treasures will we produce, to make people remember us long after we have moved on?"

"I have never had such an ambition," she admitted.

"Well, I have," Chenglei said. "And a girl like you has as much right to change the world as a man like me."

She was filled with a sudden excitement—he was right! *Anyone* could make an impact on the world—followed by the swift realization that such sentiments were not quite as popular in

Shenglang as they might be back in her own iteration. She cast her eyes down. "My aunt does not encourage such thinking," she said in a low voice.

"Well, your aunt might not know as much as I do," Chenglang said, sounding amused. "I have had experiences that Xiang could never hope to match."

Before Daiyu could answer that, a servant was stepping through one of the red-curtained doors and bowing low. "Prime Minister," he said, "Chow has arrived to speak to you on a matter he calls very urgent."

Chenglei sighed. "And if it is the matter I asked him to investigate for me, it is very urgent indeed." He turned to Daiyu. "Most honored guest, I am afraid that—"

Daiyu was already backing away toward the curtained door through which they had entered. "I will not take any more of your time! Thank you for sharing your treasures—and your thoughts—with me. I feel immeasurably enriched."

"It is I who am the richer," Chenglei said.

She was halfway out the door when she heard Chenglei speak to his servant. "I need ten minutes to read a report. Bring Chow to me after that."

"Yes, Prime Minister."

Head bent in thought, Daiyu descended the great curved staircase that led two stories down to the main foyer where they had all congregated on the night of the Presentation Ball. She was almost on the ground level when she realized that two people were coming in the front door.

"Niece, see who I found arriving at the prime minister's

house to call on you!" Xiang exclaimed, drawing Quan through the door with the air of someone about to present an expensive gift. "He is so impatient to see you that he cannot even wait till nightfall!"

"That is only partly true," Quan said with a grin. He was comfortable enough with Daiyu now to add a little humor to the ritualized conversations. "I also thought I could make myself valuable by offering to take you on any last-minute errands you might need to run. I know that women always require some final accessory to make their outfits complete."

"Oh, Daiyu is always forgetting something," Xiang said with a wave of her hand. "I am sure she will be grateful to you for your thoughtfulness."

"Most grateful," Daiyu agreed. "Aunt, may I go with him now?"

"You must first tell your host that you are leaving," Xiang said in a scolding voice. "How rude! To simply leave a man's house without a word of explanation!"

"Yes, Aunt. I'm sorry, Aunt. I will seek out the prime minister right now."

"I will wait here," Quan said.

Xiang headed straight toward the rear of the house, no doubt looking for one of the other guests to brag to about Quan's courtship of her niece. Daiyu flew back up the stairs, hoping to arrive in Chenglei's office before Chow was ushered in. Surely it had not yet been ten minutes?

She was almost at the red velvet door when she heard voices through the curtain, and she stopped, disappointed. Could she leave the house without Chenglei's permission? She crept close enough to hear, wondering if this was a conversation she could interrupt.

"And you have located the traitor Feng?" Chenglei was asking.

"We believe we have, Prime Minister," a man replied. His voice was soft and subservient; the word "unctuous" came to Daiyu's mind, though she had never used it in her life. "He has been living with a family in the *cangbai* district of Shenglang."

"And? I hope you have apprehended him, Chow."

"Not yet. He slipped away when we tried to corner him this morning. We followed him, but he mingled with the workers stepping into the river to gather *qiji* stones."

Chenglei uttered a sound of deep frustration. "And that is where he still is? Grubbing about in the mud, hiding among the stonepickers?"

"We believe so. We have men roving up and down both sides of the river, ready to catch him if he tries to leave."

There was a short silence. Daiyu could almost feel Chenglei thinking. As for herself, she couldn't think; she could scarcely breathe. This conversation made it obvious Chenglei was far more worried about the dissident Feng than he had earlier led her to believe.

"And you're positive he is in the riverbed at this very moment?" Chenglei asked.

"No," Chow replied quietly. "He may have managed to elude us. He may have escaped up the eastern bank while we were

getting men into position. But we were very fast, Prime Minister. I believe he is still there."

"Then open the gates," Chenglei said.

At first, neither Chow nor Daiyu understood what he meant.
Chow said, "Excuse me, Prime Minister?"

"Open the gates to the river," Chenglei said, enunciating
very clearly. "Let the water sweep him away."

There was a moment's silence while even the sinister Chow
seemed shocked. "Every laborer in the river will drown, Prime
Minister."

"Stonepickers are easily replaced," Chenglei said dismissive-
ly. "This is the best chance we have had in weeks to silence the
rebel. Open the gates."

There was a slight sound. Daiyu imagined Chow was bowing. "Yes, Prime Minister. It shall instantly be done."

Daiyu was halfway down the first flight of steps before she
even realized she had moved. Her heart was a misfiring cannon
booming inside her chest; her lungs were mangled sacks laboring against a vacuum. *Flood the river! Drown the stonepickers!
Murder Feng . . . and murder Kalen. . . .*

No no no no no no. . . .

She had no plan, she had no clear thought in her head except
to plunge down the steps and burst out the front door, then run
and run and run all the way to the river. She could not possibly
make it in time. However Chow had arrived at the mansion, it
undoubtedly had not been on foot. Could she catch a trolley?
Would it beat Chow's vehicle to the waterfront?

She took the final three stairs with a leap and skidded onto the patterned carpet of the foyer, almost somersaulting across the floor. "Daiyu!" someone exclaimed, and she looked up in astonishment to find Quan staring at her.

She had completely forgotten he was there.

"Quan," she said breathlessly, and dashed across the wide room to lay her hand on his arm. "Quan—my good friend—I have just realized—there is something desperately important that I need. I must have it, I must have it right now. Can you take me? Can you drive me to the riverfront?"

He had instantly put his hand over hers in a comforting fashion, but now he frowned. "To the riverfront? But what—"

"Please," she begged, tugging him toward the door. "There is no time to waste. I will explain on the way. But please, please hurry."

He hesitated only a moment—a traditional man whose instincts clearly warred with his affection for this unpredictable girl—and then grabbed her hand and started running. "Let us go!" he cried.

His car was idling in the curved driveway, guarded by admiring servants. The two of them leaped in and Quan wheeled away from the house, driving in his usual manic fashion. Daiyu clung grimly to the seat, scarcely noticing as he swerved around trolleys and wove through traffic, careening around the narrow corners without slowing down. Too many thoughts scrambled through her mind for her even to care that Quan risked both of their lives with his hazardous driving. *Chenglei is evil!* and

I should have used the bracelet and *I've been so foolish* clamored for attention, but the only thought she could really hold in her head was *Kalen will drown, Kalen will die. . . .*

"So tell me, Daiyu!" Quan called over the noise of the rushing wind and the screaming of a teenage boy who jumped out of his way. "Why are we dashing so madly to the riverfront? This is not at all what I expected."

There was no way her tortured brain could come up with a story that made much sense. "There is—something I had told Xiang I would buy—before the celebration tonight," she said. "We saw it one day in a shop near the riverfront. I lied—I told her I had it already—and I don't. And I just remembered. She will be very angry with me if I appear without it."

He shook his head, looking baffled and amused. "Sometimes you women are hard to understand."

Oh, you would have an even harder time understanding if I told you the truth. "We can only be grateful that men try to understand us even so," she agreed.

As they approached the river, traffic grew denser, and Quan was forced to slow down. Daiyu felt herself straining forward on the seat, as if by sheer will she could force the car through the tangles of vehicles and knots of pedestrians with their carts. They were close enough to the river now that Daiyu could spot the bright slash of the red lacquer gate, close enough that the streets narrowed into an almost impassable warren of twisting circles and cluttered alleys. Quan found his way blocked by a large vehicle that appeared to be delivering goods to a shop. Cursing under his breath, he whipped around a corner only to face a dead end. When he tried to back up, the exit was clogged with cars that had come to a complete standstill.

"Will you please move your cars?" Quan shouted over his shoulder. "We have very urgent business to complete!"

There was no time to waste. "Forgive me, Quan. You have been most kind," Daiyu said, and jumped down from the seat.

"Daiyu! Wait a moment! Daiyu!" he shouted after her.

"Meet me at the chocolate shop in half an hour!" she called over her shoulder. Not because she expected to join him there, but because she thought otherwise he might come after her, and she could not risk that.

She could not risk anything.

Kalen will drown, Kalen will die. . . .

Rounding the corner, she accelerated into a flat-out run. Pushing past the men and women in her way, darting into and out of street traffic if that route looked faster. Every minute counted, every second. She needed the shortest, most direct route toward the gate, toward the river, toward Kalen.

How close was Chow? How long would it take him to find the workmen to raise the gates?

She burst free of the last cluster of buildings and onto the broad stone swath of yin-and-yang symbols that separated the city from the riverfront. She could see them now, the stone-pickers bending over the great muddy expanse of the emptied riverbed, moving with slow deliberation across the littered landscape. Which one was Feng? Which one was Kalen?

Wasn't every laborer in the Zhongbu someone's friend, someone's beloved?

She'd had no plan, she'd had almost no coherent thought, but as she raced toward the river she saw the bell tower and instantly knew what she must do. She altered her course to run in that direction, calling out Gabe's name before she was even close enough for him to hear. A few people idly standing along the riverbank turned to give her curious looks, but no one seemed alarmed. No one seemed to realize that the world was about to end.

She arrived at the base of the bell tower, staggering a little, her breath coming so harshly that she felt like a knife was sawing across her rib cage. "Gabe!" she panted, then louder. "*Gabe!* Ring the bells! There's been a terrible mistake—ring the bells!"

There was no answer, and Gabe didn't poke his head over the edge of the tower. Daiyu felt a fresh surge of horror. Had Chow beaten her here? Had he murdered the bell ringers so that no one could call the stonepickers out of the river? Furiously she shook the gate, and the broken lock came open in her hand. She would have to climb to the top of the tower herself.

Forcing her trembling, exhausted legs to function, she dragged herself up the spiral staircase, gasping for air, feeling her hands shake on the railing, moving as fast as she could. "Gabe," she tried again every time she could gather enough breath, but he never answered. She dimly remembered Kalen saying that Gabe had found a girlfriend with whom he spent all his time. It was still fairly early in the morning, and the stonepickers usually worked till noon. Perhaps he had simply

assumed that he could chance arriving late . . . that there would
be no reason to summon the stonepickers out of the river before
their usual time. . . .

She heaved herself up the last step and onto the unstable
catwalk, looking around wildly and drawing in great gusts of
air. She was relieved to see no sign of Gabe's bloody body, but
dismayed to remember that the rope pull for the silver chimes
was located all the way on the other side. Clinging to the half
wall that circled the tower, she glided clumsily forward, trying
not to look down, forcing herself to ignore the fact that she was
several stories up in an untrustworthy structure. She had forgotten that there was a gap in the flooring and she whimpered
aloud when she reached it, but it was narrow, only about eight
inches across. Holding her breath and never letting go of the
ledge, she made a tiny jump and landed on the other side.

The bell pulls were in reach.

Freshly energized, she quickly unwrapped the thinner rope
from its anchor on the wall and began pulling it with all her
strength. Instantly, the little bells sent their silver trill into the
air and over the water, urgent omens of danger and retreat.
She didn't have attention to spare to see how the stonepickers
reacted when they heard this sound at least two hours before
they expected it. Would they gather their bags and hurry for
shore, would they turn to one another and wonder aloud what
was wrong? Would they notice that the eastern bells weren't
ringing and assume some young boy had climbed the western
tower to play a prank? Would they listen at all?

She pulled harder and harder on the rope, trying to invest the bells with some of the desperation she felt. But they seemed too lighthearted, too flimsy, unacquainted with doom. What else could she do? Keeping one hand on the thinner pull, she stretched her arm and began uncoiling the thicker, heavier rope, the one that controlled the large bell. When it was loose in her hand, she tugged on it as hard as she could.

The bell scarcely responded and she pulled again, seeing it begin to sway, moving with the stately precision of an elephant swinging its head around. Again she pulled, and again, almost coming to her knees to get leverage, continuing to shake the smaller bells with her other hand. And then the clapper struck the side of the metal with a sound that almost made a physical indentation in the air. She pulled again and felt the rope sweep her up, almost off her feet as the bell swung back in the other direction. Again the clapper hit—again—a dark, ominous counterpoint to the clattering chatter of the smaller chimes. *The world is upended and none of us are safe,* she willed the little bells to proclaim, while over their excited voices, the big bell intoned, *Home. Home. Home. Home.*

Now at last she risked looking over the side of the tower to see what her summons had wrought. Yes! Stonepickers on both banks were hastily climbing out of the riverbed, glancing nervously up at the gates, curiously back at the tower. In the press of people she could not make out individuals—where was Kalen? where was Feng?—and she hoped Chow's guards would have just as much difficulty as she did. Those men, she could see clearly, pacing both banks of the river, shouting to one an-

other, pointing, shaking their heads. She had a moment's spasm
of horror as she realized that she might just have driven Feng
straight into the arms of his enemies. But she devoutly hoped
that they would continue to search for Feng instead of charging
toward the tower to see who had rung the bells.

And then water began hissing out from under the gates.

She heard the collective gasp from the workers still struggling
toward safety, a great swelling murmur of disbelief that intensi-
fied as the sound of the escaping river grew louder. Now there
were shouts of fear; now she saw individual stonepickers stumble
in the mud and yield to the angry foam of the onrushing water.
At least two men were swept away. Daiyu pressed her hand to
her mouth, trying to push back her cry of anguish. Other workers formed human chains connecting the people still in the riverbed to the safety of the banks. More stonepickers were on dry
land—more—the last man was splashing up and out of the water
as the Zhongbu reached its highest, most furious peak.

Anyone who was not out of the water by now was dead.

Daiyu leaned as far over the half wall as she dared, frantically trying to make out faces and figures. She didn't waste
much time studying the Han men—she would be sorry if Feng
were dead, but he was not her primary concern—all she cared
about was Kalen's face, Kalen's fate. Her eyes skimmed over the
muttering, anxious crowd as she searched for a tall, thin, *cangbai* man with a loose, easy walk and a kind smile. . . .

She almost tumbled out of the tower when she spotted him.
He was supporting an older *heiren* woman who looked like she
had twisted her ankle in the mad dash out of the Zhongbu.

They were so close to the water's edge, they might have been the last two out of the river. Kalen was bent over her solicitously, and if Daiyu was not mistaken, he was carrying the woman's sack as well as his own. He never looked toward the bell tower.

Daiyu felt her blood thaw in her veins. Her head swam so suddenly that she almost pitched over the side of the tower. Abruptly she pulled herself back inside and collapsed onto the catwalk, fighting nausea and starting to shiver.

Kalen was safe. Kalen was alive. She had not been too late after all.

But what should she do now?

She desperately wanted to hurry down the spiral steps, push her way through the dispersing crowd of stonepickers, find Kalen, and fling herself into his arms. She wanted to pattern his face with frenzied kisses, test his breath with her own, prove to herself beyond any lingering irrational fear that he was alive, he had escaped to safety. She wanted him to hold her close, create for her a small inviolable space where she could stand without fear, sheltered by his body. But she knew that if she left this tower and ran to Kalen, she would not be able to bring herself to leave him again. She would not be able to find her way back to Quan, she would not be able to return to the palace. She would not be able to banish Chenglei, if that was what she decided to do.

She had to make impossible choices, she had to carry out dangerous plans, without drawing on Kalen's strength to support her own.

Daiyu drew her knees up and rested her face against them and tried to think through her options. She had abandoned Quan with a half-promise, not expecting to redeem it. But couldn't she? He would have no reason to think *she* was the one who had set the bells to clamoring so early in the day. Unless he had decided she was too unsteady to take seriously, he was even now awaiting her arrival at the chocolate shop, mystified and a little ruffled. She had not been gone so very long. If she could find him, if she could make up a plausible story, could she not return with him? Who would know where she had been?

She had not encountered any servants on her wild flight from the house. Xiang had not seen her race down the stairs—and even if her mad exit had been witnessed, she had said nothing incriminating. Anyone might think she had been eager to see Quan, eager to make one last purchase before the holiday. Why couldn't she return to the prime minister's house and resume her masquerade? Why couldn't she ask Aurora for the bracelet back? Why couldn't she await her next private meeting with Chenglei to send the dreadful man back to the iteration where he belonged?

But what if Chenglei or Chow had glimpsed her at the door? What if they had seen her fleeing, what if they realized what she had overheard and guessed she had been the one to sound the alarm?

She would be in mortal danger the instant she set foot in the mansion.

Daiyu lifted her head and dropped her legs so that her feet

dangled over the side of the walkway into open space. Her right hand crept to her pocket where the quartz talisman lay safely in its silken cocoon.

If Chenglei suspected she had betrayed him, she would have to go home.

If he did not, she had to play out this charade to the bitter end.

TWENTY

QUAN WAS SITTING at one of the outdoor tables, crunching on a chocolate ice and looking very ill-used. Daiyu slipped into the seat across from him, folded her hands before her on the table, and lowered her eyes.

"My most abject apologies, honored Quan," she said very formally. "I have behaved like a girl from the most backward of provinces and not like a young woman from the best family. I am ashamed. I cannot hope to be forgiven. I have come merely to tell you that I am sorry and that I will find my way back to the prime minister's on my own."

"No," he said sharply as she began to rise from her chair. And then, in a softer voice, "No. Please, Daiyu. Stay. I admit I am puzzled and confused, but I am not angry."

"Your forbearance is more than I deserve."

He signaled to the waiter, who was already bringing over a chocolate ice for Daiyu. "What I deserve, perhaps, is an explanation."

She took three bites before answering. Her mouth was so dry

from running and panting that the confection tasted divine. "I told you. I swore to Xiang that I had bought her a gift from a riverfront store, but I lied. I was afraid she would disown me if I did not give it to her tonight."

"But what is the gift?"

She risked a quick look at him, a secretive smile. "Ah, it is something only women can know about."

He blushed and looked away. He was one of those men who thought women so mysterious that they were actually a little frightening. "And why did you fail to buy it for her before today?"

She made her voice small and contrite. "Because I was unwilling to give up any chance I had to spend time with you."

It was a good gamble, and it paid off. His head came back around, and his smile was wide and pleased. "I would have helped you long before this," he said. "You would not have had to forfeit our time."

She bowed her head again, her own smile widening. "But I did not want to take the risk," she said. "I am so sorry. I have been unforgivably foolish."

His hand came up briefly to touch the back of hers where it lay on the table. "Very foolish," he said in a caressing voice, "but not unforgivably so. I am glad I was able to aid you today, Daiyu."

She took a deep breath. "And you will never know, Quan, how glad I am that you were there to help me."

✳

Xiang was in a rare state when Daiyu got back to the prime minister's house. "Where have you been? Gone so long on such an important day! You should be bathed already and sitting before your maid to have your hair styled."

"I was with Quan, Aunt," Daiyu said, her eyes wide with innocent surprise. "I thought you liked it when I spent time with Mei's son."

"Yes, but to be gone so long on *such* a day! And you did not even inform the prime minister that you were leaving, as I expressly told you to do! He came looking for you and was very surprised to learn you were gone."

"He came looking for me?" Daiyu said, keeping her voice calm. "Was he angry?"

"No, but he was disappointed. He said your talk this morning had been cut short and he wished to resume it."

"That is why I could not tell him I was leaving, Aunt. He had an important visitor. Who am I to interrupt?"

Xiang seemed a little mollified. "He asked if we might stay tomorrow after the rest of the guests were gone so that he could finish showing you his collection. So that he could show *both* of us his collection," Xiang added, sounding smug.

Daiyu tried not to take a deep breath of relief. This mark of exceptional favor meant the prime minister knew nothing of Daiyu's betrayal. This and the fact that he hadn't had his guards arrest her the moment she returned to the house. "Oh, Aunt, I hope you said we could!"

"Of course I did! *I* know what kind of behavior is proper when I am visiting the house of an important man!"

"Yes, Aunt. I apologize, Aunt. I'm sorry I have disappointed you."

Xiang fussed for a few more minutes, but really there was no time. They had to separate to their own rooms and quickly begin the ritual of readying themselves for the holiday dinner. In Daiyu's case, this involved taking a scented bath, applying body oils, getting the maid's help to put on the pearl-sewn black sheath, allowing a second maid to fix her hair while the first one brushed her face with cosmetics. She couldn't imagine how many more steps Xiang required.

Finally Daiyu had donned the finishing touches—ropes of pearls on her wrists and at her throat, pearls and studs of onyx at her ears, and flat embroidered black shoes—and she was ready to go. She shooed the maids out of the room, claiming a need for one last moment of privacy, and slipped the quartz stone in its silken pouch into her right-hand pocket.

She was ready to celebrate the holiday.

Chenglei's party was utterly charming. Even before true darkness fell, the festive lanterns strung overhead washed the back lawns with color; sweet doughs baking and spicy meats frying sent tantalizing aromas swirling out from the tents. The guests were all dressed in summer elegance, bare arms glittering with jewels, faces lifted to catch the first cool breezes of evening. The whole tone of the event was one of suppressed excitement as the privileged families of Shenglang gathered in one place to show off their beauty and revel in their wealth.

It was fairly easy for Daiyu to get free of Xiang, who was much more interested in banding together with her cronies and dropping hints about her invitation to view Chenglei's artifacts in the morning. Daiyu supposed she also managed to work into the conversation how much time her niece was spending with Mei's son. In fact, here at the party, Quan was making his interest in Daiyu quite clear as he strolled around the lawns with her for much of the evening, introducing her to his friends and offering every five minutes to fetch her something else to eat. She allowed herself, now and then, to touch him on the arm in a proprietary manner. Some of the girls her own age glared at her when they thought no one else could see their faces; some of them sighed and looked forlorn.

Daiyu had never meant for her life in Shenglang to get this tangled.

It was just on the edge of true darkness, and the technicians at the very back of the lawns had set off a few preliminary fireworks, when Mei approached Daiyu and Quan as they stood together, idly talking.

"Ah, Daiyu, how are you enjoying your first summer holiday here in Shenglang?" Mei asked in a very friendly way. "It is much different from such holidays back home, isn't it?"

"Very much so," Daiyu agreed, "though we do have fireworks. What would a summer holiday be without them? But I am sure the prime minister's will be more spectacular than any I have seen."

"Some year, if you are not invited to the prime minister's for the holiday, you should go down to the riverfront and watch the display there," Quan said. "It is a noisy and very public place, of course, but the colors overhead are magnificent."

"Foolish boy, why would there ever be a time Daiyu was not invited to the prime minister's?" Mei demanded.

Quan bowed his head, chastened, but he managed to give Daiyu a quick sideways grin. "Forgive me, Mother, that was indeed foolish."

Mei had taken hold of Daiyu's arm. "Come with me, Daiyu. One of my sisters and her daughter are here and they want to meet you. No, Quan, you find someone else to absorb your attention tonight. You do not want to be so particular that people talk about you."

Now he was grinning broadly, since it was clearly his partiality for Daiyu that was making Mei so happy. "Yes, Mother," he said. "Daiyu, I will seek you out later in the evening, when such attentions do not seem so—obvious."

She smiled in return. "Yes, Quan. Thank you, Quan."

Mei's sister, like Mei herself, was small, well-groomed, and avid for details, studying Daiyu closely by the light of the lanterns and asking searchingly personal questions. Daiyu answered serenely, giving very little away. The daughter was younger than Daiyu and quite pretty, though not particularly discreet. She stared at Daiyu during the whole conversation and asked in a loud whisper, "Is she the girl who's going to marry Quan? Why does he like her?"

It was a relief to be able to excuse herself when one of Mei's friends joined the group, and Daiyu was in no hurry to seek out Quan or Xiang again. Instead, she took advantage of the fact that full dark had fallen to wander unobserved toward the back acres of the lawn. No colorful lanterns were strung over this portion of the yard; the technicians on the fireworks stage were working by torchlight to line up their canisters and time their fuses. While Daiyu stood in the shadows, almost completely invisible in her black dress, they shot off another practice round, and this one decorated the sky with whistling spirals of red and gold. There was laughter and polite applause from the crowd.

"Do you like fireworks displays, Daiyu?" asked a voice at her elbow, and she turned in some surprise to find that Chenglei had approached her in the dark. Perhaps she wasn't so invisible after all.

"I love them," she confessed. "Not just the colors—I love the sounds as well."

"You like detonations," he said. He sounded amused, but they were too far from the lanterns and the torches for her to see his face clearly. "So do I."

She laughed. "My mother always said it was impossible to understand how such a sedate child could be so fond of loud noises," she told him.

"Perhaps you are not so sedate after all," Chenglei replied.

Daiyu considered. "Or perhaps it is the very tranquility of

my nature that allows me to endure the explosions. A woman who was more high-strung might find that all the noise put her greatly on edge."

"I would agree that you have a certain tranquility to you, but I would add that I sense an adventurousness in your soul as well," Chenglei replied. "Or have I misjudged?"

She was having a hard time believing they were having this conversation at all. She had to concentrate on the words, the bantering tone, and smother the voice of outrage in her head: *This man just tried to murder hundreds of people. This man tried to murder Kalen.* "It is only recently that the adventurousness has come to the fore," she admitted. "It is not a trait that many people admire in well-brought-up young women, and I am trying very hard not to disappoint my aunt. But you are astute, Prime Minister. That spirit is definitely there."

"I find myself wondering," he said in a soft voice, "just what adventure you were pursuing this afternoon when you went running from my house."

She turned to stone and said nothing, merely peering up at him in the dark.

Another firecracker went off, this one gold and blue. It painted Chenglei's face with vivid colors and quickly faded, but for a moment she had a clear glimpse of his unreadable smile.

Did he know what she had done? Was he merely curious about her sudden flight, willing to believe some innocent tale?

Her voice was remarkably composed. "Not so much an adventure as an insane attempt to make a purchase before the deadline of your party. Quan very kindly—and very rapidly!—

drove me to the river shops so that I could fulfill an obligation. I was only glad I remembered in time."

It was so vague as to be ridiculous, but in this polite society, it would be rude for him to press for more details. If he believed her. If he was not suspicious. From his answer, she could not be sure, and her heart began a slow, heavy pounding.

"Ah, and was Quan then allowed to know what this secret obligation consisted of?"

"It was a purchase for my aunt, and no, he was not allowed to know!" Daiyu replied. Bad enough if Chenglei suspected Daiyu, but to embroil poor Quan in this mess as well . . . !

"I was curious," Chenglei said, his voice still light and agreeable. "Because a very short time after you fled, someone broke into the bell tower on the western bank of the Zhongbu River and called the stonepickers back to shore two hours before their normal time."

Daiyu merely gaped at him, the looming shape of nemesis in the imperfect dark.

"And I wondered if you were the person ringing those bells," he went on. "And if so, why you felt compelled to do so."

She did not reply. Words would not come to her lips; air would not come to her lungs. He knew, he knew, everything was lost. . . .

She was staring at him, trying to make out his features, but even so he put his hand out and pushed her head up, as if to make sure she could not look away. "And I wondered if perhaps you lingered outside my office longer than I supposed and overheard—something—in my conversation that alarmed you."

Still she said nothing. Still she did not move. Her heart was a laboring knot of pain and her mind was a chaotic swirl of horror.

"If you do not answer me, Daiyu," he said, still in that pleasant tone, "I will consider you guilty, and the consequences will be dire."

"What consequences?" The words forced themselves past her lips.

His head tilted to one side as if he was thinking that over. "I will have you arrested for treason. I need not be specific about the act. You are practically a stranger here. No one will believe you innocent if I declare you guilty. And—I want to be very plain—no one will get a chance to ask you for *your* version of the facts."

Imprisonment—maybe torture—exactly what she might have expected from a tyrant. Exactly the reason Aurora and Ombri had given her the rose quartz talisman. She would not be incarcerated very long. But she would have to make sure she used the stone before she was bound or stripped or otherwise restricted.

She would have to use it now. Without having a chance to explain to Aurora and Ombri what she'd learned. Without saying good-bye to Kalen. At the thought, her heart protested; for a moment she didn't think she would be able to do it. But there was no choice. She flattened both hands on the front of her dress, awaiting her moment.

Chenglei was still speaking. "Xiang will be disgraced, of course. Her niece in prison! After Xiang has introduced her into every important home in Shenglang! Her property will be forfeit, she will be beggared. All because of your actions."

"No," Daiyu whispered.

"Mei, too," Chenglei added. "And her son Quan. And all their relatives. Dishonored for their stupidity in foisting a trai-tor onto Shenglang society. I already have in mind the faithful council members to whom I will award all of their estates and belongings."

"You can't," Daiyu said, her voice still faint. "Please. Don't hurt anyone but me."

"Why did you ring the bells, Daiyu?"

"You were going to let all those people die."

"Ah. So you did hear my conversation with Chow. I thought you had."

"All those people. Just to get rid of one man."

"One very troublesome man, let me point out," Chenglei said reasonably. "Feng must die, and I'm sorry that makes you unhappy, but I really cannot endure his attacks on me any longer. And, Daiyu, I cannot stomach soft-hearted girls who do not understand why I must silence the rebels."

"I don't care about Feng," she said flatly.

Another round of preliminary fireworks went off, briefly showing Chenglei's face surprised and intrigued. "Really? So it was just the scale of my reprisal that you found intolerable?"

"I don't care about any of those people," she said, her voice finding strength. Boldly, she stepped back from him, and he let his hand fall. She put her fists on her hips, tried to take the stance and tone of a mutinous girl. "My aunt would disown me if she

knew—yes, and Quan's heart would be broken!—but I have fall-
en in love with a *cangbai* boy, and he is a stonepicker who works
in the river. He is the one I wanted to save today, not your stupid
rebel, not any of those other people that I never met. You can
call that treason if you like, but I wasn't thinking of you when I
sounded the bells. I was thinking of the man I love."

"Now, that has the ring of honesty to it," Chenglei replied.
"Xiang would be justified in disowning you if she discov-
ered such a dreadful secret! What is this young man's name,
Daiyu?"

"Do you think I will tell you so you can arrest him, too?"
she scoffed. "He is nobody who will ever trouble you."

By his voice, Chenglei was amused again—possibly even delighted. "Oh, you spoke the truth when you said you admire
explosions!" he said. "How such a serene face can hide such an
addiction to danger I can hardly understand."

"We each have our secrets," Daiyu said. "You know mine
and I know yours. I won't tell if you won't."

For a moment, there was silence, as if Chenglei was considering the bargain. Then there was a sudden rapid succes-
sion of detonations as the technicians on the stage shot off the
first salvo of fireworks. Overhead, gorgeous golds and emeralds
and sapphires bloomed across the night sky, seeming to stretch
to the horizon. By their light, Daiyu saw Chenglei's narrowed
eyes and pursed lips.

"You almost persuade me," he said. "And I will miss you, I
think, when you are gone. But I cannot trust you and I cannot
allow you your freedom, so I must refuse."

It took her a second to assimilate the words, and then she realized what he had just said—and what he had implied. *You will be arrested; you will be imprisoned; perhaps you will be killed.* She must leave here, and instantly. Her right hand dove for her pocket as she spun on her heel to run.

But another burst of fireworks showed Chenglei exactly what she was doing, and his hand shot out and clamped around her forearm just as she yanked the pouch from her pocket. "A weapon, Daiyu?" he asked, amused again. "I would not have expected that from you!"

She brought her left arm around to strike at him wildly, but he easily blocked her blows with an upraised arm. "No—no— not a weapon—let me go—"

"Something you cherish, evidently," he said. His grip tightened so cruelly that she cried out in pain and dropped the pouch to the grass. More fireworks covered the sound of her voice and showed Chenglei exactly where the bag had landed. Before she could fall to her knees and scrabble for the quartz with her free hand, he twisted her right arm so ferociously that for a moment she was blinded with pain. When her eyes cleared, she saw that he had scooped up the pouch.

She was whimpering on the ground, so he obviously felt it was safe to release her. "Let us see exactly what kind of treasure you reach for at your direst moment," he said, and shook the talisman into his hand.

There was an intense flash of light, an echoing boom, and Chenglei disappeared.

More fireworks exploded overhead in an orgy of light and

sound. Not even the technicians a dozen yards away would have noticed anything unusual.

Daiyu merely stared at the spot where he had been, cradling her injured arm against her chest. She could not remember crying, but she could feel the tight streaks of dried tears along her cheeks.

The fireworks display went on and on.

TWENTY-ONE

"Is THIS NOT the most magnificent holiday party you have ever been to?" Xiang demanded a few minutes later as Daiyu rejoined her near one of the cooking tents. People were beginning to recover the use of their ears now that the explosions had finally died away, and they were laughing and talking and indulging in another round of refreshments.

"I can't remember anything like it," Daiyu said truthfully.

"Too bad we have to wait another whole year for something this good! But we will have Chenglei's collection to view tomorrow morning," Xiang said.

"I'm looking forward to that," Daiyu said. The throbbing in her arm was beginning to fade, though she was afraid if anyone touched her she would cry out in pain. She might have a bruise in the morning that she would need to explain away.

Although other explanations might soon become more pressing.

"Where is Chenglei?" Xiang asked now, looking around. "I have scarcely seen him all evening."

"Neither have I," Daiyu said, her voice steady.

Xiang waved a hand. "An important man like Chenglei often has to work even through a holiday celebration," she said. "I hope he has not been in his office all night, reading reports! I hope he got to see some of the fireworks."

"I hope so too," Daiyu said. "They were spectacular."

All around them, people were having similar conversations. *What amazing colors! What a splendid party! Where is the prime minister, so I can compliment him before I go home?* It was another ten or fifteen minutes before it became common knowledge that Chenglei was nowhere to be found, but, like Xiang, the other guests seemed to assume that he had been called away on urgent matters. A few people began to leave; others lingered by the food tents, exchanging last tidbits of gossip.

Quan found them just as Xiang had decided she and her niece should retire for the night, to be sure they were rested for their private viewing the next day. "Will I see you tomorrow?" he asked Daiyu.

"She will be too busy," Xiang answered before Daiyu could reply. "She has an appointment with the prime minister in the morning—we both do—and many things to do in the afternoon. You may see her the following day."

Quan was trying not to grin as he held out his hands, and Daiyu managed to smile as she pressed her palms against his in farewell. She had to grit her teeth against the pain in her right arm. "The day after tomorrow, then," Quan said. "The time will seem very long."

"I look forward to the next hour we meet," she replied.

She wondered if she would ever see Quan again.

Xiang chattered during the whole time they climbed the stairs and walked down the hallway to their rooms. Daiyu thought she had never seen the old woman so happy. As they paused at the door to Xiang's suite, Daiyu impulsively leaned down and kissed her wrinkled cheek.

"Thank you for everything you have done for me," she said in a soft voice. "I cannot imagine that was I lucky enough to have you as my aunt."

Xiang looked surprised but deeply pleased. "And who would have thought I would have found a niece so much after my own heart," she said. "You have proved to be a fine girl. Now, go to bed so that you will look your best in the morning."

Daiyu obediently entered her room and let the servants undress her, and she lay on her bed as soon as she was alone, but she did not sleep. Instead she listened to the faint reverberations of fireworks being shot off in other parts of the city late into the night, and then she listened to the silence. As dawn slowly whitened the windows, she listened to birds greet the morning with their usual cheerful music. She knew this was the day that everything would change.

✳

From the minute Xiang and Daiyu entered the dining room, it was clear something was wrong in the house. Daiyu took her place at the table, next to the other girls, while Xiang joined the adults standing in a knot at the back of the room. She already knew what the conversation was about, but she listened anyway to the scraps of dialogue she could overhear.

"And no one has seen him since last night?"

"But he was missing last night, too! Don't you remember?"

"I thought he had been called into the house on business."

"Did anyone talk to him at the party? Was he even there?"

"He wasn't there at all last night?"

"What do the servants say?"

"They're mystified. The head of the council has been called in, but what will she be able to do?"

"Do you think it's possible he was injured?"

"In his own *house?*"

"But if no one saw him here last night—"

Daiyu accepted only small portions when the servants came in offering food. She was not sure she would be able to choke down a bite.

Eventually, the adults joined the young women at the table, and they all ate in uneasy silence before returning to their rooms.

"Collect your things," Xiang said to Daiyu in a tense voice. "We will not be staying to view Chenglei's treasures after all."

"But, Aunt!" Daiyu exclaimed. "Have we offended the prime minister in some way?"

Xiang's mouth was tight. She was clearly disappointed, but her eyes also showed a little anger. She was not used to being abandoned without an explanation. "No," she said at last. "But it seems his plans have changed."

They were packed and out of the house within the hour. Daiyu was not surprised to find that news of Chenglei's disappearance had preceded them, for Mei was awaiting them in Xiang's overdecorated parlor when they arrived home. Xiang impatiently waved a hand at Daiyu to dismiss her, but Daiyu left the room very slowly, trying to listen.

"The whole city is talking!" Mei exclaimed before Daiyu passed out of earshot. "Where can Chenglei be? Has he fallen ill? Fallen drunk?"

"Consorted with a hired woman who poisoned his drink?" Xiang suggested. Her tone was both acid and eager—this was potentially a tragedy, but it might simply be a scandal, and Xiang and Mei lived for gossip.

"I suppose someone could have harmed him, and yet—" Mei said.

"It seems the unlikeliest of the possibilities," Xiang agreed. "I think we will find that he has either been very indiscreet or very unlucky."

"His position will be compromised," Mei said.

"Unless he has a very good story."

"But what could that story be?"

Satisfied, Daiyu continued on up to her room. She was fairly confident that, no matter what theories they proposed, they would never come close to the truth.

She pushed open the door to her room and found Aurora waiting inside.

"Daiyu, what did you do?" the blond woman asked in a hushed voice.

Hastily, Daiyu shut the door and the two of them huddled together just inside the closet, talking in whispers. They had not spoken to each other in two weeks, but all they really needed to discuss was yesterday. Aurora gasped when Daiyu related Chenglei's plan to flood the river and showed alarm when Daiyu repeated the conversation in the backyard.

"He said he was going to arrest me," Daiyu finished up. "I reached for my quartz talisman so I could go home—but he took it from me and opened the pouch. He—he disappeared. But no one saw him go because we were standing at the back of the lawn and all the fireworks were going off."

Aurora stared at her. "You sent him away—to your own iteration?"

"I suppose. I didn't mean to. Oh, Aurora, is that where he's gone? To Earth? What will happen to him there?"

Aurora shook her head in a disbelieving motion. "I have no idea. I don't even know where he might have ended up. The quartz talisman was calculated for your body, not for his. He could be anywhere—at any time."

"Will you and Ombri go after him?" Daiyu asked.

Aurora nodded. "Yes. If we don't, he will find a way to wreak damage in your iteration."

"I'm so sorry," Daiyu said.

Unexpectedly, Aurora hugged her. "Don't be sorry. You were

given a difficult job and you managed to do it, even though you didn't do it the way we planned."

"I'm sorry I didn't trust you. I'm sorry I didn't believe you about Chenglei. But when I talked to him—he was so charming—I actually liked him. And I was pleased that he liked me."

"You are not the first person who has fallen under his spell, and, unfortunately, you will not be the last," Aurora said. "If men like Chenglei were easier to resist, the world—every world—would be a less hazardous place."

Aurora patted Daiyu's shoulder and then stepped back, turning brisk. "Now," she said, "Xiang will be preoccupied with Mei for a good long while, don't you suppose? This will be an excellent time for you to leave."

"Leave? To do what?" Daiyu said. She felt her face light up. "Can I go to the aviary? Can I see Kalen? I have so much to tell him!"

"I meant, it's time for you to leave Jia," Aurora said gently. "Time for you to go back to Earth."

Daiyu stared at her, suddenly feeling stricken. "Home?" she repeated. "Today?"

Aurora nodded. "We have no time to waste. Ombri and I must go after Chenglei, and we cannot leave until we have seen you safely home."

"But I—but *now*?" Daiyu stammered. "There are so many things left to do—"

Aurora watched her steadily. "There was only one thing here you had to do, and it has been done. It is time for you to go."

Daiyu shook her head, slowly, stubbornly, even as a bubbling grief built up in her chest. "I'm not leaving until I say good-bye to Kalen."

"Daiyu—"

"I'm *not!*"

Aurora shrugged helplessly. "All right. We will return to the house before we send you on your way."

Daiyu was already hurrying out of the closet and over to a small desk stocked with writing materials. "And I have to leave a note for Xiang. I have to make up some excuse, give her some reason. She's become attached to me, and I don't want her to be hurt."

"It will hurt her no matter when you go and how you do it," Aurora said. "A note will not change that."

But Daiyu was adamant on this point as well. "It will only take a minute," she said.

Nonetheless, she sat there for at least five minutes, trying to think up a story that Xiang would accept with relief instead of pain. Finally, she picked up the elegant writing utensil and wrote with great care on the thick, pressed sheet of paper.

> *Mistress Xiang:*
>
> *I am sorry to grieve you this way, but I must leave you suddenly before I shame you and your venerable name. I have lied to you so long that I am now almost glad to tell you the truth. I am a worthless girl who does not deserve all the attention and affection you have heaped on me. I have fallen in love with a* cangbai

boy, and he has gotten me with child. Soon this will be evident to everyone. I cannot stay to dishonor you or cause distress to Mei's noble house, and so I am leaving. Knowing how angry you will be at your servant Aurora, who first brought me to your attention, I have suggested that she leave your house and never return. I beg for nine times nine hundred pardons, but I know I do not deserve one. I wish I had the right to truly call you Aunt.

Your niece-who-is-not, Daiyu

Aurora was reading over Daiyu's shoulder. "Very well put," she said. "Now, let us go."

It was heartbreakingly simple to leave the house. There was little need to pack, since the only items Daiyu had to bring with her were the gold shirt and black pants she had been wearing when she arrived in Jia. Xiang did not unexpectedly emerge from the parlor to demand where she was going; no servants challenged them at the door. Daiyu and Aurora simply walked out the front entrance, strolled down the sidewalk, and soon lost themselves in the bustle of the congested streets. They were a few blocks away from Xiang's before Aurora hailed a trolley, and they elbowed their way into the crowded aisle for the ride to the riverfront. A change of trolleys, another dreary ride, and they were in the *cangbai* district where Ombri and Aurora had their house.

They disembarked and walked the final few blocks. Aurora made no attempt at conversation, for she appeared to be deep in thought, and Daiyu just trudged along beside her, clasping her folded clothes to her chest. Compared to the streets where Xiang lived, this neighborhood seemed even more downtrodden, the tents ragged and pathetic, the standing houses decrepit. Most everyone they passed was *cangbai* or *heiren*; the few Han they encountered looked strained and miserable.

But the thought of leaving this place behind forever was pushing Daiyu into despair.

The thought of leaving Kalen behind forever. . . .

It was scarcely noon by the time they arrived at the house. Daiyu looked around eagerly, in case Kalen was there, but it was quickly evident that he was not. She felt her shoulders slump with weariness and disappointment and a mounting sense of loss.

"Are you hungry?" Aurora asked. "There's food in the kitchen."

"A little. I couldn't swallow anything this morning. And I didn't sleep at all last night."

"Well, eat something and then take a nap. I'm going to look for Ombri. I'll be back as soon as I can."

But Aurora was still gone when Daiyu finished her meal and lay down. She had automatically gone to the small room that had been hers five weeks earlier, and only now did she realize she had usurped Kalen's place. His clothes were thrown over a chair; his scent lay like a perfume across the bed. Daiyu put her head down, closed her eyes, and inhaled deeply, comforted by the smell. If she could just take a small part of Kalen back with her to St. Louis—if she could take back just one memory—

She was so tired, she fell asleep instantly, but her dreams were confused and troubling. She struggled through unfamiliar streets, running from someone who chased her, searching for someone who eluded her, while fireworks rained dangerous sparks down from overhead. It was a relief to wake a couple of hours later, feeling only a little rested. Outside her room, she could hear voices murmuring in intense conversation—Ombri and Aurora, excitedly making plans.

She turned her head on the pillow and saw Kalen sitting on the floor, watching her.

TWENTY-TWO

DAIYU WAS FLOODED with happiness, but when she opened her mouth to cry out his name, Kalen put a finger to his lips to enjoin silence. She glanced at the door then back at him, and he nodded. He did not want Aurora and Ombri to know she was awake.

Noiselessly, she moved over on the mat to make room for him, and he lay down beside her. She rested a hand on his hip, he settled his palm around the back of her head and drew her close enough for a gentle kiss. She sighed and felt a moment's utter peace.

"Are you all right?" he whispered.

She nodded against the pillow. "Are you?"

"What happened?" he said. "Tell me all of it."

"I heard Chenglei give an order to flood the river. He thought Feng had hidden there among the stonepickers, and he was willing to murder all those people in the hopes of killing Feng. I made Quan drive me to the Zhongbu, and I rang the little bells—"

"That was you?" Kalen interrupted. "Gabe came running down to the river, demanding to know what had happened. No one could believe he had left the tower empty. No one could guess who had known to ring the bells to save so many lives."

"Some people died," she said. "I saw them get washed away."

Kalen rested his forehead against hers. His hand moved down to rest warmly on her back. "So many lived. But I didn't know *you* were the one who saved us."

"I wanted to tell you—I saw you climb out of the river, help-ing some woman, and I wanted to run to you—but I had to get back to Quan. I had to get back to Chenglei's house. I thought no one would realize what I had done. I thought I could keep pretending. But then last night—at the party—Chenglei found me alone. He accused me of sounding the bells. He accused me of being a traitor. He said he would ruin Xiang, he would ruin Mei, and I was horrified at all the damage I had caused. I knew I could not be arrested, so I reached for the talisman, and he took it from me and he—and he—he disappeared."

"So Chenglei is gone and the people of Shenglang can find a new prime minister—a better one, I hope," Kalen said. He brushed another gentle kiss on her lips and she felt his mouth smiling against hers. "You have done what they brought you here to do."

"Kalen, Aurora says I must go home," she said. "But I don't want to go. Not now, not yet." She moved closer, so she was pressed against him down the entire length of his body. She felt the heat of his skin through the ragged layer of his clothing, the silken layer of hers. "I don't want to leave you. I don't think I can."

He was silent a moment, though his big hand made a slow, stroking motion down her spine. Finally he said, "You always knew you couldn't stay. And you have so much to go back to. You'll be glad once you're home on Earth."

"I can't remember my home," she whispered. "Any of it."

"Your father is a tall man with an easy smile," Kalen said, the rhythm of his voice soothing, reassuring. "He taught you to do at least one kind act every day. He works with his hands, and he makes beautiful things out of pieces that have been abandoned or thrown away. Your mother is practical and never at a loss. She could organize the world. She isn't a dreamer like your father, but she's hopelessly attracted to his dreams. Neither of them has ever loved anything as much as they love you."

"How can you remember them when I can't?" she asked him through her silent sobs.

"They're *your* memories," he told her gently. "I only held them for you."

She moved her hand up, clutched at his face. She wanted to press even closer; she wanted to crawl inside his heart. "What will happen to me, when I cross back to Earth?" she said, desperately afraid. "Will I really forget everything that happened to me here?"

"It's all right if you do," he said. "I'll hold those memories for you too."

Her face crumpled; it was harder and harder to hold back the sound of her crying. "But *you'll* be alone," she said. "All of us gone. I hate to think of you lonely and sad—oh, but that's better than not being able to think of you at all!"

"Ssshh," he said, wrapping his arms around her waist and hugging her tightly. "It will not be so dreadful. I will be happy knowing you are where you're supposed to be, surrounded by people who love you. I will be happy remembering you came into my life at all."

She could not be comforted. Her weeping grew louder, and she wasn't surprised to hear a knock on the door a moment before Aurora come in. "Is she awake then? Oh—Daiyu—this is why I didn't want you to come back and make your good-byes—"

"I'm sorry," Daiyu sobbed, though she couldn't have said what she was apologizing for. Maybe nothing more than the inability to stop crying. She heard Ombri's heavier footsteps enter the room.

"Farewells are always difficult, but there is little to be gained by drawing them out," he said in his deep voice. The tone was far more compassionate than the words. "Say your good-byes, Daiyu, for Aurora and I cannot linger. We must cross to your iteration as soon as possible. We must discover where Chenglei has gone and what fresh mischief he might have stirred up."

Kalen sat up and urged Daiyu to do the same. She knew her face was pinched and blotchy, but she didn't even care that everyone could see her in such an unattractive state. "Can't we stay one more day?" she begged. "Can't we leave tomorrow?"

"It won't be any easier tomorrow, I'm afraid," Ombri said. "For you *or* Kalen."

Kalen tried to draw her to her feet, but she twined her arms around his neck. "Come with me," she said, suddenly struck by inspiration. "You don't have any reason to stay here—follow me to St. Louis."

"You won't remember me in St. Louis," he said quietly.

"And he won't remember you, either," Ombri said. "I told you that on your first day here. There is something about the Earth iteration that erases a sojourner's memories of any place he might have been before. Even Aurora and I will need some time to regain a sense of self once we arrive on your world."

"Which is why we must find Chenglei as soon as possible," Aurora said. "Before he regains his full strength."

Daiyu turned her back on them. "Come to Earth anyway," she pleaded, putting her hands up to Kalen's cheeks. "I'll find you. I'll write myself a note! I'll tell myself to go down to the Arch—the gateway—every day and wait for someone. I'll describe you. I'll tell myself to trust you and to be your friend."

"Daiyu, it won't work," Aurora said.

"It will," she said fiercely. "Kalen, promise you'll come."

He leaned his forehead against hers again; his eyes were huge and liquid just inches away. "And what happens to me if you cannot find me?" he said sadly. "What happens to me if you do not remember to look for me, if you do not recognize me when I appear? I am alone in a place I do not understand—"

"Where you do not speak the language," Ombri interposed.

"And where I must appear like a lunatic to the authorities. What happens to me then?"

He was right. The thought was horrifying. The only thing that could make her wish him to stay behind was the fear of what could happen to him if he tried to follow her. "Then you must stay in Shenglang," she whispered against his mouth. "And I must try to live without even the memory of you on Earth."

"Come, Daiyu," Ombri said. "We must get you home."

Not surprisingly, it took a few more minutes to get ready. Daiyu had to change into her own clothes, so that she would not be startled, back on Earth, to find herself suddenly wearing a wholly unfamiliar outfit. In addition, despite Aurora's disapproval, she had to write herself a note trying to explain her adventure. But what could she possibly say? In the end, she merely put down the most important part: "You were briefly transported to another world, and you fell in love with a boy named Kalen. If you ever see him again, he won't remember you and you won't remember him, but you should trust him and let him into your life." She wondered if she would believe the words when she saw them.

She had managed to keep the silken pouch she had carried the whole time she was in Shenglang. Chenglei had dropped it as he was flung to her iteration, and she had retrieved it from the grass before she rejoined Xiang. In it was the other note she had written to herself, which she discarded now, and the precious drawing Kalen had made of the riverfront. This, of course, she kept. Now she added the smoky brown rock Kalen had found in the river one day, the one decorated with bits of orange and cobalt. He had given it to her; maybe it would help her remember him.

"I'm ready," she said finally in a quavering voice, although she wasn't ready, she would never be ready, she didn't think she had the strength to make this final journey. But "Good," Aurora said, and Ombri nodded, and Kalen smiled at her and took her hand.

"Then let's go to the gateway," Kalen said.

He continued to hold her hand as the four of them walked to the nearest trolley stop, and he held her hand as they sat together on one of the hard wooden seats. His grip was reassuringly tight as they disembarked from the trolley and picked their way across the yin-yang border of stones until they were standing in front of the tall red-lacquer gate.

"What do I do now?" Daiyu asked, her voice roughened by the tightness of her throat.

"It's simple," Ombri said. "You will take this gem and step through the gate, and you will be back in your own iteration."

Aurora handed her a silver necklace hung with a pink stone pendant. It was a piece of rose quartz much smaller than the talisman she had carried all these weeks. Apparently, since she was using it in conjunction with a gateway, it didn't need to be as powerful.

"And no time will have passed since I left?" Daiyu asked.

"A second, maybe two," Aurora said. "Nothing you would notice. You will probably feel dizzy. You might feel nauseated. You'll be a little confused. Nothing you can't explain away by sunstroke or heat exhaustion."

She had left St. Louis on the evening of a scorching hot day. Sunstroke and heat exhaustion would be entirely believable.

"Are you sure I won't remember?" she asked.

Ombri put his hands on her shoulders, even though Kalen continued to hold her hand. "We're sure," he said. He leaned down to kiss her on the forehead. "Travel safely, Daiyu. You have been a splendid companion."

He stepped aside, and Aurora hugged her, kissing her on the cheek. "You have such courage and grace," the older woman whispered. "Those will serve you well no matter what world you call home."

Aurora drew back, and now there was only Kalen to say good-bye to. Daiyu wanted to fling herself into his arms, cling to him and refuse to let go, but she knew such a display would hurt him far longer than it hurt her. If ever there was a time to show courage and grace, it was now.

"I love you," she told him, speaking steadily despite her falling tears. "Remember that for me, in case I forget."

"I love you, too," he said, kissing her on the mouth and finally releasing her hand. "And that will be true as long as either of us lives in either of our worlds."

There was nothing else to say. Daiyu clutched the cool pink stone in her right hand, gave them all one last brave smile, and stepped through the red-lacquer gate.

TWENTY-THREE

DAIYU TRIPPED ON something and fell to the ground on the other side of the Arch, landing awkwardly on her hands and knees. The pendant flew from her grip to land a few feet away. For a moment, the breath was punched out of her body; for a moment, it was hard to see.

"Are you all right?" someone asked, and she looked up to see a pair of middle-aged women bending over her. One wore jeans and a Cardinals shirt, and the other had on a long sundress printed with palm trees and flamingos.

"I think so," she said cautiously. "But I feel a little dizzy."

"See if you can stand up," said the Cardinals fan, offering her a friendly hand. The one in the Florida dress reached over to pick up the necklace from the grass.

"I think you dropped this," she said, handing it over.

"Yes. Thank you," Daiyu said. She felt unsteady on her feet, as if she'd spent too long on a carnival ride. Maybe she was dehydrated.

"You don't look so good," said the woman in the Cardinals shirt. "I think we'd better find first aid."

Daiyu's first instinct was to say, *No, I'm fine,* but the dizziness was getting worse and she was starting to see little spots in front of her eyes. A sizzle and boom overhead made her jump, though she knew it was just more practice fireworks being shot off. "Maybe we should," she said. "But I have to give this necklace back—it belongs to that old woman at the booth back there—" She gestured behind her. At the moment, she didn't have the energy to try to figure out which other vendor had been interested in buying the necklace from the old woman.

The flamingo woman said, "I'll take it to her. You just wait right here. Katie, if you see any cops, you might flag them down."

Ten minutes later, Daiyu was sitting in the air-conditioned first-aid trailer, drinking bottled water and having her blood pressure taken by an emergency medical technician. He also examined a bruise on her arm that Daiyu couldn't remember getting—maybe she'd landed on it when she tripped and fell—but since she clearly had no broken bones, he quickly lost interest. A few other people were in the trailer, lying on cots or sitting on hard plastic chairs, holding ice bags to their foreheads.

"I think you'll be okay," said the EMT, "but you ought to go home, and not on your own two feet. Is there someone we can call?"

"My friend Isabel is here working at the voter-registration booth. I think she'll give me a ride home."

The EMT picked up a walkie-talkie. "Then let's find Isabel."

It was another twenty minutes before Isabel was located and had brought her Lexus to the rendezvous point on Broadway where the EMT insisted on accompanying Daiyu. "I'm *fine*," she said about a dozen times, but he just grinned and kept walking.

"Daiyu, good heavens, what happened?" Isabel exclaimed as Daiyu climbed into the car and slumped against the seat. "Did you faint?"

"Not quite," Daiyu mumbled. "I just fell down, and then I felt dizzy, and everybody made a big deal about nothing. I'm sorry to drag you away from the booth."

"I don't mind at all," Isabel said briskly, setting the car in motion. "I was looking for an excuse to get away. I hate fireworks."

"I love them," Daiyu said.

And then she started crying.

Isabel wouldn't leave the house until Daiyu had called her father's cell phone, and he was home minutes after Daiyu had changed into a long T-shirt to sleep in.

"I'm *fine*," she repeated, when he sat on the edge of her bed and quizzed her about how she felt. "I just got too hot. And it was such a long day."

"Do you want me to take you to the emergency room?"

"No! If you ask me that one more time, I'm going to call Mom and tell her you're driving me crazy."

He laughed and pushed the hair back out of her eyes. "Well, did you at least have fun today? Before you got sick and fainted?"

"I didn't faint! The job fair was pretty boring, but I had a good time at the riverfront." She extended a hand. "I bought a ring. Isn't it pretty?"

He gave it a cursory look. "Very nice. Are you going to wear it to bed?"

She smiled at him. "I think I will. Do you have a problem with that?"

He kissed her forehead and pushed her back against the covers. "Not at all. I'll check on you before I go to church in the morning, but you should sleep in."

"All right," she said drowsily. "I will. Good night, Dad. I'm glad to be home."

She and her mother talked for about an hour the next morning while her father was gone. Daiyu was still wearing her sleep shirt as she sat at the kitchen table and spoke into the cordless phone. Her mother, never an alarmist about health issues, had done a quick rundown of Daiyu's symptoms and then seemed perfectly satisfied.

"So what else is going on?"

"I had the weirdest dreams last night," Daiyu said. "But it was like the same dream that kept going on and on. You know how you're dreaming, and you wake up, but when you fall back asleep, you're back in the same dream? It was like that."

"What was the dream about?"

"Well, now I can't really remember it. Maybe I was in China, because there were a lot of Asians there. And all the buildings had those kind of flirty edges to them, you know, like pagodas. And there was a river, except sometimes it wasn't a river, it was just this big patch of mud and people were walking around in the mud picking up rocks. Oh, and there was this really scary guy talking to me, but I gave him a rock and he went away."

"One of the rocks from the river?"

"No, a *different* rock. One I had in my pocket. And there was a cute boy there, and he kissed me."

"Sounds like a pretty exciting dream," her mother said.

"Yeah, the second or third time I woke up, I told myself I should write it all down so I'd remember it this morning—but—I was too tired, so I didn't."

"What are you and your dad going to do today?"

"I think he and Edward are going to keep working on the third bedroom," Daiyu said. "I'm just going to lie around and watch TV."

She could hear the smile in her mother's voice. "It's not often you get a free pass from your father," she said. "Take advantage of it while you can."

In fact, Daiyu got bored fairly quickly flipping through channels and paging through some of her favorite magazines. Once her father and Edward were back at work on the bedroom, she headed out to the Soulard market, where she picked up fresh fruit and salad ingredients for dinner. When she was home, she gathered up clothes from her closet and her father's so she could start the laundry.

She was checking pockets for forgotten coins and tissues when she found something in the black pants she'd been wearing the previous day. Mystified, she pulled out a small red silk bag closed with a golden drawstring.

"Where in the world did *this* come from?" she said out loud. When she opened it and dumped out the contents, a stone bounced onto the floor, followed by a couple of slips of paper.

She picked up the rock first. It was caramel colored and walnut sized, lined with streaks of orange and crowned with a smudge of blue. "Aren't you pretty," she said, holding it up to the light. "I wonder where I got you. I don't remember ever seeing you before."

Laying it on her desk, she examined the first piece of paper, which featured text that appeared to be written in the complex, stylized Chinese alphabet. "No idea what that means," she said, and balled up the paper and tossed it in the trash.

The last item seemed to be a piece of scrap paper on which someone had doodled times and dates and maybe a grocery list—also in Chinese. The reverse side was a little more interesting. It showed a poorly drawn scene that might have been workers laboring in a very muddy field, picking some kind of crop to throw into their shoulder bags. But there were a lot of strange architectural elements that bordered the field—a couple of bridges, a tower (maybe a silo?), and some kind of hugely disproportionate garden gate. Daiyu hesitated to throw this away too. Bizarre as it was, it looked as if someone had struggled over the image for a long time, erasing and redrawing lines to try to perfect them.

"I'll just put it aside for now," she decided, and laid it in her desk drawer where she put everything she couldn't figure out what to do with. After a moment's thought, she returned the rock to the silk bag and dropped it into the drawer as well. She decided not to let it bother her that she had no memory of acquiring these items; they didn't really seem important enough to worry about.

Monday morning came around way too soon. Daiyu was still feeling just a little under the weather and strangely emotional. She'd been watching television Sunday night and a stupid Hallmark commercial had made her start crying. She didn't even *have* any long-distance friends to send cards to. The only person she missed who was currently out of state was her mother, and Daiyu talked to her every day.

By Friday, though, she was pretty much her old self, working with her usual efficiency at the Executive Edge agency. Isabel came out of her office at noon, looking harassed.

"Are you going out to lunch? I'll buy yours if you'll bring something back for me," she said.

"Sure," said Daiyu, already on her feet. "I'll go get us sandwiches."

When the doors to the elevator opened, there was already one woman inside. She appeared to be in her late forties, stylishly dressed in a gray business suit and pink shell, with white-blond hair pulled back in an elegant chignon. She wore tiny, glittering studs in each ear, some kind of gems that looked like they might be opals crossed with rose quartz.

"Hi," Daiyu said. "I like your earrings."

The blond woman smiled back. "Thanks," she said. "So this is my first week of work here, and I have no idea where to go to lunch. I just want soup or a sandwich. Any place you'd recommend?"

"There's a great place called Edible Difference just a few blocks away. That's where I'm going, in fact. You can walk with me."

"I'd really appreciate that," the woman said, following Daiyu out into the lobby. "I have a feeling I'm going to be working through dinner, so I'd better get lunch."

"What kind of work do you do?"

"International law. I travel a lot."

"That sounds glamorous."

The woman laughed. "Like most jobs, more work than glamour. But I always enjoy a chance to visit different cities and live in different places. What do you do?"

"I'm a summer intern at an employment agency," Daiyu replied. "I'll only be here a few more weeks."

"I'm glad I met you while you were still here. My name's Dawn, by the way."

"I'm Daiyu."

They chatted easily during the short walk, then parted at the lunch counter of Edible Difference. Dawn stayed at the restaurant to eat, while Daiyu headed back to the office with the carryout bags in hand.

Right outside the doors to the Met Square Building, an itinerant musician had begun to perform, a guitar strapped over his shoulder and a case open at his feet. He was African American, older than her father; his short gray hair was a vivid contrast to his dark skin. His fingers coaxed a strange, syncopated melody from the strings, and Daiyu paused for a few minutes to listen. She thought she almost recognized the tune, but she couldn't place where she might have heard it before.

She dropped all of Isabel's change into the guitar case alongside a few one-dollar bills he'd already collected. "That's pretty," she said. "Did you write it yourself?"

He smiled at her, his fingers never pausing in their intricate motions. "No, but this is my own arrangement," he said in a deep and surprisingly beautiful voice. "I call it 'Sunshine and Shadow.' My name is Shadow," he added.

"I like that. I'm Daiyu. Pleased to meet you."

"Pleased to meet you as well."

She rode the elevator up to the office, her feet tapping out the steps to a dance she made up on the spot. For the rest of the afternoon, she found herself humming Shadow's melody and occasionally smiling.

The next few weeks flew by. July somersaulted slowly into August—which was, impossibly, even hotter than July. The agency continued to be so busy that Isabel rarely had time to take a lunch break, although once in a while Daiyu convinced her to leave the office long enough to eat. These outings were always entertaining but a little exhausting, since Isabel would spend pretty much the entire hour ranting about the excesses and mistakes of the current crop of politicians. Twice Daiyu had lunch with Dawn, which was a little strange. They had nothing in common to talk about, so conversation was somewhat stilted, though filled with goodwill.

More often she would bring her lunch and eat it outside. On these days, she found herself drawn to the riverfront by a longing she couldn't understand. She would sit on the top step of the stairway that led from the Arch down to the Mississippi, situating herself so she could see the monument swooping skyward on one side of her and the river sparkling southward on the other. She always felt excited and hopeful as she hurried toward the Arch grounds, as if expecting to meet an old friend or see some rare treasure on display. She always felt a little lonely and depressed as she walked back, as if the endless unrolling of the water had carried away her last, most precious dream.

By mid-August, Isabel was bemoaning the fact that Daiyu would soon be gone. "I know you have to go back to school, but please tell me you'll come work for me next summer," Isabel said one afternoon when Daiyu stayed late to finish typing up letters. "You're the best intern I've ever had."

"I'd like that," Daiyu said. "If I get into St. Louis University, I'll be able to work here part-time when I'm in college, too."

"Excellent!" Isabel exclaimed. "And if you're open to weekend work during the school year, I know I'll have a lot of projects you could help me with."

"Sure. Just call me."

"And if you have any time to do volunteering," Isabel added, "I'm trying to find workers for the Carnahan campaign."

"Mmmm—I don't think so," Daiyu said.

It was as if Isabel hadn't heard her. "We *have* to defeat Charles Lee," Isabel said. "If that man is the next governor of Missouri, I'm going to have to move to Illinois. Or move to Canada! I don't know that I can live in any country that would elect a man like him to any office."

"What's he done that's so terrible?" Daiyu asked.

"What's he—Well, here, let me just give you a little literature," Isabel said, disappearing into her office. She reappeared a moment later with a stack of magazines and what looked like photocopies of articles from a dozen more. "You can take these home and read them, and then tell me why he's so terrible."

"Great," Daiyu said, flipping through the pages of the *Time* magazine on top of the pile. Maybe there would be a good movie review toward the back. "Something to read on the bus."

"If you wait five minutes, I'll give you a lift home," Isabel offered.

"That sounds good," Daiyu said, and settled back into her chair.

Isabel vanished into her office again. Daiyu sighed and turned to the political section of the magazine. It seemed like the proper payment for the gift of the ride.

The article that was marked with a yellow Post-it note was

titled "America's Next Governors" and featured a rundown of promising candidates in ten states. Daiyu skimmed until she found the section called "Battle for the Heartland: The Carnahan Legacy or the Upstart Lee?" She tried to concentrate on the pros and cons of both contenders, but the arguments didn't really register with her until she turned the page and saw a photo of Charles Lee.

She just stared at him.

She couldn't have said why, but she had an immediate reaction of dislike so strong it was almost panic. He was a handsome biracial man, with strong Chinese features partially molded by a Caucasian heritage. His hair was as black as hers, except for a sexy streak of gray that waved back from his forehead, and his eyes were bright with intelligence. Even from the printed page, he exuded an intensity that was almost electric. In the photo, he was smiling as he extended his hand to a crowd of wellwishers. Everyone in the mob surrounding him looked worshipful and awed.

Isabel came bustling out, her purse over her shoulder. "What did I tell you? He's a horror, isn't he? He fails on every single issue! The environment, the energy policy, national defense, immigration—"

Daiyu closed the magazine, disturbed by her strange antipathy toward a man she'd never even heard of until five minutes ago. "I guess I should read about him a little more," she said.

"Him and every other candidate!" Isabel agreed. "Your best defense in an uncertain world is to arm yourself with information."

Isabel continued in much the same vein as they walked to the car, exited the garage, and began driving south on Broadway. Daiyu didn't have to do more than murmur an agreement from time to time. Traffic was clogged by baseball fans heading to the game, and they were stopped for a long time in front of the new stadium. Through two light changes, Daiyu stared at the Cardinals logo emblazoned all over the stadium and traced the lines of the arched metal accents that rose like a half-finished cage above the brick of the massive structure. A memory struggled to surface from the depths of her mind. Then the light changed and Isabel drove on.

As they pulled up in front of the townhouse, Isabel said, "You think about volunteering for the Carnahan campaign. We could use your help."

Her hand on the door handle, Daiyu surprised herself by saying, "You know what? I think I'll do it. Let me know when you want me to be where."

TWENTY-FOUR

ONE WEEK LATER, there was only a single day left in Daiyu's summer internship. Daiyu figured Isabel would treat her to a nice lunch, even though it wouldn't really be her final day at the agency, since she'd agreed to work one Saturday a month. She was already thinking about what outfit she would wear in case they ended up at one of the fancy downtown restaurants like Kemoll's or Mike Shannon's.

"Daiyu, I have to run," Isabel said, hurrying from her office while simultaneously trying to fix an earring. "Can you turn off the phones and lock up? I hate to ask."

"Not a problem," Daiyu said. "See you tomorrow morning."

"Thank you!" Isabel called and disappeared out the door.

Daiyu routed the phone system to the night message and powered down her computer. Then—because Isabel was notoriously neglectful of small details—she went to Isabel's office to turn off the computer and switch off the lights. She was just picking her purse up from her desk when a shy knock drew her attention to the door.

"May I help you?" she asked.

The visitor was a young man, her own age or a year or two older, tall and thin and scruffy-looking. His brown hair fell in curls to his shoulders, and his clothes looked like they'd been slept in for the past five days. Still, she couldn't immediately smell any unpleasant body odor, so Daiyu guessed that he'd cleaned himself up recently in the fountain at Kiener Plaza or maybe the bathroom at Union Station. He looked lost, but not at all scary. At any rate, she wasn't afraid of him. She gave him a friendly smile.

He smiled back. "I thought—it said on the sign—this is an employment agency?"

"That's right."

"Do you think you could help me find a job?"

She kept her voice compassionate. "It's not that kind of agency," she said. "We only find jobs for people who already have jobs and want better ones."

"Oh. All right."

He made no move to leave, just watched her with a slightly hopeful expression. She said, "What kind of work can you do?"

He hunched his shoulders in a shrug. "You know. Whatever needs to be done. Manual labor, mostly."

"When's the last time you worked?" she asked.

He shook his head. "I've been looking for a while," he said.

"When's the last time you ate?" she said even more gently.

"Oh, I had a meal this morning. There's a church a few blocks away where they'll feed you. Let you sleep. But I want to get hired on somewhere. I don't like this drifting around."

"How long have you been in St. Louis?"

"A couple of weeks."

"Where were you before?"

He didn't answer, and she came a step nearer, studying him more closely. The clothes were a little strange, sloppy black pants and a brightly colored shirt that didn't fit like American clothes. Maybe he'd picked them up from the trash bin behind a theatrical shop. He wasn't wearing a watch and didn't have any tattoos that she could see, but both his earlobes were pierced, and he wore small black hoops that looked like they might be made of jet or even black jade. He was thin, but his forearms were wiry; wherever he'd been before, he'd been used to hard physical work. He was probably strong enough to lift her over his head or strangle her with his bare hands.

Many girls, she knew, would have been terrified to be caught alone in an upper-story office with a strange man who looked like a drifter. But Daiyu wasn't afraid in the least. Something about this lost young man appealed to her—a sweetness in his smile, a kindness in his expression. "Where were you before?" she repeated in a soft voice.

He gave her a lopsided grin. "I don't really know. I'm having trouble remembering things. Maybe I hit my head or something."

"Could be the effect of drugs or alcohol."

"No," he said swiftly. "I remember that much. I don't do that stuff."

She didn't think he was old enough to be a veteran suffering from post-traumatic stress—then again, a car accident, a fall down some steep steps, any number of catastrophes could have left him with a case of partial amnesia.

"Do you think you need to see a doctor?"

He shook his head. "No, I feel fine. I feel pretty good, in fact. I just—woke up one morning and I was here in St. Louis, sleeping under the Arch. I've been trying to figure out what to do ever since."

"There are a couple of homeless shelters I can tell you how to get to," she offered. "Maybe they'll have a social worker who can help you. I suppose you don't have a Social Security number or a driver's license or any kind of I.D."

He grinned. "I suppose not."

"Do you know your name?"

He looked surprised, as if it hadn't occurred to him that he ought to have one. "It begins with a 'K,'" he said at last.

"Keith? Kevin? Kelly? Karl?"

"I don't think so. Karl's the closest."

"Caleb?" she added, even though it didn't really start with a "K."

He looked pleased. "Caleb," he said. "Or—mm—almost."

"Well, Caleb, I've got to lock up the office now and go home. I can tell you how to get to Larry Rice's place, but I'm afraid there's not much else I can do for you. I'm sorry."

"That's all right," he said. "Thanks for being so nice."

He pushed the button for the elevator while she locked the office door, and they rode down in silence. Once they were outside, she took him to the corner of Olive and Broadway so she could give him directions to Larry Rice's New Life Evangelistic Center. He listened closely and nodded every time she named an intersection, so she was reasonably certain he'd be able to find his way. But before saying a brisk good-bye and running for her bus, she hesitated and asked one last question. "What brought you to St. Louis? Any idea?"

"I've been trying to remember that, too," he said. "I think a friend of mine is here somewhere."

"Maybe he's looking for you."

"I don't think so. I'm pretty sure I said I wouldn't come."

"Why'd you change your mind?"

He smiled. "Got too lonely, I guess. Seemed worse to stay behind than make the journey."

"Did you come a long way?"

"I think so. I can't remember."

She tilted her head to one side. "Are you sorry you came? All that effort and then—you don't even know why you're here?"

"No, I like it in St. Louis. I think this is where I'm supposed to be."

"Well, good luck, Caleb. I hope you get your memory back. I hope you locate your friend. You think you can find the shelter now?"

"I think so. Thanks again."

He smiled at her again and set off west on Olive, against the direction of the one-way traffic. She only just now noticed the heavy cloth bag hanging over his shoulder and probably holding all his worldly possessions.

On impulse, she called after him. "Caleb!"

He turned. "Yes?"

"Listen, my dad's rehabbing our house. He's always hiring a couple of guys to help him with the heavy work. If you want a job for a few days, there's plenty to do at our place."

He stood there a moment, his hands clasping the strap of his bag. "Really?"

She smiled. "Yeah, really. I'll even make you dinner."

"I don't want to get in the way."

"My dad'll be glad to have you. Come on."

He hesitated another moment, but she waved him forward, and he joined her again, ducking his head to hide his shy smile. "Look, there's our bus!" she cried, and grabbed his arm to pull him quickly down the street to where the Soulard bus was wheezing to a stop.

She had to dig for her own bus pass and then fish out enough change to pay Caleb's fare, but she did all of that one-handed. Her fingers were still crooked around his elbow, and she kept her hand on his arm as she pushed him ahead of her down the aisle and onto one of the empty sets of hard plastic seats. She held on to him once the bus lurched forward; she kept her grip as she began pointing out all the sights he might have missed during his brief stay in the city. She didn't even question the fact that it seemed so natural to be sitting so close to him, her fingers wrapped around his arm. She held on to him as if afraid he might disappear if she were foolish enough to let him go.

SHARON SHINN has won the William C. Crawford Award for Outstanding New Fantasy Writer and was twice nominated for the John W. Campbell Award for Best New Writer. Her Samaria novels have been *Locus* bestsellers, and her novels *Summers at Castle Auburn* and *The Safe-Keeper's Secret* were named ALA Best Books for Young Adults. Her book *Angel-Seeker* won the Reviewer's Choice Award for Best Science Fiction novel from the *Romantic Times,* and her books *Mystic and Rider, Reader and Raelynx,* and *Fortune and Fate* were all named finalists. A graduate of Northwestern University, Sharon Shinn also works as a journalist for a trade magazine.

Visit her Web site at www.sharonshinn.net.